HALO
SILENTIUM

SILENTIUM

BOOK THREE OF THE FORERUNNER SAGA

GREG BEAR

BASED ON THE BESTSELLING VIDEO GAME FOR XBOX®

G

GALLERY BOOKS

New York | London | Toronto | Sydney | New Delhi

G

Gallery Books
An Imprint of Simon & Schuster, Inc.
1230 Avenue of the Americas
New York, NY 10020

First Gallery Books trade paperback edition March 2019

GALLERY BOOKS and colophon are registered trademarks of Simon & Schuster, Inc.

For information about special discounts for bulk purchases, please contact Simon & Schuster Special Sales at 1-866-506-1949 or business@simonandschuster.com

The Simon & Schuster Speakers Bureau can bring authors to your live event. For more information or to book an event, contact the Simon & Schuster Speakers Bureau at 1-866-248-3049 or visit our website at www.simonspeakers.com.

Manufactured in the United States of America

10   9   8   7   6

Library of Congress Cataloging-in-Publication Data is available.

ISBN 978-1-9821-1181-6
ISBN 978-1-9821-1182-3 (ebook)

To my son, Erik—my Vergil
throughout these three books

SILENTIUM

This document is a translation of thirty-nine strings of Forerunner data, converted to text/audio. They have been abstracted from two sources: the shell or carapace of Forerunner remains #879 ("Catalog") and a damaged monitor associated with a single fossilized "Juridical," a hitherto unknown Forerunner type, presumably a legal functionary.

The "Catalog" carapace enclosed a highly specialized Forerunner that apparently served as an amplified collector of data. The misshapen body within has almost entirely rotted away.

No attempt has been made to restore or reactivate either the monitor or the carapace.

CONTEXT: At the very end of the Forerunner empire, as the Flood made major inroads and both Builders and the revived class of Warrior-Servants prepared their last defenses, the

Juridicals were given free access to all citizens and personnel throughout the ecumene.

Their mandate: to investigate the circumstances alluded to in the "Bornstellar Relation" ("Destruction of Orion Complex Capital World," ONI File CR-537-21), but also to investigate the delicate question of human and Forerunner origins, and the fate of the Precursors, who allegedly created both species.

When the ship that collected, repaired, and debriefed Forerunner monitor 343 Guilty Spark is recovered, more of these issues will doubtless be illuminated. For the time being, some matters must remain obscure.

The fragments are arranged in a temporary logical order. Chronology of some fragments cannot be established, but all were recorded in the last decade of the Forerunner empire, before the apocalyptic discharge of the energies of the Halo rings.

Tactical translations in this report incorporate audio strings associated with the names of places, ships, and individuals. Some of these have been transliterated, with their modern equivalents in parentheses. All other translations follow colloquial style for quick comprehension. [TT] denotes Tactical Translator note.

ONI takes no responsibility for command decisions based on inferences made from these translations, particularly with regard to the Didact or the Librarian.

—ONIRF Investigation Team

Welcome, Juridical. The Domain is especially clear this evening. I presume the transport of all those brutish wheels has come to a pause. Where may I guide you?

"Thank you, Haruspis. I am empowered by the New Council to investigate the matter of the Precursors and possible crimes against the Mantle. Grant me access to that beginning."

A unique request—and not a welcome one. That region of the Domain has long been sealed. For you, it does not exist.

"The Master Juridical orders it be opened."

Not even such a One has that authority.

"Who does?"

Ten million years have passed. Back then, Warriors were not yet servants and stood highest. Perhaps the greatest of your Warriors might persuade the Domain.

"I am authorized to remove the Haruspis and access the Domain directly, should you refuse."

I see the authorization is legitimate. That does not make it virtuous or wise.

"Forerunners are rapidly moving beyond virtue and wisdom. The evidence is essential to judge testimony gathered by Catalog regarding the Flood, the Master Builder, the Old Council, and the Didact. Surely you've stored other materials relevant to those cases."

They have been refused by the Domain.

"How is that possible? The Domain is the soul and record of all things Forerunner. Is it judging and correcting before history is made?"

Since the destruction of the Capital world, the Domain is frequently off-line now, and even when it is available and clear, it does not always respond to timely storage or retrieval.

"Individuals and their ancillas have reported difficulties—but you?"

What I know suggests the possible influence of an immense event yet to come. Do you anticipate such an event, Juridical? Does your request seek justification, or preparation?

"That is beyond my scope."

You have come to remove me. Please do. I have been so long with the Domain that I will quickly pass into it—and I can think of no more suitable fate for Haruspis.

"I would prefer of course to rely on your experience. I plead with you . . . !"

Do not hesitate or your courage will fail. Wait.

Wait.

"Is there a problem?"

The Domain is making its own request. The Domain wishes to testify to a Juridical.

"The Domain is not a recognized class of being. It is not in any way a citizen—not even an *awareness*!"

How little you know. Haruspis is standing aside now. Are you recording?

"Yes . . . Unprecedented! But recording."

All paths are clear. Signal strength is remarkable, even willful . . . Harupis has never seen it like this.

"Recording . . . too fast! Too powerful! Can't absorb it all . . ."

You asked for it, Juridical. The Domain is here, the Domain is wide open—and it is not happy.

idday and the skies grow dark with ships. Lightning flashes along the far horizon. We stand on the rim of a promontory overlooking a wide, flat plain covered as far as the eye can see with dry grass—three Lifeworkers and me.

The Lifeworkers have been tasked with the selection and collection of but a few of this planet's living things, that the coming Halo desecration may one day be forgiven when our lives are summed at the end of Living Time.

The planet is called Erde-Tyrene. Ships great and small sweep over the continent where humans may have first evolved.

I am Catalog. I record all that I am called upon to witness. I am filled with evidence and testimony related to the cases at hand. Accessing investigations conducted on other worlds, I study many histories: clans and families and partners split apart by the Flood war, cities destroyed, star systems scoured to prevent infection. All that terror and hatred burn inside me like so many flame-carved scars. These events echo through the Domain, and inevitably attract the attention of Juridicals. The Juridicals then dispatch Catalog.

I am one of many.

We are all the same.

In theory.

Once my presence has been mandated, no one can refuse me. In the investigation of a possible crime, Catalog determines what is passed along to the Juridicals. Nobody wishes to be accused of crimes against the Mantle. But that is just one of the potential charges on which I gather testimony and evidence.

The three Lifeworkers beside me have finished early surveys and activated the beacons that in turn have told all humans imprinted with the Librarian's *geas* to settle their affairs and gather. The evacuation has been going on for many days. The plain before us is alive with an incessant, dreadful noise—the screams of frightened humans and other animals, cowering as ships swoop down and Lifeworkers emerge to collect.

Everywhere on Erde-Tyrene, across the prairies and over the mountains, between the islands, even across a thick northern cloak of glaciers, terrified humans leave their hunting grounds, their farms and villages and towns. The animals so summoned have no choice. By the grace of the Lifeworkers, many will be preserved. Most will not.

The Librarian, it is said, favors humans. But as Catalog I am aware that she has studied and favored one hundred and twenty-three technologically capable species across three million worlds within the explored regions of our galaxy. How many of these she will seek to preserve, it is not my job to predict or even to understand.

The Lifeworkers have sworn to carry out the commands of the New Council, reconstituted from survivors found deep beneath the ruins of the Capital world. Most of the Old Council was killed by the metarch-level ancilla known as Mendicant Bias when it unleashed the killing power of Halo, possibly at the instigation of the Master Builder.

That is one of the cases Juridicals will examine and decide. But that is not why I am here.

The three Lifeworkers stand silent and solemn beside me. Their white armor provides them with information from around Erde-Tyrene. I receive similar data from Juridical probes spread around the ecumene in anticipation of new cases. At the moment, however, only the local network is available to me.

Across the thunder-booming plain, out of the bellies of the great ships, thousands of lesser ships drop and spread like mosquitoes, their engines a distant, buzzing whine. Many trail yellowish curtains like tainted rain. This is solute, which will cause every animal killed by Halo action to instantly decay into component molecules. This will avert an ecological miasma. But it could also be construed as a way to hide a tremendous crime from later investigators.

Very interesting to Catalog.

Lifeworkers have time and resources to preserve less than one out of a thousand of Erde-Tyrene's large species. A great extinction will follow. Very soon, this world will be quiet. This may not in itself constitute a crime against the Mantle. Deliberate and total extinction would qualify, and this is not that.

Not yet.

The chief Lifeworker, a mature third-form named Carrier-of-Immunity, receives a signal from our ship, a seeker transport parked on a rocky promontory a few dozen meters behind us.

"The Lifeshaper is in the system," he says.

"Are we to meet with the Lifeshaper?" Celebrator-of-Birth, a young first-form, asks hopefully. There are billions of Lifeworkers but only one Lifeshaper.

"Not yet. The community of Marontik has yet to be processed." Carrier adds, "I have new orders, however. Catalog will be removed from Erde-Tyrene. I will accompany him to the Lifeshaper's ship."

"The Librarian interrupts my investigation?" I ask, suddenly on alert. Crime ever multiplies and grows!

"That's all I know," Carrier says. "Please come with me." He walks toward the transport. I have no choice but to follow, leaving the others on the rim rock overlooking the evacuations.

We enter the ship and are swiftly conveyed to low orbit. I withdraw my external sensors and go silent on all channels and frequencies. There is no reason to discuss matters with this Lifeworker. He has little power and less culpability.

We dock with the Librarian's ship and I am released onto the passenger deck. Carrier-of-Immunity withdraws, no doubt with relief, to return to Erde-Tyrene. I am alone. The deck is wide, empty, dark. Despite the power of the Juridicals, I am apprehensive.

The suspects in our investigation are legendary: the Librarian, the IsoDidact, and the Master Builder. All have yet to be deposed. The Librarian has been granted a temporary waiver due to her pressing duties.

The IsoDidact is an ingenious copy of the original Didact, who imprinted a Manipular named Bornstellar-Makes-Eternal-Lasting. He has assumed control of Forerunner defense and oversees the security of Lifeworker activities. The Librarian maintains this copy is still her husband. He calls her wife.

As the minutes pass, I hear echoing noises in the gloom. Then, through an opening port, sunlight flows like burning gold and splashes against two shadows, one ominous and bulky, the other smaller and slender.

The IsoDidact's form nearly overwhelms that of the Librarian. He is a Promethean, the most honored class of the old Warrior-Servants, wide and thick and strong, with great arms and massive hands. His broad face, piercing eyes, and flat nose have a classically Forerunner yet brutish aspect. There is little hint of the Manipular that took the Didact's imprint. The segments of his battle armor hover just above an inner shell of hard light that outlines him in lines of pale blue. One can often tell a Forerunner's mood by the color of his or her armor. This armor is dark with displeasure.

"It is not right to interfere with Juridicals," he murmurs.

"There is no interference," the Librarian insists, stepping forward. Smaller, more delicately constructed than the Promethean, her eyes seem larger, all-seeing. She wears blue Lifeworker armor, narrow grooves and slots along the arms and torso concealing persuaders, scanners, sample bays, subcutanes, biopsy probes, and other instruments of her profession.

"Your escorts did not explain their reasons," the IsoDidact says. Culpability for the actions of his original could become an interesting point of law.

"They were following orders," the Librarian says. "They could not know my intent."

She turns her full attention to me. Lifeshaper is her title among Lifeworkers—a term of extreme regard. Her slender body and careworn face, with those great, dark eyes, revive emotions I might have felt before assuming the carapace. I once had an eye for beauty among all rates. Yet the Librarian's beauty lies neither in youth nor in physical perfection. She is in many ways flawed: a tilt of one eye, slanted lower lip, unseemly whiteness of teeth. She seems to have deliberately adopted a few characteristics of those humans she now collects. I wonder if that makes her more or less beautiful to the IsoDidact.

"I am solely to blame," she says, and walks around me, her gait light as air. Her eyes study and soothe at once.

For a moment, I am unhappy being Catalog. There is no particular reason for either the Librarian or the IsoDidact to show me favor or even civility. Recent history has not been kind to them—nor have the Juridicals.

I rotate my carapace to track her. "My work has been interrupted," I say. "I am here on a Council-approved investigation."

Now the IsoDidact makes *his* circuit, hand to helmet's chin, as if studying an adversary. "Builders supplied your carapace," he says. "Your colleagues have been subverted in the past."

"Subversion is most unlikely," I say, measuring the situation.

"What Builders have done to undermine your integrity, they can keep secret even from you. It has happened before."

There is nothing I can or would wish to say to justify the crimes committed under the Master Builder's centuries of misrule. "Those times were unfortunate," I say. "They ended before I assumed the carapace. Those who strayed were punished."

"Even so . . ." the IsoDidact murmurs. The Librarian gives her husband a look of mild reproof, but with a hint of admiration. Are they about to shut down my investigation, sequester me? The probability, my ancilla tells me, is rather high.

"I have been cut off from my remotes," I protest. "I insist on gathering evidence without interference."

"We have no intention of interfering," she says. "Husband?"

The IsoDidact lays his hand on my carapace. "Our diagnostics find no evidence of Builder tampering. Full access will resume."

I send out queries. The ship's ancilla cooperates. I receive new data from my remotes. They fill in gaps in my continuous record. But communication with the greater Juridical network is still problematic.

The IsoDidact keeps his hand on my carapace. I am not sure of his intentions. "Juridicals are investigating the destruction of the Capital world," he says. "I was there, you know. Ask *me* what happened."

I was not aware of this. Had he been present as the IsoDidact, or as the Manipular?

Into my silence he continues, "Catalog must also report new crimes—crimes in progress—to the Juridicals and to the New Council, correct?"

"That is my duty," I say.

"Would it not be efficient to take our testimonies now, while Lifeworkers preserve this system's life forms? There is no crime *here*, Catalog—only mercy and pity."

I had never expected to be brought before these two, or to take their testimony on any matter. I could make a request to expand the scope of my investigation, but with communications so sporadic, the response may be delayed.

"I have little power in the matter. I must obtain permission. . . ." Very embarrassing.

The IsoDidact and his wife link hands and engage in silent conversation. When they finish, the Didact faces me. "I see by your manner that you were once a Warrior-Servant. Why diminish—why *abandon* your rate for *this*?"

Strange for this one to speak of such! Yet once, I had been almost as large and nearly as strong. Why did I give up that strength? Because of my own crime, before I assumed the carapace. Going against the creed of my rate. Against the express command of my mentor. Allowing anger to overwhelm judgment.

The strength of Catalog lies in personal awareness of the nature of guilt.

"Be not so bold, Husband," the Librarian cautions.

The IsoDidact raises a massive hand and gives it a half-turn. I know the meaning of the gesture: command received. He clenches thick fingers, then loosens them. Their offer may be withdrawn. And what they may have to say does seem relevant to many cases under our review.

"I am not presently in contact with the Juridical network," I say. "Until such time as communication resumes, I will take your testimonies."

"Wise move, Catalog," the IsoDidact says in an undertone. But we are suddenly interrupted by alarms. A group of Life-workers and Warrior-Servants gathers protectively around the Librarian and the IsoDidact. The deck has gone weightless; we all float. Field activators flicker across the bulkheads, co-ordinating with armor and carapace, as if in preparation for a quick journey to interplanetary orbit—an emergency jump. Images of looming Forerunner squadrons dance around the IsoDidact.

I am for the moment irrelevant.

"We're in danger," he growls. "Flood-infested ships have broken through our defenses, spread thin out here. We are ending operations on Erde-Tyrene. The Flood may be in this system in a few hours. You are far too important to risk, Wife."

"But there are many more species to be saved!" she protests.

"These will have to suffice."

Another silent communication between them. Husband and wife will be parted yet again. The Librarian's expression turns deeply sad. Her beauty increases and my objectivity is once more threatened.

The IsoDidact directs that he be delivered to the only fully armed dreadnought in the system. After conducting defensive operations, and insuring the safety of Lifeworker ships, he will make his way back to the heart of the ecumene; his force here is far too small to go on the offensive.

"You'll travel with the Librarian," he tells me.

Between us, as between Warrior-Servants of old—the rate I once was, the rate he grew into so suddenly—there is a current of request, bequest, demand.

Protect her.

Strangely, I am happy to comply. "It would be my honor," I say.

———

Their last moments together are spent in private, in a secluded angle of the bridge. Outside, the limb of Erde-Tyrene is serene, brown and blue and beige, capped in the north with great sheets of ice and all over deckled with clouds. All seems peaceful. The Lifeworker collection ships are withdrawing with the last of their specimens.

The Lifeshaper indicates I should follow her. "We will do what we can to save those we have collected," she says. "I hope we can reach the greater Ark and deliver them to safekeeping. . . ."

Down a corridor, I see the IsoDidact conferring with other warriors. Their armor grows thicker and sturdier. A port opens and they push through into the dreadnought.

The ships separate.

The Librarian and I drop deeper into the collection hold, through layer upon layer of stacked zoological compartments, each hundreds of meters wide and equipped with illusions of sky, sea, land, whatever the animals carried therein will find relatively soothing. We are descending to the compression and storage chambers at the ship's core.

"My husband has long held controversial views on Flood defense," the Librarian says. Her eyes are stoic, but I sense reflections on an even deeper loss. "You may have guessed, he is skeptical about any Juridical investigation into the Master Builder."

"I detect that opinion."

"He is old-fashioned, you know. He expects you to do your best to protect me . . . even though you are no longer a Warrior-Servant."

That stings, somehow.

The flexible tube deposits us in a weightless maze of storage cylinders attended by hundreds of monitors. This part of the ship is not accustomed to visitors. We drift a moment before an environmental field draws us down to a platform and courteously supplies breathable air.

"He presumes that any investigation should have begun centuries earlier—does he not?" I ask, absorbing these details.

"Had the Juridicals been *vigilant*," the Librarian says, "my husband might not have had to go into exile. He might have blocked the Flood's most recent incursions—and we would have avoided all this." Her hand sweeps around the broad inner chamber. "We will save less than one-thousandth of the larger species."

"Animals," I say, and then, to an arch of her brow, add, "Animals *and* humans, on Erde-Tyrene, due to your grace, Lifeshaper. Will saving fewer humans disappoint the IsoDidact?"

"I have heard Juridicals hold conservative views," she counters. "Do you?"

"Before I took the carapace, I absorbed the attitudes of Warrior-Servants. I never fought humans, however. As for the Juridicals—their conservatism comes of long experience with the Domain. The cosmos, Lifeshaper, is highly conservative, don't you agree?"

"The cosmos brought life into existence. Life is ever changing," she says. "I have seen it open itself time and again to change, down to its living heart. But fascinating as these matters may be, I am here to testify about other events. Events that have yet to come to the attention of a Catalog."

Implication that Catalog is many and not unity is a forgivable rudeness. Few understood the oaths and training involved in taking the carapace—or the singleness of purpose it brings. "Defense of your husband's efforts is not to the point of our present inquiries," I say. "Not now, at any rate. We have sufficient testimony about the Master Builder." I am forbidden from telling her that the Master Builder is still alive and active in Flood defense. That is not my role.

"My husband and I were separated for a thousand years," the Librarian says. "Much happened during that time. The Didact, while fully functional, currently possesses less than a third the active memory of . . ." She can hardly bring herself to say, "the original."

"Understood," I say. I am also forbidden from telling her that the Ur-Didact is alive as well and has been returned to the ecumene. Why does she not yet know?

"That may change in time," she says, "as his imprint continues to flower. Yet he does remember some very disturbing things."

"Strange you have not been called to give such evidence before now."

"I was, when Juridicals were instruments of the Master Builder," she says. "I rejected the request. You, however, *are* pure," she says. "Are you not?" Her eyes shine with a sentiment mixing curiosity and, could it be, humor? This change from sadness energizes me. I am beginning to understand the power this Life-worker has over those who share her labors.

All I can answer is, "I have to presume your diagnostics are accurate."

"Good. What I will testify to is no longer of any use to the Master Builder, alive or dead, or to my husband's opposition in the New Council."

Alone, we have made our way to a closeted space away from the grim reduction. Only a few intact specimens will be kept in stasis; the rest will be reduced.

"It will be secure at any rate from political interference," I say.

She thinks on this. "The Didact swore to protect the Mantle. And that is the primary duty of Lifeworkers."

"Observing the rule of the Mantle is *our* primary duty as well," I remind her. "All our laws rise to that brilliant glow."

The bulkheads shape rudimentary furnishings. The Librarian's armor unwinds from her upper torso. She stretches lithe arms, flexes her fingers, exhausted perhaps not so much from recent labors as the long burden of her story. Catalog has seen this before. Catalog can lift such burdens.

It is my duty to bear witness.

"A thousand years ago, my husband and I did not part on the best of terms. Now I am blessed to make peace with him. But as with all things in our lives, along with this gift comes something more.

"When the Didact left his imprint on a young Manipular, and returned to me in that way, a memory he had withheld for ten thousand years surfaced again to haunt him." Her face loses some color. "Forerunners assert our duty to the Mantle. Yet on more than one occasion, our survival, pride, and arrogance took precedence. Forerunner humility gave way to desperate anger. Once, we rose up against our very creators. . . ."

I know nothing of this. A fable, perhaps?

I do not judge. I record.

was not always called Lifeshaper. That title came to me just before I walked among the defeated humans at Charum Hakkor, in the company of the Didact, ten thousand years ago. And that is a kind of beginning.

Despite my husband's triumph over these broken wretches, I felt like weeping, remembering fallen friends, colleagues . . . family. But not for them alone would I weep. These pitiful humans, wounded and fallen, were also *my* children. So the Rule of the Mantle instructs.

Forerunners have always thought themselves especially mindful of their responsibility to all living things, even should they bite and scratch and claw—or kill. But threaten us with utter destruction? Humans had fought *too well*. And evidence of their own cruelty and arrogance was overwhelming.

While pushing back human forces, Forerunners had come upon system after system where humans had wiped out entire species and civilizations, or subjugated them to their own schemes—as they had with the decadent and beautiful San'Shyuum.

The final triumph at Charum Hakkor had brought with it mixed spoils, mysteries, perhaps not so much treasures as curses passed along by the defeated, as if knowing they would distract us, sap our will to fight, drain us of our conviction . . .

The most important of these was a human timelock, kept at the center of a vast Citadel. Within this device, humans had preserved, or imprisoned—or both—an ancient being found just beyond the last thin star clusters at the margin of the galaxy. They called it the timeless one.

The Didact called it the Primordial.

My husband forced knowledge of the timelock's workings from a damaged human servitor—a version of our ancillas. The Didact could not unseal the timelock, nor release the occupant, but he did conduct a brief communication with the creature stored therein.

The Primordial was six meters wide and almost as tall, an unnatural mix of ancient arthropod and mammal, head flat and broad and low, overlapping sloping shoulders, wide-spaced compound eyes glittering like raw diamonds, its compressed body that of a many-limbed, corpulent ape, while down its spine crept a segmented, sea-scorpion tail—all packed tightly inside the container.

The Didact's first opinion was that this time-suspended horror was a clever fake—perhaps a psychological weapon. But it was much more than that.

This encounter changed the Didact. He told me what he saw, ten thousand years ago, but not what the creature *said* to him. *That* he withheld from me—or any other. I think he wished to protect us. He could not, of course. Not long after securing the Didact in his Cryptum, I made a journey to Path Kethona and discovered the Primordial's secret on my own.

More on that in its proper place.

———————

As the human-Forerunner war twisted and stumbled to its conclusion, Builders supplied even more weapons and ships than were needed. They acquired greater and greater wealth and power. With this power came a drift away from the old ways and attitudes. Under the Builders' growing influence, the Old Council also underwent a transformation—becoming more and more vindictive and wealth-driven.

Facing apparent evidence of our enemy's rapacious cruelty, the Old Council decided that humanity as a species was guilty of crimes against the Mantle. I agreed—at first. Later, when we realized humans had made great efforts to fight the Flood, and that many of their so-called atrocities had been carried out with that in mind, I changed that opinion. But Lifeworkers were ignored. Politically weakened, we could not push our case.

Some Warrior-Servants objected as well. Peculiar notions of honor and duty ruled their lives. Humans had been worthy opponents. Subduing them was honorable—extinction, not. Yet they, too, were ignored.

The Builders single-mindedly made plans for a final human solution. Forerunners were sliding down a steep path to committing just the sort of alleged atrocity for which humans were to be punished. The paradox was dizzying. Yet despite the cruel contradiction, not even Juridicals objected.

But another, far greater concern quickly came to the fore: the Flood. Our earliest encounters with that shape-changing and all-consuming plague had been shocking. The Flood ripped through hundreds of Forerunner battle fleets and dissolved their crews into crawling, agonized muck, or grouped them into amazing collectives we called Graveminds. Warrior-Servants methodically destroyed the infected fleets, leaving only scattered remains to analyze—damaged monitors and broken bits of armor. A few of the recovered monitors were beyond repair or even interrogation. They had been subjected to a hitherto unknown *philosophical* corruption—much like the perversion later observed in Mendicant Bias. They quickly spread their corruption to other AIs.

It was obviously not healthy for an ancilla to match wits with a Gravemind. The same might have been true of organic beings. But with them, the Flood leaped over any subtle perversion or persuasion.

It simply absorbed, converted, *used*.

The earliest antecedents of the Flood had appeared among humans centuries before they engaged with Forerunners—long before we ourselves faced the plague. The infection was first delivered into their midst by small ships, very old, of unknown origin, carrying a peculiar and apparently lifeless powder. The powder-bearing ships had originated outside the galaxy—perhaps from Path Kethona [TT: the Greater Magellanic Cloud].

The powder first produced desirable mutations on the Pheru, a type of pet humans particularly favored. I have long wondered through what devious process the pet's masters discovered this. But ingenuity is often indistinguishable from foolish play, and foolish play is one of those traits I find most endearing about humanity.

The Pheru came from Faun Hakkor, in the same system as Charum Hakkor, one of the key centers of human culture, as well as an amazing collection of massive Precursor artifacts.

Centuries before the beginning of our war, the mutated Pheru entered a new phase and produced spores that infected their masters with the first stage of the Flood. The infection spread rapidly, evolving quickly in its new hosts and weakening humans so severely that early Forerunner victories came with surprising ease.

Humans were, in effect, fighting on two fronts.

But within decades, that situation changed. Humans surged back. Their strength redoubled. Our fleets came upon strong, healthy human populations residing in Flood-infested sectors of the galaxy, apparently unmolested. Humans had obviously found a way to immunize against the Flood, or had developed a natural resistance—or possibly even found a cure.

Yet despite this rebound, Forerunners had taken sufficient advantage of the earlier, troubled period to organize our forces and distribute them to key positions, great in both strength and strategy.

My husband's fleets and warriors made tremendous gains.

The Flood no longer seemed to infect humans, but along the galactic margins, in many other systems, it held its awful sway over thousands of worlds. Wherever the Didact's forces came upon pockets of infection, they burned them out—cauterized them by sheer firepower. The Flood seemed to be quelled—for a time. The Didact and I knew these piecemeal efforts should not have been enough. Lifeworkers calculated that given its virulence and adaptability, the Flood should have overcome our entire galaxy within a few hundred years.

Yet before our eyes, even as humans were being defeated,

the Flood was evaporating like frost on sun-warmed ground. It seemed to deliberately retreat, as if it had established a *pact* with humanity and was sensitive to their change of fortune. Forerunner fleets soon squeezed humanity into a few redoubts. Charum Hakkor held out to the very last.

It seemed for a time that our two greatest enemies were being defeated. But Forerunners could not afford complacency. We knew what the Flood was capable of. There was an overpowering conviction, and not just in the Old Council or among the Builders, that it would return with renewed virulence. And we had no immunity.

We desperately needed to learn how humans had survived the Flood. Captured humans could not be forced to divulge these secrets. Analysis of dead humans revealed little. But the Old Council became convinced a vaccine or cure existed.

And yet they had ordered the destruction of the human race. It was obvious this contradiction had to be resolved.

Already some Builders were laying their own plans for a solution if there was ever a resurgence of the Flood. The culmination of those plans would come thousands of years later, and would be called Halo. Even so, it seemed appropriate—and politically expedient—for a Lifeworker to be put in charge of Flood research.

At that time, my star was rising in line with the Didact's victories. He was a triumphant hero. I was his constant companion, and I had studied Flood-ravaged worlds in detail. I was given the title of Lifeshaper and put in charge of a renewed effort. Understanding the Flood became my responsibility. The Didact approved. It would strengthen his hand in the Council to be allied with me in this matter. And he was always proud of my accomplishments.

His confidence was boundless.

I was ordered to the Capital planet to meet with the Council. Although I had originally supported aggressively dealing with the humans, now I made the Lifeworker case that erasing this species was not only a potential crime against the Mantle, but might impede Flood research. I told the councilors—truthfully enough—that the greatest resource might not be human genetics or even human memory, but the inherent qualities found only in intact populations. Culture, language, population-wide exchanges . . . the subtle discourse of an entire species could ultimately reveal a cure, if any existed. We had to preserve as much of humanity as we could—as much as still remained, most of them suffering through the last stages of resistance on and around Charum Hakkor.

The Old Council saw my logic, but the war had already cost Forerunners much blood and treasure. The councilors insisted that we must balance our quest for a solution to the Flood with other concerns. We had to safeguard against human resurgence.

The Didact as well had mixed feelings, though he rarely expressed them to me—not then. He supported the rule of the Mantle, but as a Promethean he had sworn to preserve Forerunners at all cost. He knew what fierce enemies humans could be, should they escape our forces and rise again to power. Yet even to the Didact, it was obvious preservation of one sort or another was necessary.

The Builders finally came around and agreed with me—in part. They combined forces with Lifeworkers to push hard for a program of relentless research. The Flood, after all, might return and endanger the systems we had captured—reducing Builder profit following the war.

In the end, the Old Council and I struck an awful bargain.

Humans would be reduced to a powerless remnant of their former selves. And Lifeworkers were commanded to use any means necessary to discover the secret of human resistance. There was a strong component of punishment in our instructions—that much was obvious. Our grief burned. It burns still.

The human-Forerunner war ground on to its inevitable conclusion. While the fate of the humans was being finalized, Charum Hakkor held out to a bitter end, sacrificing tens of thousands of ships and millions of lives on both sides.

Then—Forthencho, that awful name, that awful, magnificent presence! Forthencho, Lord of Admirals, the Didact's greatest opponent—surrendered his fleets, disbanded his forces, and awaited whatever we might bring.

———

And so it was that at Charum Hakkor, the Didact and I moved among the captured commanders and warriors and their families, surrounded by those who had fought against us for decades, often bravely, more often still with unique treachery. We could not avoid bitterness—we are only Forerunners, after all. But the cost the humans had paid, and would continue to pay, was horrendous.

The debris of battle lay all around, ruins of human structures but also, visible through the haze and smoke as long slender streaks in the sky, the untouchable and perpetual star roads of the Precursors, placed there more than ten million years before. These gray, eternal whorls stretched to middle orbit, where their rotating bands drew constantly and silently from the neurophysical energy of raw space in ways we still do not understand.

Life—achingly beautiful, impossibly difficult.

What we brought for Lord of Admirals and his last warriors

were the Composers. These large, ugly machines had originally been designed by Builders in a failed attempt to attain immunity against the Flood. Composers broadcast high-energy fields of entangled sympathies to gather victim mentalities—essences—and then translated them into machine data. In the original scheme, new bodies were constructed, and the subjects' essences were imprinted over them—minus any trace of Flood patterns.

The results were not at all satisfactory. In fact, they were horrible. The Forerunner bodies so treated did not live very long. None survived outside of mechanical storage.

But here—Composers were all we had. All we were given. Builders and vengeful councilors made sure of that.

The hundreds of thousands of humans still alive on Charum Hakkor were handed over to Lifeworkers to be studied, probed, analyzed molecule by molecule, thought by thought, down to their very cells—and then subjected to the wide-ranging, rippling fields of Composers.

After the Composers had done their work, draining these last survivors, these exhausted and dying warriors, of their memories and patterns, their remains were reduced to scattered atoms. It was manifest holocaust. Once the second greatest fighting civilization and species in the galaxy, humans were stomped down, reduced, effectively eliminated as a threat.

Throughout, the hardest part was processing the human children. They had been formed into their own cadres, given their own defensive orders. Raised in times of continuous war, they seemed to understand what was about to happen better than their elders. I remember their wise eyes, unafraid, terrible.

CATALOG NOTE: The Lifeshaper's ancilla transfers sensory data recorded at the time described. What Catalog glimpses of Composer procedures is disturbing. I have never directly witnessed such events. And yet, even this does not rise to the level of a crime against the Mantle.

Not yet.

LIBRARIAN

Despite our feverish preparations, Builders and the Old Council had kept the Flood's existence secret from the great centers of Forerunner population, ostensibly to avoid panic during time of war.

Most of the ecumene celebrated a newfound security, unaware even of the existence of the Flood.

The second part of my deal with the Council, to preserve humans as a potentially renewable species, required a selection of intact and vital specimens. Thousands more were extracted from hiding in shattered redoubts around the conquered human territories and carried to Erde-Tyrene, which even today exhibits the fossil remains of humanity's most ancient ancestors.

Yet while honoring my request, the Old Council insisted that the last surviving humans were to be *devolved*. Human epigenetics would be played backward, reversing their time-enriched evolutionary music. Individuals, the Council mandated, would be forced to consciously experience this reversal, as a reminder and balance for their arrogance and cruelty.

Each and every day, for months, my specimens felt their bodies lose memory, complexity, mass—and finally, intelligence.

The Council and the Builders then put another, even stranger twist on my hopes to preserve human cultural patterns. As the humans devolved, the Composer-gathered personalities and memories of their fellows at Charum Hakkor would be holographically stored within their changing flesh. Not active, but dormant—thus avoiding the consequences of Composer decay.

Each devolved human would in effect carry the memories of tens of thousands of their kind, preserved for future study and investigation—and passed along to their offspring.

Those same memories and personalities would also be transferred to machine storage and subjected to constant rote interrogation—creating a library of enslaved ghosts subjected to mechanized torment for thousands of years to come. Thus, the Council believed, the secret to human resistance to the Flood would eventually be found.

Our perverse nod to the Mantle exhibited cruelty far beyond simple extinction. The Builders had gained practically everything they wished for. But that did not stop another and very different war from breaking out—between my husband and the Master Builder.

Powerful forces within the Council and among Warrior-Servants still supported the Didact's strategy for containing the Flood: hundreds of enormous Shield Worlds, placed at key locations around the galaxy to both survey for Flood incursions and conduct carefully chosen, system-wide operations. The Didact had worked with me to provide these huge constructs with a tremendous capacity to preserve imperiled species—on a localized basis.

Thus, he said, his defenses did not violate the Rule of the Mantle. Unlike the Master Builder's proposed Halos, the Shield Worlds did not require a great extinction, and in fact they could be used as immense refuges in time of crisis.

In response, the Master Builder ordered that his Halos also

be adapted to support and preserve species. Playing politics better than any of us, the Master Builder knew that this removed the Council's last objection to his Halo strategy—the threat of violating the Mantle, of destroying the galaxy in order to save it.

Worse, in asking me to design these sanctuaries, a request I could not refuse, I was perceived as working with the Master Builder, against the wishes of my husband.

The Master Builder, sensing a winning strategy, now volunteered that the great extragalactic factory used to manufacture Halos, known as the Ark, would also safely carry protected populations—at tremendous expense and great profit for Builders. Builders heartily approved.

And he suggested that a second Ark be constructed, in secret, to expand that role. More species could be saved, more Halos could be made. Additionally, all of the problems now apparent with the first Ark could be addressed.

The choices my husband and I faced were narrowing. Politically, our paths would soon diverge.

———

Life roils with competition, death, and replacement, from the tide pool borders of our natal ocean to the farthest stars. Its cruelty and creativity are interwoven.

And yet this was a time—far from the first time—when Forerunner defiance of the dictates of the Mantle pushed us perilously close to tyranny, desecration, and—I use the oldest of our words here—*outrage*.

We had the excuse that Lifeworkers and Warrior-Servants were not in supreme power, that the Old Council was being managed by Builders, that even the Juridicals were under their sway . . . And that the Flood might again place the entire galaxy in peril.

But was even all of that justification enough?

———————

The Builders made the first Ark and the earliest Halo installations . . . large revolving rings, thirty thousand kilometers in diameter, capable of sustaining millions if not billions of organisms on their inner surfaces. Paradises for research, in one way—but designed ultimately to destroy all life for hundreds of thousands of light-years around.

The Old Council had the wisdom at least to delay construction of the second Ark. No need to make the Builders too powerful to be controlled.

The last physically intact humans arrived on Erde-Tyrene. They were very few, much fewer than I had planned. Almost immediately, I began my program of rebuilding their populations—away from the critical eye of the Master Builder, the Council, and even the Didact.

In this familiar environment, my humans thrived. In fact, they demonstrated an astonishing, almost supernatural resilience. To the shock of my Lifeworkers, the reverted humans bred to more and more advanced forms over just a thousand years, diverging into distinct varieties like a bush blooming with a thousand brilliant flowers. Their numbers grew as well, from thousands to hundreds of thousands to millions.

I could not explain this effect. I sought for it in their genetics, and found nothing. Was there something else at work here—something that had somehow remained hidden from us?

My humans soon gathered into bands, tribes, villages. Tilled the soil and raised crops. Took wolves and goats and sheep, cattle, birds, and charmed them into domestication. Made many tools, developed crude trade and industry.

Within a thousand years, some of them reminded me of the Lord of Admirals.

Others—of the wise-eyed children . . .

I kept their extraordinary progress hidden from the Old Council and the Builders. I did not tell my husband. Erde-Tyrene was far outside the usual runnels of Forerunner commerce. I removed my Lifeworkers, trimming their numbers to a few, and then, to none. The planet became a forgotten backwater.

Every now and then, I dropped by in person to study their progress. I gave them all my *geas*, my mark of instruction, utility and pride. I wished to be remembered. My own existence seemed so frail, after what we had done. When I worked with the humans, studying their genetics and personalities, I could almost forget the larger conflicts that loomed.

But that time was also spent away from my husband, and his difficulties were growing. The Didact continued to stubbornly promote his Shield Worlds, demonstrating their effectiveness again and again to Council audiences. He continued to make dangerous enemies.

As for the memories of his victories . . . they slipped into the past.

They dimmed.

The Master Builder brilliantly chipped away at the Didact's remaining base of support. The political war between Builders and Warrior-Servants came to a head. Warrior-Servants were reduced as a rate. Many moved to the Builder rate, taking on the role of Builder Security. The insult was obvious—but at least they survived, found prosperity, and became of value to the new regime.

And then came the final blow. Juridicals ruled against my

husband. The Didact was found in contempt of the Council, ordered to stop making Shield Worlds, turn over his records and ancillas, end his planning, and submit to the authority of the Builders—and in particular to Faber, the Master Builder.

The Didact refused.

Even as my humans revived classic forms, then flowered into new and unexpected variations, the possibility grew to certainty that I would have to proceed alone, because of the my husband's pending exile—or execution.

last saw the Didact on our estate around Far Nomdagro, a small orange star seven light-years from the Capital system. We shared this world with a million Warrior-Servants. Many of our neighbors were already pulling up their estates and families, abandoning their birth rate to enlist in Builder Security.

Nomdagro was temperate, ancient of birth and low of mountains, half-ocean and half-land. I suppose by comparison our estate was humble, but I had never lived anywhere more luxurious. Unlike Lifeworkers, Warrior-Servants were not inclined to live frugally.

The Didact, when he designed our nuptial house, demonstrated a style some would call severe, but still inclined to majesty. I have seen ancient fortresses with less grandeur. Our central quarters were cut from blocks of lava filled with the fossils of Nomdagro's only indigenous species, a lovely variety of silicon worm, long since extinct. They seemed to have swum through the lava before it cooled, but that had likely not been the case; more true to imagine them having died in great, contorted coils, their immensely strong cuticles and cartilaginous members resisting as the lava washed over, entombing them until masons split the solid blocks.

The Didact had picked those stones with me in mind, and they *were* lovely, in a forbidding sort of way. The fossils bore enough residual thorium and uranium to glow softly at night, lighting our way as we went to that last supper before he entered his Cryptum.

I remember those hours with crystal clarity. An associate of Haruspis had been called and had arrived the night before. Those were brilliant nights indeed. An unstable star on the far side of the Orion complex had supernovaed one hundred years before. That long-traveling radiation was now, to our eyes, lighting up the vast nebula, washing over the far-spreading clouds and wisps of gas as if in preternatural warning.

"A well-chosen occasion. The delay of space is profound," the Haruspis's associate intoned. Its attitude—it was a self-gelding like all associates—irritated the Didact. More so was my husband annoyed by the implication that we might have chosen this occasion to highlight the occasion, to *grandstand*.

Still, he controlled himself, and faced off with the associate under the burning streamers of yellow and orange and deep purple. At the associate's signal, the Didact's armor lifted from his hard light under-sheath, uncoiling and separating, protruding wedges and spikes as if preparing for battle—and then slumped into a compact egg.

The Didact lifted his hands to receive the cup containing the first full measure of *inchukoa* and drank it back in one swallow.

This began the process of living desiccation.

Our conversation around that spare supper was mostly gentle and loving. The Didact and I had been a highly unsuitable match, and yet we had been married for thousands of years. What some might have interpreted as disagreement, debate, barely contained irritation or competition, was in fact the fire of our deepest love. We still took delight in the sparks we struck.

I remember this so clearly. . . .

Household monitors arranged towels and cups around the Didact's chair as his skin wept salty drops. The skin of his broad, noble face stretched tight.

Face glistening—shedding his water—flesh turning to leather, blood a glassy gel.

His speech became slow and precise; he had difficulty moving his lips. "I hate to abandon you," he said. "If there was another way . . ." He shook his great head and reached to massage a shrinking shoulder. His skin, normally gray and rich purple, had darkened to reddish brown.

And then he smiled—most unexpectedly. I had not seen him smile since we had been Manipulars, and did not know he still had it in him. Perhaps the mature musculature was being liberated by this awful process. Perhaps he was simply expressing a final ironic amusement.

"I know you've made plans best carried out in my absence," he said.

"Our own plans are not finished," I said.

"There will be many voices," the Didact said. "The Master Builder may not find me, but that does not mean he won't find a means by which to invoke my support."

"He will hold off such treachery for a good long while," I suggested.

"And if he does not, still you'll carry out your pact with him."

"Probably."

"To save your beloved species."

"Yes."

"And your humans."

"Those as well."

"Even those who killed our children."

"You told me it was honorable, that they fought well—and you agreed this was our best strategy."

"You agreed too quickly." Again that odd, tightening smile. The Didact meant his words kindly. The pain we had suffered during the long war—and the loss—had inured us to such recrimination. Our children had followed the way of their Warrior-Servant father. They had proved themselves capable and courageous. It was the Warrior's creed within the Mantle to honor one's finest enemies, and humans had been that. "I sometimes wish you were more bloody-minded, more vengeful, Wife."

"Not the way of the Warrior or of the Mantle—and of course not mine."

"Of course."

The Didact's discomfort increased. He swallowed half of the second cup of *inchukoa,* then lifted the cup and turned it in his fingers. "The ecumene has become confused. The Council steeps itself in lies and dishonor. But . . . you foresee my return, in one form or another, and the resumption of our struggle."

"There is often a sickness before the purge."

"That sounds gross *and* bloody-minded." He returned the cup to his lips and swallowed the last measure. "I am reminded of why I sought our love in the first place."

"*You* sought it?"

"I did."

"That isn't how *I* remember it, Warrior. An unlikely love, at any rate—so your fellows said."

"But we knew. As you have instructed me often, we play out our parts in Living Time and accept all that life brings, and all that it takes away. So we support the Mantle: *Daaowa maadthu.*"

His use of that human phrase, so ancient and fraught with meaning, caught me by surprise.

He added, "The humans . . . Had they been willing to acknowledge their crimes, they would have made a great civilization, worthy to join our own. But they did not. I hope that what remains of them, in your care, does not disappoint you. My anger would then be impossible to control."

The Didact's aide returned with the Haruspis's associate close behind. The associate peered around the hall with a critical squint. Display of wealth and power was exquisitely distasteful to those who served the Domain.

"Didact, you must recline and complete the vitrifaction, before we move you to your Cryptum," the aide said. She stood in a submissive posture that could be interpreted as the first stage of mourning—something the Didact had forbidden. But he could not bring himself to correct her.

Monitors brought forward a hovering bed, shaping to support his shrunken frame. He rose with some difficulty. I could hardly bear to look at him. But I knew this was nothing close to death—though it would bring a separation of centuries, while he lay in a meditative trance and while that awful political purge worked its way through the Forerunner body.

While the Master Builder ultimately overreached, as we knew he would, and the return of the Flood would compel the Didact's revival.

I walked beside my husband as he was carried to the Cryptum.

The glow of the far supernova had dimmed, as all had known it would. The farther one is from astronomical events, the less surprise.

The Haruspis's associate spoke the words, in middle Digon, which would help the Didact focus on his long meditation: enchanting, musical words we all hoped might open access, if the Domain was so disposed, if the Didact was so disposed, to higher experience and greater awareness.

The words penetrated my husband's discomfort. He tried to reach for me. I saw his effort and stroked his face, his naked arm. Already his flesh, rapidly cooling, felt like rock. His eyes tracked with increasing difficulty the shadowy figures around him. Soon he would see and hear and feel nothing of this world. He would be connected to us by the barest metaphysical thread.

One step away from death itself.

One step from knowing all.

We delivered the Didact to the elliptical hatch, opening wide like the mouth of an eyeless fish; only we who were flesh. Neither monitors nor ancillas were allowed to participate.

The Didact stared straight up as he vanished from our sight.

CATALOG

The Librarian pauses.

We have traveled inward to the central hold. There is much activity here. Ancillas are delivering a new selection of humans. The Lifeshaper watches closely as they are aligned shoulder to shoulder in restraining fields. Male and female, young and old, they are briefly roused and released.

"They believe they have been transported to a better place," she says, in the same tone of voice she used to describe the Domain: reverential, but with a shadow of deeper guilt.

I can barely discern the luminous edges of the environment projected to keep them calm. "An afterlife?" I ask.

"They believe so. I came to all of them at birth. They believe when they see me next, I will lift them from trouble and pain. In a way, that is true."

A light appears over her head. The humans in the hold turn as one and behold the Librarian. Their faces transform. The hold is filled with echoes of wonder as they crowd forward, trying to communicate their joy, their hope.

The light above the Librarian dims. The fields return, separate the humans, and again numb them, at this high moment of joy, to their plight.

"Life is resilient—particularly human life," the Lifeshaper says. I can barely hear her, she speaks so softly. "They will be taken to the Ark."

I cannot stifle a sense of awe and even affront. Such power—such hubris! And yet, without the Lifeshaper's intervention, all humans would have died long before.

She does what she can.

"They feel no pain, no distress. Composers are no longer used by any of our teams. Their memories and genetic patterns will be carried in the flesh of all their descendants, when Erde-Tyrene is repopulated. In that way, they will touch eternity. But their existence here is ending."

The humans rise like bubbles in a pond and swing around an immense, glowing blue flower, undergoing deep examination. Their faces go slack. The bodies are then consumed by brilliant purple flares, and the remains compacted to be returned to the oceans of Erde-Tyrene—not as ashes, burned and degraded, but rich nutrients that will feed minute organisms in the sea during the great sweep of Halo radiation.

When the hundreds of thousands of humans collected in the last few hours are processed, she lifts us from the hold and wraps us both in cooling darkness.

"I pity future scholars. They will notice nothing here to explain what happened—neither an increase in the fossil record nor any other evidence of a great die-off. Now . . . the time has come to describe what I found in Path Kethona. May I tell that story?"

No permission is necessary. I am Catalog.

I listen.

THE LIBRARIAN

Things did not improve after my husband vanished.

The Master Builder regarded my partnership as a liability. To maintain our status, such as it was, and to uphold our few remaining privileges, we needed to remain essential to both the Council and Builders.

I proposed to the Council that we seek out the truth about the Flood: its origins, its vulnerabilities, its motivations—if any.

For thousands of years, based on where the Flood struck in our galaxy, many had theorized it originated in one of the smaller local galaxies, Path Kethona, and in particular a huge, filamentary nebula ripe with birthing suns called the Spider [TT: Tarantula Nebula].

According to legend, Path Kethona was first visited by Forerunners during our greatest period of exploration, over ten million years ago. Yet there was substantial doubt that voyage had ever happened. Records had long ago vanished. Not even Haruspis, entrusted with studying the Domain, could access those memories.

In any case, the Domain, in time, converts history into truth beyond the understanding of most Forerunners. To establish the kind of truth we could understand, we would need to recreate that first great voyage.

We would need to go there.

I am not comfortable with the spaces between suns, much less between galaxies. My love and expertise lies in the immensity within—the unbounded inner roil of a cell, the tight-packed jostling of hundreds of thousands of molecules cooperating and competing at once, all unaware that their activities, massed together, open doorways to even greater immensities: you, me, all living things.

The greatest galaxies are nothing without our inner immensity, which opens our eyes to their light, our senses to their warmth, and our minds to their challenge.

Stars I understand. They shed light and give life. It is the emptiness between that haunts me. Space has its own textures and mysteries. Forerunners draw power from the perpetual rise and fall of ghostly particles that have no true existence—until they are harvested. We draw power as well from the interstices of space itself, where space and time form the tiniest little knots of uncertainty and dimension.

But emptiness without sensation, the unobserved vastness between suns, brings me nightmares. I am happiest on a teeming planet, surrounded by aggressions and consumptions and births and all the colliding webs of observation and fixation. Reality for me begins with the small. . . .

But inevitably it must end with the very large.

Soon after the Didact was safely hidden, I went before the Council with a plan for an intergalactic fast transport, a vessel so extraordinary it would enrich Builders across the Forerunner galaxy.

I had learned well how to play this particular game of Council politics. For Builders, contracts meant everything, and my challenge combined elements they found irresistible: re-creating the greatness of our past, harnessing new technologies, and accessing the immense resources of the ecumene to stuff Builder coffers.

As well, the mission's goal was direct and compelling. This would be a Lifeworker-sponsored expedition. Neither the Builders nor the Old Council could deny that Lifeworkers were most devoted to preserving and understanding life. However strange, the Flood was a living thing, or mass of things, and so it was well within our purview to study it and try to understand.

And so my expedition—whether it was the second, or the first—was designed to once and for all confirm the extragalactic origin of the Flood. That sealed the deal with both the Old Council and the Builders.

Builders have always been superb shipwrights. The construction took ten years. Permission from the Old Council to make the journey took another ten.

I understood their delay.

Travel across even a few light-years through a portal or jump requires mending breaches in causality. Forerunner ships crossing between systems create a buildup of space-time resistance, a polluting effect that gradually limits both transport and communication—and may also interfere with access to the

Domain. When the buildup is eliminated—as reconciliations are made and aftereffects fade into the quantum background—more journeys become possible.

But moving even a single small ship over one hundred and sixty thousand light-years in just a few jumps, without long pauses, creates a monumental backup. The journey to Path Kethona could slow or even halt transportation throughout the ecumene for over a year. Nevertheless, the intrigue of making history and solving one of the greatest mysteries was irresistible. Builders worked hard to forge consensus, as I knew they would.

That a Lifeworker was in command—worse still, a Lifeworker associated with the Didact—was an irritation, but not insurmountable. Who else was more qualified to study the origins of the Flood? Or understand the nature of Precursor beginnings? For of course the Precursors themselves were believed to have traveled to our galaxy from Path Kethona, billions of years ago.

We christened our ship *Audacity*. Less than one hundred meters in length and thirty across the beam—modest, lightly armed. A crew of seven, including me: one Miner, three adventurous Builders, and two Lifeworkers were selected from well over a million volunteers.

No Juridicals joined our crew. At that point, there was no reason to suspect we were about to uncover the greatest crime in Forerunner history.

———

Our ship emerged from its second jump, the middle distance—eighty-seven million light-years from the Orion complex, sixty million light-years from the irregular margins of our galaxy. I stood on the transparent bridge, surrounded by the dim specks of far galaxies, and for a horrid moment, imagined my spirit set free to wander home at a walking pace, utterly alone, barely recognizing the impossibly distant and freezing haze of our home galaxy.

The Didact would have reveled in such vastness. Perhaps in his Cryptum, he was even more isolated, more directly in tune with the singing whine of the indescribable that flows around our lives.

Emptiness.

Vastation.

Nothingness.

Humans believe in nothingness, in zeros. It is one of their distinguishing traits. They keep inventing nothing. Forerunners know otherwise. Even where there is very little matter, each cubic centimeter of space is crossed by a crucial density of radiation, fundamentally linked with far places and ancient times.

Audacity paused before its next jump, giving those external feelers, those entangled ray-traces, a chance to adjust to our intrusion. To reconcile. We had all heard stories of bold journeys ending badly. Space-time, we've been reliably informed, forms something like a bruise or clot around ships that consistently outrace their own reality. We were certainly in that category. We dared not even attempt to communicate our success—that might have tipped the scales.

For that and other reasons, objectively—within our frame— the journey would take far longer than one might think, considering our jumps could in theory have been instantaneous. We were at the mercy of healing space-time.

We would not know how long we had been gone, from our old frame's reference, until we returned.

Months. A year.

Longer.

The last half of the journey I spent in slumber, wrapped in a slowly rotating cocoon of loose sheets. Occasionally I would rise from this dreamless sleep and try to remember my husband's face. Then the faces of our children. I would fail on both counts.

An ancilla could have refreshed that memory. Armor could have supplied me with all our time spent together. I availed myself of neither.

My crew wisely set their slumbers to last until near the end of the journey.

———

A chiming sound.

Time to come to full alertness.

I ignored the alarm for as long as *Audacity* allowed. Then, small monitors entered my cabin and snipped away the silken layers of my cocoon.

We had not yet arrived. One more jump would be made.

My fellow travelers were making themselves useful in an antechamber to the bridge. I stepped between darting sounds and flowing images, a bird swarm of diagnostics and discoveries, revealing the ship's relief at surviving so far, over so few long jumps.

The crew also celebrated, threw aside their armor, embraced, slapped flesh awake, confounding the little monitors trying to assess their health.

The seven slowly became aware of me and grew quiet as I moved forward.

Keeper-of-Tools, an arrogant young Builder, came up to assure me all was well. Clearance-of-Old-Forests, a Miner of one of our most ancient clades, passed out cups of celebratory nectar dosed with restoratives. He doubled the dose for my two Lifeworkers, Chant-to-Green and Birth-to-Light. Somehow, they looked less fit than either the Builders or the Miner. No surprise. I felt it, too. Out here, the aura of Living Time—the sea within which Life-workers swim like fish—was very thin indeed.

"Apologies, Lifeshaper," Clearance said. "You've had a hard journey."

I accepted my own double dose of restorative. "Do I look sickly?" I asked.

"You do," Clearance said with that blunt lack of decorum common among Miners.

"No apologies," I said. "You must feel lost as well, out here."

"I do," Clearance admitted. "No planets, no stone or magma— nothing! Watched by a trillion tiny eyes in the dark." He shuddered.

We sipped until all seemed well enough, though exhausted.

"We are farther from other Forerunners than anyone in verified history," Keeper said. "All honor to those who crafted *Audacity!*"

We toasted these Builders with the last of our nectar, and the crew resumed armor. Birth-to-Light was already evaluating the fresher light from Path Kethona. A second-form Lifeworker, she was capable and experienced; we had worked together many times before.

"Looks barren," she said.

A practiced eye can detect the effects of advanced civilizations on a starfield, as technologies harness and affect the raw radiation emitted by so many stars. And fresher light carries more information, more detectable entanglements. The light from these stars was less than a thousand years old.

"Perhaps," said Chant-to-Green, our youngest. "But it'll take time to know for sure." I had taken a special liking to Chant; earnest and focused, with an intensity that hid her naivety, she reminded me of my own daughter, lost at Charum Hakkor. That one had of course been a Warrior-Servant. Still, Chant-to-Green was like the daughter I might have had, had I not married outside my rate. . . .

I made my own measurements. The stars indeed appeared untouched, color shifts entirely natural. I could not be as sensitive as the instruments wielded by *Audacity,* but my instincts told me that this small satellite galaxy was as close to lifeless as any region of stars I had ever experienced.

"It *feels* young," said Dawn-over-Fields, our second Builder, the quietest of our group and the oldest, other than myself.

"Youth can last billions of years for a galaxy," I reminded them. "Civilizations burn like grass fires on a dry prairie. Suns explode and kill. Nebulas spread new elements and seed new suns . . . and it all begins again. Our own galaxy has gone through many such cycles. We are just the latest."

I had been about to say "the last."

The last leg of our journey, a few thousand light-years, was accomplished without incident. But the most strenuous phase of *Audacity's* reconciliation forced us back into armor and sleep for many hours.

That completed, Keeper and Dawn confirmed the ship's fitness.

A detailed sensor sweep of the satellite galaxy's billions of stars again revealed no communications of any variety known to Forerunners. Path Kethona appeared free of technological civilizations, and based on a close-in analysis of the few planetary systems, free of most forms of life as well.

The focus of our probing expedition was to be a star deep within Path Kethona, on the outskirts of the Spider nebula. This star had over a million years ago attracted the attention of a female of the now-subsumed rate called Theoreticals. She had been called Boundless. Soon after her death, her rate had been forcibly merged with the Builders.

Boundless had persisted in her studies throughout her long life, in defiance of Warrior orders. The reason why Warriors wanted this particular star left unstudied was never explained. Perhaps they didn't themselves know. She was finally prosecuted for her defiance—I assume by Juridicals.

Perhaps you know of her case. No? Conveniently lost or forgotten, I suppose. Those millennia were harsh times indeed.

Her studies were suppressed, and she herself forced to enter a Cryptum that turned out to be defective, perhaps sabotaged. A thousand years after she entered, her Cryptum was opened, her death discovered, and her remains quietly disposed of by a small group of former students.

There is an odd story that for tens of thousands of years after her death, Haruspis kept finding her suppressed information floating to the fore in Domain studies. The Domain was favoring her, some claimed—but those tales are now considered legendary.

Still, I have always wondered.

A century before the Didact entered his Cryptum, I found a hard copy of Boundless's studies preserved in the collection of a former Theoretical on Keth Sidon. Reading this copy, I was curious as to how all the odd facts Boundless had compiled about Path Kethona seemed to fit into a hypothesis emerging from my studies of human genetics.

Humans very likely originated on Erde-Tyrene. But they long ago abandoned that world and moved outward, setting up population centers around two other suns dozens of light-years away, then stringing outposts across almost thirty thousand light-years, out toward the margin of our galaxy.

Forerunners were aware of humans, of course, and tracked their growing populations, their predatory colonial habits. At that time, our boundaries did not merge. Humans were likely to be very troublesome, many thought—but not then. Not yet.

In just a few centuries those human outposts became very populous indeed and would later, during the following conflicts, absorb the brunt of early attacks by the Flood.

But who else had been aware of humans long before the Flood—of humans and perhaps also of Forerunners?

Keeper approached me and said, in a low voice, "We are on the lookout for neural physics architecture, true?"

"True enough."

"We're assuming that Precursors also reached out this far."

"Assume nothing," I said. "But search . . . yes."

We now made six closely spaced jumps of a few light-years apiece. At the last jump, *Audacity* opened a small portal from which we might later choose, at will, a wide conical selection of future jumps.

In case we needed to depart Path Kethona quickly.

For many hours, we drifted in and out of the shock wave of our chosen star's plume of ionized plasma, waving and furling over ten billion kilometers like an immense candle flame dancing in a soft breeze, as it intersected the more diffuse but steady output of a local cluster of suns.

"Four rocky planets," Keeper announced. The small crew showed little outward excitement. Young and self-impressed, I thought, but still keeping taut discipline.

"And five anomalous masses," Dawn added, pointing them out in virtual perspective.

"You theorized these masses existed before the sensors reported them," I said. "How?"

"Slight deviations in the starfield. Very slight."

"And perturbations in the orbits of two planets," Keeper said, nodding in admiration at his crewmate's sensitivity.

"They're uniform in mass, appear to be uniform in diameter. . . . Could be failed stars," Dawn suggested.

"Perhaps," Keeper said. "But failed stars still release heat, if not visible light. These masses are colder than the interstellar void."

The quiet that followed was properly respectful. We were thinking the same thoughts. We had seen similar masses before—in our schooling. Only a few still existed in our home galaxy.

"Precursor anchors?" Keeper asked.

"No visible bridges or threads linking them, or out between the stars," Dawn said. "Not in this system. Not now."

Even dormant, such constructs were thought to be unstable—perhaps dangerous. *Audacity*'s ancilla supplied us with records of previous Forerunner encounters. They were not encouraging. Ships vanishing . . . Surviving crews requiring extensive protogeometric therapy to return their minds to a proper neural topology.

My crew was unsettled, but undeterred.

"We'll approach with caution," I suggested.

Keeper and Dawn linked their armor to mine, and together with *Audacity* we plotted a fine course across the two billion kilometers that separated us from the closest dark mass.

As a precaution, our armor locked our positions and reduced our chemistry. During the next few days, as our vessel followed a long hyperbolic orbit to the nearest cold, dark mass, we allowed *Audacity* to refresh our memories on Precursor architecture and all the other mysterious artifacts Forerunners had encountered, some of them billions of years old.

Assuming nothing . . . and yet knowing, as if by instinct, that we were close to the heart of a controversy that had perplexed Forerunners for hundreds of thousands of years.

Was Path Kethona the source of the Precursors? Or had it been the birth galaxy of another great, more primary race, active even before the Precursors . . . Or a race before *that,* on and on back through time to the great Glow itself?

Minds simmering under the tutelage of our ancillas, our bodies moved slow as glass as our ship plunged deeper into the system.

The Juridical Network briefly opens, and Catalog takes the opportunity to send what it has gathered, then to supplement its understanding of the Librarian's testimony.

In another system, Juridicals have deposed the Ur-Didact. Catalog is provided selections relevant to the Lifeshaper's testimony, but she cannot be informed of his survival.

UR-DIDACT

After the capture of my ship in the San'Shyuum quarantine system, the Master Builder locked me into a weapons-grade stasis bubble, like some dangerous bomb.

I have no awareness of the time between.

Then: the deafening peal of a great bell, followed by a smoky ozone stench. The bubble collapsed. All the years of pent-up time rushed in at once and singed my outer skin. That is the way of such bubbles; they are designed to contain and render harmless more than to delicately preserve.

Dropping to the floor in a heap, I wiped a thin layer of ash from around my eyes and tried to estimate, from my weakness, how long I had been in the bubble. My eyes would not focus. My arms and legs trembled. I could barely rise to my feet.

At least a year.

I was aboard a ship—not small, apparently deserted. The bubble had been abandoned in long-term stowage. The compartment had a physical hatch, not locked; lighting dim. Sounds not encouraging: ratcheting, ragged ticking, distant, mournful scraping. An old vessel in poor repair.

Still gathering my wits, I stumbled out of the compartment and down a curving hallway to a transit tube. The tube refused to work. Pressing against the tube's sides, I twisted and wormed my way to the next open compartment—another stowage area.

Here I found four more military-grade stasis bubbles shoved into a corner. By the thin whine they made, and the flickering view of their contents, I judged they would soon collapse as mine had.

I pulled and shoved the bubbles apart and stood between them on the deck, watching their opacities flow like clouds in a sky.

Gradually, I dimly made out a Builder, still wearing armor. The second, possibly a member of Builder Security, without armor—caught halfway between Warrior-Servant physiology and a newer pattern.

The third, in its carapace: Catalog. A Juridical gatherer of information. Of little use in the present circumstance. Juridicals and I have never gotten along. They dogged our every movement in the last phases of the human-Forerunner war.

No sign of the Manipular I had imprinted, nor of the two humans who had accompanied us. Given the Master Builder's temper and his obsession with fighting the Flood, I suspect they were delivered to one of his research centers and met a bad end.

For the moment, I left the bubbles where they were and made my way to what I assumed was an inboard helm, a compartment ill-lit, bleak, and filthy with layers of organic debris.

Deserted.

Worse and worse. An unauthorized trading ship or some piece of confiscated junk. At least it was Forerunner. I climbed to the next level, the main bridge.

A restless unease in my gut warned me that gravity on these decks might fail at any moment. Very dangerous—gravity gradients are not to be ignored. I could be slammed up or thrown sideways, smashed to a pulp. As any warrior will tell you, unbalanced gravity is a [TT: expletive, possibly sacrilegious, untranslatable].

I walked around the bridge. The equipment was older than the ships we had fought with at Charum Hakkor. The Master Builder was nothing if not frugal with the way he disposed of his enemies. I wondered where he had found this one—perhaps in some surplus yard on an outlying planet, or a salvage orbit around one of his construction facilities.

I shouted instructions. No response. No ancilla presented itself either to assist or to deny me access.

Pushing aside dust and desiccated scraps of what might have been flesh, I spit onto a clear panel to clear what looked like dried blood. Clearly this vessel had seen desperate action. But what sort?

Through the smeared panel, lights faintly glowed. I swiped the surface again. The lights brightened—then flickered, threatened to go dark. The ship was still functioning—but just barely.

At least the air was not freezing—and still breathable, but dense, stale.

How far had we traveled, for how long, and from where?

To where?

A disquieting thought . . . That we had been sent on a long journey to no system in particular, moving at less than light speed, without benefit of jump or portal. When the power to the stasis bubbles declined, mine opened—to release me into a limbo of slow decline and death.

Was it possible I had underestimated the moral degeneracy or the raging fury of the Master Builder?

The panel lights glowed brighter. I danced my fingers over the panel and managed to summon a grainy display of what lay forward of the ship: a planetary limb, reddish and angry. I thought I recognized a distinctive swirl of continents, like paint stirred with a stick—a unique tectonic formation. This could be Uthera Midgeerrd, on the extreme outer reaches of the Forerunner ecumene, less than a hundred light-years from the unpatrolled borders of the galactic margin.

Before I entered the Cryptum, Uthera had been regarded as a far-flung outpost of Forerunner culture and design, distinctly anti-Builder in its sympathies, populated by half-renegade Miners and others who had deserted their rates. Perhaps the Master

Builder found delicious irony in sending a Promethean to this undisciplined place.

Movement behind me. I turned to see a face peer over the rim of the transit tube. With a slow, cold shock, I recognized a fellow veteran of the human wars, a commander of one of my tactical squadrons—known at the time as Sharp-by-Striking.

"Distinguished company!" he murmured. "Is this the veritable Didact, come to join me in exile?" He pulled himself into the compartment and stretched his arms. He appeared much reduced by hardship—paler, very thin. "There are still two others . . . Harsh stasis. Doesn't look good down there."

We approached each other warily, then crossed arms, caught up in ancient emotions—not all of them pleasant. Sharp had opposed my grand strategy and been instrumental in convincing the Old Council my Shield Worlds were unworkable.

All that, of course, meant nothing now.

He peered at the display. "Is that Uthera?" he asked. "Not encouraging. I've served on Flood watch on one hulk after another for almost a century, a thousand light-years and more from here. Now . . . Uthera! My well-deserved reward for serving Builders. But you! I had heard rumors. Released from your Cryptum . . ."

"Our situation," I interrupted, with the gentlest command voice. "Tell me what you know."

"Well, for one, we're in a Burn," he said with an unhappy click.

"I don't know what that is."

"No ancillas, no armor . . ." He examined his hands and curled his fingers as if they were unfamiliar. "Weak as newborns. A Burn is a thema or margin arc lost to the Flood. This entire system is infested. Likely every surrounding system as well, for dozens of light-years." He dropped his shoulders. "Once you trained me, Didact. I have failed. I am yours to punish as you see fit."

I have difficulty forgiving those who have brought harm to those I respect and admire. But Sharp-by-Striking was a pitiful shadow of what he had once been.

As for myself—

Little better.

"Looks like we're stuck with each other," I said. "You know this hulk and what it's capable of?"

He drew himself up again and took a deep breath.

"A Builder reject, stockpiled against direct orders to scuttle and send to salvage. It should have been recycled long ago. Instead, it's been put to use where success was unlikely, to replace newer, far more expensive ships. I've served on several. Hard duty, Didact." He swallowed and grimaced. "Builders are ever driven by power and profit. I did my best to serve the ecumene."

"No doubt," I said.

Now Sharp turned his own self-loathing into cold, outward anger, an old tactic among Warriors who had survived defeat. "Someone has to have ordered this one into the Burn, against any sensible plan. If there are other vessels . . . they might have all been overtaken, commandeered by the Flood, used to spread contagion." His eyes narrowed and he groaned deep in his chest. "We're on a plague ship!"

The look of utter horror on his features unsettled my innards even more than the fluctuating gravity. "We don't know that," I said.

"The others . . . Still in stasis. They might be infected!"

"We don't know *that,* either."

"In the early stages of infection . . . all you might see would be a tiny patch, a blemish, a single tendril!"

He coughed and then doubled up in a spasm. Clearly he had been treated badly before being discarded. The air was getting worse. My own lungs and throat felt tight.

Sharp's spasm subsided. "My weakness has passed, Didact," he said. "It is good to serve you again. If you will have me."

We regarded each other for a somber moment. Sharp-by-Striking in his best days had been a serviceable commander. Something of a talker, however.

"We are where we are," I said. "Let's learn what we can."

He went to the controls and, muttering Warrior curses, pure and sweet to our ears, began to slam and cajole the controls, until the balky old hulk grudgingly did its best to respond. The direct view panels opened and we looked across the full expanse of Uthera.

"Not good," Sharp said.

Slowly, an old ancilla struggled to revive, appearing first as a spinning disk, then as a headless torso with floating, staring eyes. "Pardon me," it said. "I am designed to represent the combined intelligence of four vessels. I will respond only to a flotilla commander."

"A flotilla sub-metarch is common," Sharp explained in a weary undertone. "None of these ships had the resources to fight alone."

"None of our other ships are responsive," the ancilla said. "I am no longer functional. I am merely an incomplete residue—"

"Obviously," I said. "Never mind that. What can this ship do?"

After an unpleasant interval, during which various portions of the ancilla's anatomy reappeared, only to disappear again, the residue did its best to diagnose our situation. "We cannot leave the system. This ship cannot formulate a slipspace jump—the necessary components are far too worn, and besides, there is no longer any means to establish a legitimate request."

"We could ignore protocol," Sharp muttered.

The fragmented ancilla continued, "There are no local portals.

All have apparently been withdrawn. I am only partially aware of this system's status, but it appears that fifteen nearby suns and their attendant worlds have been quarantined. Perhaps years ago. This much can be recovered from ship's history."

"Check on the other two bubbles," I murmured to Sharp. "Maybe they can tell us something . . . if they survive release."

He agreed. Before he entered the transit tube, he looked back at me and said, "I may have some of the attributes of a Builder, but I renounce them. I would like to return to being a Warrior-Servant . . . in *your* thoughts, at least."

"So observed," I said.

"Thank you, Commander." He vanished into the tube.

At least we knew where we stood with each other. A better way to die.

I focused my full attention on learning what the ancilla might still be capable of. It was reluctant to test the ship's scanning capabilities. "I am not attuned to direct control of this vessel," it said. "Anything I attempt may damage it."

Uthera seemed unchanged from the last time I had visited this system, but without enhanced sensory input, there was no way I could learn more.

"I'm willing to take that risk," I said.

"Yes, but I do not have you in memory as an authorized commander."

"Then locate the commander," I suggested.

"That will require activating ship's internal and external sensors. And that may damage our systems. We seem to be at a stalemate."

Its staring, floating eyes irritated me, so I suggested it revert to the spinning disk or no visual whatsoever. It chose the latter and its responsiveness immediately improved.

"This ship answers a light query. It tells me it no longer remembers its name or number," it said. "It also informs me an internal report on operability will not damage equipment. That's a relief, no?"

"Maybe," I said, paying more attention to the world below, as if staring hard might reveal something I had not noticed to this point.

And it did.

"Ship says external sensors are corroded and barely operable," the residue continued. "But properly coaxed, they may still supply some information. Shall I coax?"

I pointed to a grayish patch on Uthera's limb, even now sliding into darkness—but still, as it did so, shaping a visible bump against the thin starfield beyond. "Try focusing on *that*," I said.

"It is of considerable size," the residue said. "Yet it does not appear to be a natural feature, nor a Forerunner construct. Ship will take a closer view."

That view—grainy and shimmering, as if through a rising column of hot air—revealed what I had dreaded most and seen only once, ten thousand years before: a spore mountain.

The Flood.

"The object rises fifty kilometers above the planet's datum and measures four hundred kilometers across the base, at its greatest diameter. It intersects many Forerunner constructs and appears to have arisen at the center of a major city, which city is, if memory serves—if this is truly Uthera—"

A matter of little importance to me at this moment. "Will ship respond to my commands? Will *you*?"

The residue considered, then flashed a geometric shape—a complex polygon. "Do you have proper codes for assuming command?"

The codes I carried in memory were over a millennium old—but they might appeal to this poor remnant, or the ship with which it was so delicately linked.

"Try this," I said, and spoke a string of four hundred intricately looping nonsense words and numbers of the sliding, nonintegral varieties favored by Builder systems.

"Checking," the residue said.

Sharp-by-Striking came up through the transit opening, but this time in proper fashion, rising slowly, accompanied by a sigh of freshening air. "Tubes and conveyors are working, sort of," he said. "What did you do?"

"We're waking up," I said. "What about our comrades in the hold?"

"Murky, but clearing a little. Not long until they burst. One appears to be a high-ranking Builder," Sharp said, confirming my observation. "Still has armor."

"Not Faber—?"

"Not the Master Builder." He grimaced in disappointment.

"Too bad," I agreed. We shared a moment of darkness, touching the sixth fingers of our left hands in vengeful sympathy.

"But possibly one of his subordinates, fallen from favor," Sharp said. "If the armor still functions, perhaps it can help control the ship."

"And the other?"

"Catalog," Sharp said grimly. "Carapace looks damaged. It may not come out alive."

Here again, the Master Builder's ironic touch was evident. No doubt Catalog had been sent to him by Juridicals to conduct an interview—only to be frozen in stasis and dumped here with the rest of Faber's garbage.

My wife had supplied me with fully updated armor after I left my Cryptum. That had been taken from me, so my knowledge of more immediate events was spotty at best. I had no idea what might have forced the Master Builder's hand. Having captured me, he should have been inclined to bring me to trial before his corrupted Juridicals. He had not. That implied that even before my capture, his situation had already started to decline.

If Catalog came out alive, if it could still hook up to a Juridical network—and no doubt it would want to, after what it had experienced—we might reach out to the ecumene and report our status.

Uthera was infested. Any attempt to land and conduct repairs would end in disaster. None of the worlds here would be of use. How had it gone so far wrong?

"What do you know about the last few years . . . or however long I've been out of action?" I asked.

"Without armor, my knowledge has huge gaps," Sharp said. "In the end, Faber took no one into his confidence. Except Mendicant Bias."

"You know about that?"

"The Master Builder was under arrest, on trial. Without warning, Halos conducted an attack on the Capital. Some said Mendicant Bias was trying to rescue Faber, but I think not."

The details were coming together. Sharp's expression told me as much.

"Faber escaped. You went with him," I said.

He marked a Y over his forehead and the bridge of his nose, a Warrior's admission of guilt. "With the help of the Warden, who removed Faber from the capital and delivered him to me. I commanded a fast frigate, one of six that may have been carrying high-ranking members of Builder Security. . . . We were ordered to flee the Capital system, even though it was under attack."

"And?"

"The Master Builder's personal security overwhelmed our crew. I recognized them by his sigil. They killed all but me. That's the last I remember."

"I must have been on that frigate as well. Did you know?"

"None of our crew knew."

Perhaps everything was already lost. Perhaps the Burn extended across the entire galaxy. If so, surely the Master Builder would have fired off his beloved wheels, his Halos! Unless they had all been damaged or destroyed while attacking the Capital.

Sharp said he knew nothing about that, or how many Halos might remain active. His ignorance of events that must have transpired while he fled with the Master Builder was not convincing. But we had little time to argue.

He pointed to the displays. "We're attracting attention." Tracking symbols flocked around tiny points of light moving into position along the limb of the planet, coming up from behind its curve—and then appeared far out in the system. The symbols blossomed into readouts of size, class, capability.

"Forerunner vessels," Sharp said. "Newer. Powerful. Hundreds of them."

The new ships were communicating with our own—perhaps trying to take command.

"They say they're in control of this system," Sharp interpreted from the battle displays. "They welcome us—invite us to join them." He looked at me dubiously. "To surrender. What are they still doing here, in the Burn?"

"We need to release the others," I told him. "They're our last hope."

The remaining stasis bubbles were in the final stages of depletion and decay. Sharp and I worked out means of forcing the issue. Warrior-Servants, exerting all their strength, can wreak real havoc—and we did just that. We grabbed for heavy, hard implements. Fortunately, the ship was old enough that its re-shaping capabilities were minimal, and it soon yielded pieces of interior framing, furniture, and console supports with sufficient mass to be swung with real effect.

We battered. Fully energized, a stasis bubble can resist almost any imaginable force. But weakened, they shimmered and radiated in the ultraviolet with each of our coordinated blows. We were desperate. And for once, we were in luck. The fields blackened, then *popped* with a burst of brilliant blue light.

We had just enough warning to avert our eyes.

The Builder sprawled across the deck—female. Her armor spasmed and she lay curled up like a dying insect, face beaded with sweat, skin dark and blotchy.

For a moment, we wondered whether she was infected. . . .

Her eyelids flickered, opened. We backed away. Then Sharp moved in and turned her over, gently twisted her head around, looked into her eyes.

"She's not sick," he concluded.

Catalog lay on the deck, twitching, unable to raise its five limbs. Its carapace was scarred and crazed. It had suffered a lot of punishment.

Neither looked strong. Nevertheless, Sharp grabbed up the Builder and I took Catalog, and we dragged them to the main bridge.

The ship was still working to revive and return to full duty. The effort was both noble and pitiful.

"Very old . . . hulk," the female Builder observed, struggling weakly to free herself from my grip. I let her go, then caught her again as she fell forward. "How did I get here?"

"We were dropped into this ship and sent to a Flood-infested system."

To this she responded with an unbelieving glare. "They wouldn't do that!"

"Look for yourself."

Sharp lifted Catalog, tried to set all its limbs under it, then let it down gently. Three of the legs held, the other two folded. It fell back with a heavy thud.

"I was giving testimony...to *that* one!" the Builder said, standing without help. Her skin color was also improving. "Faber's personal security found us. They tried to stop a Juridical deposition! I couldn't believe it—"

"Where were you?" I asked.

She struggled to concentrate. Her ancilla was not being much help, I guessed. "On Secunda," she said. "An emergency Council. Many Builders were facing extradition and arrest. I was among them."

"You were turning Council evidence to protect yourself," Sharp suggested. He glanced at me and shrugged.

"What happened?" I asked her.

"We heard there was an assault on the Capital system. The most powerful Builders scrambled to find protection. Monitors turned against them. The last thing I remember is Catalog being thrust into stasis. I must have been next."

My worst fears about the ascendancy of the Builders had never imagined this level of perfidy.

The female examined my face in disbelief. "You're the Didact! We've spent a *thousand years* looking for you. You betrayed us in our time of greatest need."

I have had long experience controlling anger. Mostly my efforts succeed. "Is your ancilla still working?" I asked, voice steady.

She closed her eyes. "Weak—still there."

"What was your function?"

"I helped design installations to fight the Flood," she said.

"Halos?"

"Yes. In their later stages."

I could not help myself, hearing this. I pounded my fist against a bulkhead and produced the strangest, most demented of grunts.

"You're *laughing*!" the female said indignantly. "Only animals do that."

"And humans," I said, covering my mouth as another fit came upon me.

Sharp looked aside, ashamed for me.

At the last, Forthencho, the greatest human general, my most challenging opponent, as the Lifeshaper and I had prepared for his reduction at Charum Hakkor, had smiled—and then had made just such sharp, grunting noises.

In later years, I dreamed about that sound, that emotion. I came to understand and even appreciate it. Something had brought forth that human-like rictus, had made me *smile* as I entered the Cryptum, causing my wife to fear for my sanity, I suspect.

But why now? Something churned in the back of my thoughts . . . A dark complex of evidence and induction. Part of me understood something my intellect found repellent. The Primordial's last statement to me from the timelock. The puzzling development of human resistance to the Flood. The Lifeshaper and the Council collaborating with the Master Builder to preserve human personalities, human memory and history, in part through the use of Composers . . .

The unprecedented destruction of Precursor artifacts at Charum Hakkor.

Before I could voice my suspicions, fortune turned direction.

"Ship is waking," the Builder said, looking down at her hand as if it might be deceiving her. "We won't have to rely on the damaged ancilla. I think my family may have designed this class of vessel—thousands of years ago. I'm asking it to survey its capabilities."

———

The female Builder's name was Maker-of-Moons. She came from an old family long involved in the manufacture of fast, heavily armed ships.

"I knew your father," I told her. "He served the Master Builder—performed his dirty tricks. Your father was directly responsible for forcing me into exile."

Sharp gave her a rueful glance.

Maker's armor took an automatic stance, a defensive mode, but she stared me down and forced it to relax.

"He died ten years ago," she said. "Assassinated at the orders of the Master Builder."

"I did not know."

"How could you, Didact? You *abandoned* us."

I held back another useless grunt. Obviously, while waiting for the ship to assess, and our enemies to close in, there was little more we could do.

This was the time for stories.

Maker was less than two thousand years old. The Master Builder's strengthening grip on the Council had led to difficult times even for Builders, especially those who, unlike her father, were not part of the general corruption.

Maker's first assignment had been to improve upon existing plans for Halos. But she found a fatal flaw in the Master Builder's original design. "They were too damned *big*," she told us. "Transporting a Halo produces an enormous debt in reconciliation. There was no way the original Halos could all be sent to where they were needed with sufficient speed and flexibility. I could not follow through."

This flaw, she said, had been discovered only during final testing of the first installations. Worse, the Ark built to manufacture them was not capable of making smaller Halos. A few of the deployed Halos were theoretically capable of shedding segments and thus mass and size, but for all their power they were remarkably delicate. Self-reduction entailed too many dangers—instability and collapse being the most obvious.

Nobody had listened to her. After decades of work and frustration, getting nowhere, she had resigned in protest.

She gave me a stern, searching look. "For my obstinacy, I was brought up before the Juridicals. My father intervened. On Faber's orders, Builder Security executed him." She nudged Catalog with her armored foot. It reacted like a sleepy insect. "*This* was my confessor. The Master Builder ordered us *both* placed in stasis."

With a quivering groan, Catalog attempted to stand on three limbs and managed to extend a number of complicated looking eyes.

"I am Catalog," it announced.

"We know," Sharp said.

It looked around and wobbled before us, making those peculiar internal clicking and slopping noises common to Catalog and disgusting—to my sensibilities, at least.

This one did not look especially strong. It slowly rotated, two of its limbs tangling, and leaned toward Maker-of-Moons. "My assignment . . ." It nearly fell over, but righted itself at the last moment. "My assignment is this Builder." It made stuttering noises for a few seconds, then apologized. "I appear to be damaged," it said. "Something has attempted to access my processes."

"Did it succeed?" Maker asked.

"Not that I am aware of. I may no longer be secure, however, and should not take testimony. As a precaution."

"Wise," I said. "Can you add anything further to this Builder's story?"

"Is this ship capable of communicating?"

"No," Maker said.

Catalog's voice gained some strength. "There *are* Juridical channels available even out here. Unfortunately, their use for extra-Juridical traffic is forbidden."

Obviously we would have to supply persuasion. I assisted Catalog as it rotated its carapace again and focused its many eyes on the approaching ships.

"Those are not allies, are they?" it asked.

"Almost certainly not," I said.

It turned its eyes and other sensors on me. "You are the Didact, against whom the Council and the Master Builder lodged a formal complaint over a thousand years ago."

"I am," I said.

"That case has been dismissed," Catalog said. "There are no longer proceedings against you." It paused. "There have been dramatic developments since I was removed from the Master Builder's presence. Many indeed. The Old Council was nearly destroyed by an attack on the Capital system. There is a New Council. But there is also . . ." It examined me more closely, with a suspicious backward lean. "Are you *sure* you're the Didact? Because there is another, working with the Lifeshaper and given full authority."

So Bornstellar survived!

"I imprinted a Manipular in case of my capture. That is likely him."

"So much to catch up on . . ." Its voice dropped and its words slowed. "Oh, my. Juridicals have reorganized. We have been found wanting. There was corruption."

"Indeed," I said. I left Catalog to its catching up and asked Maker if this ship could be convinced to move to a more secure location while we studied our options.

"I'm working on that," she said. "It's murky. The main ancilla was decommissioned, but whoever did it was sloppy. Emergency backups could still be cached. . . . I'll need time."

In my experience, this was a statement expected of any Builder faced with repairs. Somehow it encouraged me. I was starting to like this Builder despite myself.

"Oh, my," Catalog announced again, and jerked itself to full attention. Its voice rose in pitch. "The Flood has entered over five hundred systems and infected thousands of worlds and entire fleets."

"Tell us something encouraging," Sharp-by-Striking grumbled.

"All of those systems have fallen silent, and it is assumed that their defenses have been placed at the disposal of the Flood."

"That isn't what I meant," Sharp said.

Maker came up from her tech-reverie to announce, "The central ancilla is online! *Still* a classic Builder vessel."

"What about weapons?" Sharp asked, approaching the control display.

Maker stood back to allow him access. "Stripped out before we were sent here. If the Master Builder dumped the Didact into a Burn, defenseless, I'd say it was personal."

"There were few kind words," I agreed.

Maker tried to sound optimistic. "It's possible we'll be able to maneuver within this system, but only for a short time. And no great distance—less than a hundred million kilometers upstar, twice that downstar. Better sensor response is now possible, however."

A sharp tone rang out as a small gray circle appeared in the display, above the limb of Uthera but in line with the plane of the ecliptic. The circle surrounded an almost invisible blur emerging from star-specked darkness. Neither we nor the ship could discern what this blur might be. Nor did it become more obvious as both the blur and the gray circle expanded.

All we knew was an unidentified mass was closing fast from a distance of about two hundred and fifty million kilometers.

"It's a dark sun," Sharp said. "Has to be."

"Nowhere near enough mass," Maker observed.

The object was at least fifty thousand kilometers in diameter. Not solid. The closer it approached, the more compact it appeared.

"Some new form of Halo?" I asked Maker.

"Much too large," she said. "Also not enough mass. The mass reading is puzzling. It *changes*." She listened to her ancilla. "No fresh light signatures. No entanglements. It's not made of ordinary matter. But it isn't trying to be deceptive." She held up her arm as if to move the circle—and succeeded in spinning the display around and magnifying it.

Now we could make out thousands of slender, interwoven threads, none more than a few kilometers thick. The threads squirmed slowly, majestically, and then compacted, like a snarl of snakes trying to stay warm in the cold.

Maker frowned. She tapped the circle with an extended sixth finger, as if she might flip it out of the system and away from this planet, the ship, our orbit. "*Probably* not made of matter," she said, second-guessing herself. "But it does resemble . . ."

She looked at us. At me.

She and I were thinking the same thought.

"We've seen its like before," I said.

"Neural physics," she said. "Precursor structures."

"That's impossible!" Sharp said. "They've been dead for millions of years!"

I knew otherwise. I had interviewed a being that claimed to have survived from those hidden times. A being that had sworn vengeance against Forerunners for the extinction of its kind.

"Dead or dormant," Maker said, her armor darkening.

As if astonished into new vitality, the ship made an awful sound, like the clamor of broken bells. "Unknown construct approaching at one-third light-speed," it said. "Instructions!"

Sharp still refused to believe. The expanded gray circle outlined an irregular ball of coiling and twisting star roads, Precursor artifacts that had been around for as long as any Forerunner could remember—unchanging, unresponsive. Revered by both Forerunners and humans as the remnants of our Creation.

"It's going to arrive here about the same time as those ships," Maker said.

"Can we outrun it?" I asked.

"No," she said.

"Try," I said. "Make it chase us. We'll learn more that way . . . and maybe it's not looking for us. We are, after all, very small."

[TT: A later dialog, date unknown. Not contigous with previous string, but seems to belong in this sequence.]

MASTER JURIDICAL: Juridicals acknowledge a decommissioned Catalog opened a link from a Flood-infested region. But all portals there had been closed, all citizens and vessels placed under extreme interdiction. Why did you not take advantage of the open channel and announce your presence? There might have been a rescue attempt.

DIDACT: Doubtful. I was curious. I believed we might be of more use where we were.

MASTER JURIDICAL: Truly?

DIDACT: And I've never trusted Juridicals. I trust nobody, except perhaps my wife. And even she might have had plans she did not divulge. It was also possible she had learned something crucial after sealing me into my Cryptum. Had she?

MASTER JURIDICAL: This is your testimony.

DIDACT: You'll stick with your protocols even should it mean the ecumene dies, and all history and your precious law with it?

MASTER JURIDICAL: Juridicals have considered the state of law in a Flood-occupied civilization. We understand that Graveminds are vast combinatorial repositories of memories and information. Living libraries, as it were. How much that is essential to civilization is lost under those conditions, really?

DIDACT (DISGUSTED): Now you understand why I don't trust you. You supported that defeatist attitude for thousands of years. . . . Did the Lifeshaper ever agree?

MASTER JURIDICAL: Not to be divulged one way or the other.

DIDACT: Then my testimony is at an end.

MASTER JURIDICAL: Unfortunate. Can you at least reveal to me the fate of Catalog in the Burn?

DIDACT (AMUSED): Only if you tell me whether my wife had anything to do with sending us there. I was about to leave the game board, and her moves had to become her own. Did she make her own deal—another deal—with the Master Builder?

MASTER JURIDICAL: Searching . . . Searching . . . Precedent tells me that crucial testimony can be encouraged by an exchange of information irrelevant to the case of the testifier.

DIDACT: Even if it goes to motive?

MASTER JURIDICAL: Are you arguing for or against having your request granted? I am not empowered to make subtle legal distinctions.

DIDACT: Out in the Burn, that's exactly what Catalog did—make subtle distinctions. And it saved my life, very likely.

MASTER JURIDICAL: Perhaps.

DIDACT: Pique your curiosity?

MASTER JURIDICAL: I have no personal curiosity.

(Brief lapse in record)

MASTER JURIDICAL: I have found precedent. To cut through the casuistry, I am allowed to give you that small bit of information.

DIDACT: Do so, and I'll resume.

MASTER JURIDICAL: It was not her plan.

DIDACT: It was the Master Builder's plan, then.

MASTER JURIDICAL: No confirmation possible. But that is a logical conclusion. How and why did Catalog take action outside of its instructions?

DIDACT: It saw what I saw. It found its courage. It became a true Forerunner once more.

G ravitation on the control deck had been turned off to save energy and avoid accidents. As we drifted within the flickering displays, I began to feel confined. The direct view was no less oppressive, but I preferred using my eyes to relying on the ship.

All hulks sent into the Burn, including ours, according to Sharp, had been decommissioned and listed as salvaged or destroyed. None of them officially existed. We were abandoned, thrown aside . . . But it turned out I had been afforded quite a clever crew. Clever, and deeply motivated.

Even more motivated as the Precursor snarl loomed.

Yet as fast as Maker worked, she was not fast enough; the ship's systems were still balky and the revived ancilla showed alarming signs of autonome dementia.

"Ships are taking up formation around the tangle," Sharp observed.

How could we have ever presumed to understand such ancient technology? Even to the extent of believing it to be inactive. It was not dead; it had simply bided its time, waiting for the proper moment. The same thing might be happening throughout the galaxy.

I replayed in memory what we had seen at Charum Hakkor, the aftermath of the Master Builder's insidious Halo test: the disintegration of all Precursor structures, including the star roads. Halo radiation disrupts neural physics, and the theoretically analogous process of neural physics is often invoked to explain Precursor technology. . . . Space-time as a kind of organism within itself, apparently subject to the destructive radiation of the Halo.

"Whatever that thing is, it may not be invulnerable," I said.

Maker gave me a skeptical look. "It's bigger than any space-faring construct *we've* made," she observed.

"If it *is* space-faring," Sharp said, doubt and hope mixed.

"It's *faring* well enough toward *us*," Maker said, backing away from her labors.

Catalog pushed up its many eyes and wands. "I have transferred my report and received a response. The Juridicals would very much like for all of you to survive to testify. To that end, they are extending communication privilege to this ship. We may be able to arrange a direct link to the Capital and the Council, or to anybody you think is better equipped to advise us on how to return to the Orion complex."

"How kind," I said. "Are you certain the Juridicals aren't still in league with the Master Builder? Certain we weren't sent here just to die or be absorbed by the Flood?"

Catalog grew sleek, like an animal dropping its ridge fur.

Sharp watched me closely. "You have that *look*," he said.

"I'm curious as to your reasoning, Didact. If I may be allowed a glimpse."

"Not yet," I said. The others regarded me with concern. "We need to learn who's in charge of those ships."

"The Juridical link may not be open much longer," Catalog warned. "There is a tremendous amount of traffic throughout the ecumene. Massive evacuations. If those *wheels* begin to move again," it added, "all bets are off."

For a moment, all of us were lost in even darker thoughts. Billions of Forerunners fleeing the Flood in millions of vessels . . . Before my exile, I had helped plan just such evacuations.

Sharp's chest muscles gave a brief quiver. "The Flood may have us in a few hours," he said. "I'd like to face that believing there is purpose to our sacrifice."

"Of that I'm not yet convinced," I said. I looked out across the night-dark orb of Uthera—switching from display to direct view, as if one or the other might hold answers to questions I was reluctant to ask.

I focused on Catalog. "Very well. Your channel is open. How did the Flood take over these systems? Query the Juridicals about *that*. Did they depose the commanders in charge of this zone's defense?"

At first, my request seemed too much for Catalog. Again it withdrew its eyes and sensors and its carapace became smooth. But then it bristled. "All those answers are available, if they will be of service in removing us from this danger. Your testimony is most important."

I turned to Sharp. "You were *here*, weren't you? That's why you've been returned. Why don't *you* tell us what happened?"

Sharp drew up his knees. His face worked through a variety of expressions. Finally he said, "This system lies outside of the

Jat-Krula protected boundary [TT: "**Maginot Sphere**"]. All systems beyond Jat-Krula have been left to fend for themselves. The ecumene—last I heard—was focused on preserving what lies inside the boundary."

I was all too familiar with Jat-Krula. During one of our interminable civil wars, half a million years before my birth, Jat-Krula had been a formidable strategy of fortified defense, designed to control frequently traversed manifolds in the Orion complex.

Key to Jat-Krula was vigilance over all conceivable slipspace entries and portals—the necessary and most efficient avenues of slipspace travel. Millions of fixed fortifications had been spread like beaded curtains between hundreds of systems, standing vigil over a collective of jump solutions, protecting historic routes that supported trade as well as offensive and counter-offensive maneuvers.

Any major assault force, it was reasoned, must pass through this hyper-spherical boundary. And the boundary, so planners insisted, could at a moment's notice be rendered impassable, solid—impregnable.

Then a legion of revolutionary Warrior commanders decided to forego crystal-mediated slipspace and instead flew twenty attack squadrons "naked" through a non-manifold array, bypassing the Jat-Krula defenses. The passage was savage. Their squadrons suffered fifty-percent losses—but the remaining ships emerged within the boundary and quickly overwhelmed fourteen key systems.

This brave and catastrophic act should have forever changed Forerunner strategy. Jat-Krula became a sobering object lesson taught to Warrior-Servants at all levels. There was no such thing as an impregnable defense.

Yet if I were to believe this former Warrior-Servant, what had

once been old and outmoded was again novel and exciting—
ignoring the deadly lessons of history.

"We're ruled by idiots," I murmured.

"It gets worse," Sharp said. "The Master Builder seemed to believe that by demonstrating the force of the Halos, out in the open,
the Flood—by which I suppose he meant Graveminds—would
see we were willing to suffer total destruction rather than defeat."

That *could* explain what had been done at Charum Hakkor. A
tactical demonstration—like threatening to cut one's own throat if
an aggressor came too close. Jat-Krula . . . combined with suicidal
intent.

I felt my skin grow hot. "Madness!"

"I warned them," Maker-of-Moons said quietly.

I could not absorb all of this for many minutes. Maker did her
best, with Sharp's help, to bring the ship back to cruising power.
But multiple systems failed just as they were engaged.

We were overtaken by the vast weave of reawakened star
roads, spinning and churning like serpents in a huge nest—the
graceful and haunting structures of our deep past now made fell
and horrifying. The tangle looped around Uthera, deftly avoiding
intersecting the planet. Then, incredibly, the planet itself began to
crack and shrink, as if squeezed by a huge fist. The resulting shift
in our orbit thrust us farther into the mass. An entire planet was
being destroyed—just to draw us closer.

"This is the way Precursors moved stars," Maker whispered.

The ships escorting the tangle were near enough to reveal their
outlines. I recognized roughly four classes of vessels. The newer
designs were unfamiliar, but they were all Forerunner.

"Channels for communication still open," Catalog said. "There
is still time left for testimony. . . ."

"Oh, shut *up*," Sharp said.

I had to look upon this fate as one way—not the best way, to be sure—to learn what was really happening in our galaxy. The others, I decided, should try to make their escape, if such was possible, while I offered myself as bait. I at least had the consolation of knowing that my imprinted duplicate was capable of handling most of the challenges I might have faced, had I survived. Some part of me would live on, free and unmolested.

"Can the stasis bubbles be re-energized?" I asked Sharp-by-Striking.

"The ship should be able to generate that much power. But why—" And then he understood. "The bubbles leave no sensor profiles. We could blow up the ship and still survive. They might not capture us . . . right away. Or even know we exist."

"Lost forever in orbit," Maker said.

"Better that than part of a Gravemind," Sharp said.

"I wonder," Catalog said.

"Go," I said.

Just before Maker descended into the transit hatch, she looked back at me.

"You're not coming?"

"Not yet," I said.

She knew. "You'll give yourself up to them?" she asked.

"A poor plan, probably my last. Don't even think of joining me."

She watched for a moment. "You never did like Builders much, did you?"

"Not much."

"Well, you'll need this," she said, and removed her armor. It unwound and floated free of her limbs and torso, still quivering, as if reluctant to leave her unprotected. She pushed the compacting bundle my way. "It won't be much use to me in stasis. But . . . you knew I'd leave it for you, didn't you?"

"I hoped as much. It's tough to survive an exploding ship in one's underwear."

"I'd rather stay with you," she said.

"No doubt."

"Or *you* can enter stasis, and I'll direct the ship."

"Not an option."

During our exchange, Catalog had not moved. "I have been instructed to stay with the Didact at all costs," it said. "My carapace is capable of surviving vacuum and other inclement conditions. It may be tougher than your armor."

Spoken with real courage. Despite myself, I was touched.

"We are shamed by this example," Sharp said, eyes downcast.

"We all serve," I said, and to Catalog, "Stay, then."

"I will tell them what you did, if I live," Maker said.

"Do that," I said.

The slithering, sibilant noise of grapplers surrounded us. Maker vanished down the hatch, followed by Sharp, who lifted his hand and touched his chin.

"An honor to serve, Didact."

"Go . . . friend," I said.

I never saw them again.

Catalog remained. I was suddenly glad not to be alone. For the first time in many thousands of years, I felt real fear. No shame in that. I had seen what the Flood did to Forerunners.

Together, Catalog and I set about finding a way to destroy the ship.

Audacity inserted itself into a wide elliptical orbit around the first great mass . . . over a perfectly reflective surface. We came out of our glassy slowness to see a faint, greenish glimmer moving deep within the sphere, tracking our close approach.

It then leaped ahead, as if asking to be chased. . . .

Obviously, this was not just a reflection of our ship.

Keeper spoke first, face glowing with excitement. "It could be a probability mirror," he said. "If so, it reflects light within a narrow stretch of time as well as space. If it treats our immediate light so . . . Reforming our traces, correcting our short-term entanglements . . . The spheres might be an early method of reconciliation!" Keeper said.

"Precursor?" Chant asked.

"No, I don't think so," he said. "Precursors seemed to have other ways to deal with causality."

"About which we know nothing," Clearance added.

Keeper shrugged this off. His excitement was too great to allow the Miner's reminder of Builder limitations to bother him.

The image flickered, grew larger, than shrank. A clear outline was impossible to fix. We might be looking down at our ship, seconds later—or at another vessel only vaguely like ours, from billions of years before.

Clearance apologized for presumption, then floated close to me on the translucent bridge. "Lifeshaper, I have an idea . . . Not a very good idea, I'm afraid . . . but interesting."

Keeper joined us.

"Let's hear it," I said.

"If these masses are indeed time-phased mirrors, then they could have been used as blunt-force counterbalance for a series of massive portals. Not the techniques we use now, yet, there is something familiar about them."

"Of course!" Keeper said. "Brilliant. Reconciling and anchoring all at once."

"They may have been used by Forerunners . . . our ancestors," Clearance said.

Dawn and Chant tapped his shoulders. In the face of this approval from higher rates, Clearance shook his head in a not very convincing display of humility. "It's just an idea. I don't know where it came from."

"Wouldn't that mean moving an exceptionally large number of vessels?" I asked.

"Hadn't thought of that," Clearance said.

Keeper murmured, "They could hold all the causal burdens of our far-traveling ancestors. Great middens of contradiction . . ."

I felt like I was being led into shadows. Or led *by* shadows. The huge black sphere did not respond to probe or signal—merely echoed what we sent down, shifted it ahead and then backward a few seconds, but giving no clue to the sphere's composition or internal structure, if any. Very likely, I thought, the other spheres in this system would behave the same.

"These stars are haunted," Chant-to-Green said softly. The others looked at her with some distaste.

I suggested that *Audacity* make the bridge opaque. The object below was too distracting. Dispiriting.

"For the moment, we'll move off and focus our study on the planets," I said. "If the spheres are Forerunner, then this system may hold other surprises."

"Something *Audacity* can't see?"

"Possibly."

Our armor slowed us again as we traveled downstar several hundred million kilometers. I had instructed *Audacity*'s ancilla to monitor changes and wake me—but not the others—if something significant occurred.

It did.

After reviving me, *Audacity* revealed that, less than seven hundred million kilometers from the star, sensor readings were abruptly and erratically changing. From our upstar orbit, significant details had been veiled. We were able to see more clearly the nature of the inner worlds.

Some Builders believed, as an article of faith, that Forerunners had once possessed superior technologies long since lost. If ancient Forerunners had created those spheres, then placed a veil over this system, a veil that had persisted for ten million years, then that tradition seemed entirely justified.

All very intriguing. But the larger questions remained unanswered: What happened here, so long ago—and why? And how did it end?

My crew and I had come here to study Flood origins. But mysteries were piling upon mysteries.

The crew again rose from slowness. *Audacity* had taken up a nearly circular orbit around the fifth planet, a murky gas giant surrounded by seven rings of icy debris.

"A star road!" Clearance said in awe. "And huge!"

From the seven rings, a narrow great band dropped inward to touch the planet's slushy, cold outer layers. As we moved around to the opposite side, we saw another, very slender road rising below the rings, then sweeping downstar in a smooth, tremendous curve, like a single strand of spider silk strung between neighbors— neighbors only in the sense that they were a mere forty million kilometers apart.

As we watched, the star road slowly flexed, automatically adjusting to changing forces, all the way downstar to the last tiny, sun-skimming chunk of rock.

And it was not alone. Many more star roads had been strung around the inner system, forming a great web—but with substantial gaps, deletions where automatic adjustments had not sufficed, where not even Precursor technology could correct the chaotic imbalances, and the web had crumbled. All the planets had once been connected, strung together. At opposition, some of the webs would have had to loop up and *over* the star, like swinging ropes in a child's game.

But these children played enormous games.

The web was doubtless Precursor, far more impressive and possibly more ancient than anything seen in our galaxy. But just as dormant. Just as dead and abandoned.

Or so Forerunner scientists assured us. How many times had skeptical Lifeworkers attended the mandatory Builder lectures on this dogmatic assertion? The many explanations of how a structure could adjust and adapt, yet have no real inner life or process . . .

And because star roads and other Precursor artifacts merely adjusted, and never changed in other significant ways, we accepted. We believed.

Keeper was jubilant. "Forerunners must have collaborated with the Precursors, long ago! More glory to Builders—glory to all!"

I could not follow his reasoning—but it might not be wrong. All things seemed possible here: time-shifted probability mirrors, upstar veiling, massive complexes of star roads.

Chant, Keeper, and Clearance moved to the opposite side of the bridge to carry out their own analyses. Not all were heartened by what the deeper evidence was telling us.

"Downstar, around the middle rocky planets . . . We see vessels of a very different design," Dawn said. "Much smaller."

"Forerunner—I'm sure of it," Keeper said. "They appear to be dead hulks. No activity. Undoubtedly prehistoric. I've seen their like as symbols in Builder rituals." He glanced at me, embarrassed to be telling secrets. "The teachers told us such ships were sacred vessels. Nobody ever thought we might actually *find* them."

"There are no energy signatures. All are inactive," *Audacity* confirmed. "Dormancy possible but unlikely."

The look of awe and longing on Keeper's features was instructive. Clearly he had been schooled in Builder mysteries. He was being prepared to move high in Builder society. Which was likely why he had been sent on this mission.

Reluctantly, as if unveiling a new nakedness, he magnified and shifted the images for all to see. Thousands of ships were arrayed in clusters around the wide-vaulting star roads. These old ships were massive enough—most in the range of one or two kilometers—yet sleek in their obvious power, and, to my eye at least, thoroughly aggressive, deadly looking. Yet indeed of an oddly familiar pedigree, as if even what the most ancient Forerunner voyagers had wrought was still recognizable to their descendants millions of years later.

"It must have been horrendously expensive to bring them here," Chant-to-Green said.

"Almost certainly—if just moving our tiny ship nearly bankrupts the ecumene!" Keeper said. "But why? What were they doing here?"

"Cheaper to abandon them once their work was finished," Clearance said, breaking from his trance.

"But what *was* their work?" Keeper asked, clearly frustrated, conflicted.

"Any dozen of them could have surveyed an entire system," I said. "But we see hundreds of thousands."

"A tremendous fleet—and clearly a battle fleet," Clearance said. "Sent here to kill on a massive scale."

Indeed, a fleet of this size could have targeted myriads of stars and planets—and how many of those worlds had once been inhabited by Precursors?

Keeper flashed from frustration to anger. "We don't know that! Builders would never have ordered such a thing!"

Clearance took this opportunity to agree, but with a twist. "Rates weren't the same back then," he said. "Warriors might have served at the top. Builders would have worked for them."

"And Miners?" Keeper prodded. "Where would *they* fit in?"

Clearance did not take the bait.

"This is *not* what we came to study," Chant-to-Green said. "We're here to learn the origin of the Flood. Forerunners are not responsible for that . . . are they?"

Silence.

"We have to get closer," I said. "Ship, move us downstar to within a safe distance."

"How safe?" *Audacity* asked.

"Ten million kilometers. Send greetings in earliest Digon. Perhaps Keeper can instruct you in some sort of clandestine Builder grammar."

Keeper agreed before he caught himself. Our eyes met. Curiosity trumped any fealty to secret societies. "Builders will want to know the truth as much as any of us," he said.

"If those vessels turn out to still be active," I said, "jump us back to the outskirts of the system. If necessary, jump us to the margins of the cluster."

"You don't trust our ancestors?" Chant asked.

"She understands Warriors," Keeper said in an undertone. I do not enjoy having my thoughts spoken for me, but could not disagree.

The things around us that do not change may be of the greatest efficiency, but least capable of refinement. All their options are burned into design and instinct. They react swiftly and without thought.

These ancient vessels appeared extremely efficient. We could only hope they were truly dead.

———

Audacity carried us farther downstar. The magnitude of the Precursor structures overwhelmed all. Compared to this system's artifacts, Charum Hakkor seemed a primitive village. And yet wherever those great interplanetary bridges stretched, ancient ships—Forerunner ships—gathered in disciplined rows, as if still on alert, still watching, waiting.

Chant-to-Green stated clearly what we were all thinking. "These ships may be older than any recorded language. We have only a vague idea what Forerunners were like then. The most ancient records have long since disappeared."

Those had likely been eras of *digital* storage, the least enduring and the most subject to centralization and disastrous failure.

But we had much larger concerns.

"We need to select a likely-looking vessel and find a way to board," I said. "It isn't impossible these ships came here on a similar mission."

My crew soberly assessed the implications.

"We'll send monitors," I said.

Clearance was not convinced. "Our machines are less likely to be recognized than one of us," he pointed out. "We have changed less than they have."

"Did they even wear armor back then?" Chant asked.

"Unknown," I said. "Builders keep the deepest rituals. Something Keeper knows might stretch back to those times. Ancient phrases, meaningless today."

"I was just beginning that degree of induction," Keeper said, uncomfortable once more at being singled out. "Other rates have traditions and rituals, too."

"Warriors were purged of their rituals during the civil wars," I said. "As for Miners . . ." I looked to the one Miner in our crew.

"Also lost," Clearance said. He glanced at Keeper. "Builders suppressed them."

"Lifeworkers have never accepted the greatness of the past," I said, hoping to forestall debate about who did what to whom. "There was never an age of perfection."

"You say that, even in the face of *this*?" Keeper asked as we passed over a sweeping segment of star road. Extremely light, immensely strong—and totally unresponsive. Star roads surrounded the inner worlds like a highly attenuated bird's nest. "Half the mass in this system was converted to Precursor constructs. It's like being inside a huge puzzle."

"Greatness is not always measured by size," I said. "The smallest lives rule."

"I wonder what our ancestors thought, seeing this," Dawn said. "Maybe they came here to worship. . . ."

But none of us could be convinced that so many ships represented an attempt to reach out and show appreciation.

That left us with the choice that already seemed most obvious. Forerunners had come here in force to react to an extreme challenge—or to exact some form of vengeance. Then they had abandoned their ships. Had they sacrificed their own lives in the process? If the challenge they faced had involved the Flood, or *what the Flood might once have been* . . .

All possible. But if Forerunners were still here, they were well hidden.

We chose an outlying group of seven vessels and cautiously approached. The flotilla did not respond, even when we were easily within threat range. It consisted of two first-order ships, each about a five kilometers long—dwarfing *Audacity*—and a number of sixth- or seventh-order ships, four hundred meters in length, slender dark hulls, possibly logistics support or interdictors designed to protect the two larger vessels.

We had no idea what sort of arms they had once carried.

Audacity continued closing. We came within a kilometer of one of the sixth-order vessels and kept station in a negligibly higher orbit.

"No response," *Audacity* said.

Chant and Keeper continued to focus on the near ships, refining whatever might be gleaned from immediate light.

Nothing significant. No change.

My ancilla and I had been together for over two thousand years. On this journey, I had requested that it express low-level running commentary on our situation, including crew behavior.

But now—it surprised me. For the first time in decades, it suddenly appeared in personified form, blocking my view, and requested my complete attention.

"Statistical analysis of long-range entanglements may have found life in a nearby system," it said, and revealed a star about ten light-years away, little more than a slow-burning orange blot in the middle reaches of the Spider. "Three small, rocky worlds and one very cold icy giant. Life only on the innermost world—very faint. Ambient surface temperature so close to the star allows liquid water for all of that planet's orbit. Oxygen, methane, sulfur compounds, the slightest hint at this distance of chlorophyll."

"What sort of life?" I asked. "Surely not technological."

"No. The nature of combinations point to a highly unusual circumstance."

"Unusual in what way?"

"Organically active, but with uniquely Forerunner profiles. No other genetics."

"That's all?"

"Our search has been thorough. There are no other organic signatures within the Spider or all of Path Kethona."

Beyond curious! Life arises wherever there is the right chemistry and an outflow of energy, a wet haven that radiation can warm before fleeing to the darkness of space. A cluster of stars this great should have thousands of organically active worlds, from ice-wrapped moons to rocky planets to self-warming gas giants. Yet Path Kethona—but for one system—was dead.

In a way, that made our job easier. . . . But it also disturbed me.

If the faint traces around the small orange sun were purely Forerunner, then it seemed most likely whatever lived there descended from those who had arrived ten million years ago.

And that meant Path Kethona had either undergone a tremendous extinction event, or indigenous ecologies had never evolved.

Keeper drew my attention back to the nearest ship. "Still inert. Likely safe to approach and board."

The ship's surface bore a haze of micrometeor scratches, like sand-tumbled quartz. The erosion had blasted away centimeters in some locations, giving relatively useless insight into the dusty sweeps of comets through which the ships had passed again and again.

Old things wear down.

"There's a possible seamless hatchway forward of the drive nodes," Keeper said. "Observe the deeper strike grooves. Hatches probably served as rescue ports and may not have been as hardened as the rest of the hull."

Audacity outlined a proposed point of entry.

"Send out monitors," I instructed.

"Should we withdraw while they work?" Dawn asked.

"No need," Keeper said. "Any effective trap would set up a perimeter throughout the system."

I agreed that such caution was impractical under the circumstances. We were committed to our plan. A group of ten monitors left *Audacity* and slowly approached the ancient craft. At any sign of revival, the monitors would back off and attempt to return— or, if danger presented itself, act as decoys while we made our retreat.

Two of the monitors extended manipulators. The first manipulator lightly brushed the craft's worn surface.

"No response," *Audacity* announced.

Within the flotilla, and throughout the ancient fleet, no ship, large or small, showed the slightest reaction.

For machines, ten million years is a very long time. But ten million years is just a brief trek for a living planet. And so even as our monitors opened the vessel, I turned my thoughts toward the small orange star and its single living planet.

That was where we would find answers.

Ten centuries I spent in meditative solitude, while the Life-shaper completed her duties for the Council—and for the Master Builder—and arranged her own biological traps and releases. Very clever, my wife. I miss her deeply. She was ever my balance and my goad—ever my conscience. But despite her cleverest efforts, providing me with a fast ship, loyal ancillas, and a mixed bag of comrades, she could not prevent my ultimate capture.

Strange that recounting all this brings back my time in the Cryptum, so close to the Domain . . . Memories that until now I had thought lost. Or discarded. I have never been prone to either solitude or meditation. Up until now, I could barely remember the state I had lain in for so long. Yet watching as our near-derelict hulk was drawn deeper and deeper into the writhing nest of star roads, with Catalog close by but silent, there was little to do *but* remember, to *stew in my own juices,* as Forthencho, my greatest human adversary, had so aptly described his own capture and imprisonment. Before a Composer brutally sucked away his patterns and memories.

"It is invigorating," Catalog said.

"What is?" I asked.

"Awaiting the inevitable. I am an individual truly now."

"What were you, before you became Catalog?" I asked.

"Not a proper question," it replied.

"I've heard that each Catalog has a certain *history,*" I continued, feeling less than proper as my fear mounted.

Catalog regarded me with its many sensors. Was it affronted? "That is no secret," it said after a pause. "Juridicals are chosen from those who have done wrong. Awareness of the nature of guilt is our strength."

"And what was your crime?" I asked.

"Not to be revealed. Expunged. I serve."

"We're not likely to survive," I said. "You know *my* crimes, don't you?"

"I am aware of your prior acts. Catalog does not judge. I observe."

"So tell me. We'll be equals."

"You mock me."

"Not at all."

The sensors on its carapace shifted, and a low humming sound came from within.

"Before I assumed the carapace, I was a Miner," it said. "I improperly set forward a planet's destruction, to reduce it to spaceborne rubble. Before a crew containing my crèche-mate could evacuate."

"Crèche-mate . . . What did you have against him, or her?"

"Him. He was destined to bond with the heir to a powerful

family, highest in our rate. I had been passed over. It was not just, so I felt."

"You blew him up?"

"Utterly. And twelve of his crew."

This put my stalwart companion in an entirely new light. "The Juridicals chose you anyway?"

"They did."

"You must have a very special quality."

"Yes." Again the hum. "Depth of depravity."

"I once tried to destroy an entire species," I said.

"Perhaps you are destined to become like me," Catalog said.

"Perhaps. I don't judge. You don't judge. We're here to observe. And to do our best to survive."

"Correct."

"Glad to have that resolved." I held out my hand and gripped one shoulder. Catalog raised one of its hands and we clasped palms, then each of us drew a Y with a finger, me, over my nose, Catalog, over the front portion of its forward sensor. A Warrior's awareness of shame.

"Now, you're an honorary Warrior-Servant," I said.

"If you insist, Didact."

We waited.

"You're still connected with the Juridicals, aren't you?"

"No," it said. "All our channels have closed. The Domain is also blocked."

"They're moving Halos again?" I asked with a shudder.

"A possible explanation," Catalog said. "Or *that*."

We were approaching the middle of the tangle, nudged along by a coiling ribbon of star road, shoved toward an assemblage unlike any Precursor structure I had ever seen.

The star roads had combined to sketch out a great, parallel double-arc, like two arrow-shooting bows pulled from an ancient armory. And at the center of each double bow glowed a brilliant ring surrounding a pit of blackness deeper than space.

"It's not a ship," I said.

"Is it like the Ark?" Catalog asked.

"I don't know."

"Maybe they hope to collect us, as the Librarian collects her beasts?" Catalog withdrew most of its sensors. "Before all connections closed, Haruspis supplied me with a number of records. I have conducted a search and can now recognize the structure."

"How?"

"Testimony from the Lifeshaper and others across the ecumene," Catalog said.

"She was deposed?"

"Yes."

"And you received her testimony?"

"Before the network closed, yes."

The double bow overwhelmed our visual field.

After a long, agonizing moment—Catalog no doubt luxuriating in its knowledge but utterly silent and still—I asked, "Willing to share?"

love planets—those agglomerations of rocks and volatiles found around most stars throughout the galaxy, and even between the stars.

Most living things are born on gas-infused, stony orbs. Still, the exceptions are fascinating. I have long studied those ice-bound moons where blind scuttlers arise in secret oceans to stack rocks and burrow deep. Stifled beneath kilometers of mineral-cold ice, they rarely if ever get to see the stars, living out a dreaming existence in perpetual, sulfur-rich darkness.

Three times I have liberated icy moons—opened crevices in the deep frozen shields and freed the inbred scuttlers. They climbed up and out, were astonished by the depth and emptiness of the unbounded void of space—and then fell back, terrified and discouraged, to seek refuge again beneath the ice. They wiped their minds and their histories of what I had shown them. Now, they do not remember anything about Fore-runners.

I do not know if their ice will protect them against the Halos. Likely not. However, a great many were small . . . less than the size of my hand. That might save them.

How much like those scuttlers all young species are! The empty greatness of space is a thick wall erected between lovers, harsh and cruel.

When Forerunners were young and bound to our natal planet, we must have wondered who and what we were, how we would measure up if we met our peers—or our superiors—out there in the void. But the challenge of simply crossing the void was so tremendous that for millennia after we acquired speech, fire, art, machines, we still clung to our rock and shunned the endless vacuum.

Inexperience—naivety—hope and fear.

Young wisdom.

———————

Hulk after ancient hulk we carved open without resistance, with-out reaction. All records within the equivalent of our ancillas—primitive memory stores, huge and bulky—had decayed to random patterns of binary garble.

Binary! After our great memory catastrophes, digital stor-age had been given way to substrates of quantum foam. Yet on these ships, the last dim hope of log and history crumbled at a touch.

Ten million years is a long time for machines.

We finished knowing little more than when we began—a vague recognition of shared heritage, a realization that these ships, gathered about the star roads like so many flocks of dead birds suspended in a silent gray cathedral, reminded us of archaic designs in Builder ritual. No more. And no less.

"They were Forerunner, that's all we may ever know," Clearance said.

"We could transport the best Builder technicians out here," Keeper suggested. "We could set loose our finest researchers to go ship by ship . . . *Then* we would learn!"

But Keeper's enthusiasm was not convincing. Back in our home galaxy, where nearly all of Forerunner history had played out, preparations to fight the advance of the Flood would certainly take precedence.

The one thing we could all surmise about the great fleet we were leaving behind, mute and pitifully old, was that no species had ever mounted such an effort except to save itself. No species had ever gone to such great lengths for any purpose other than all-out war.

And what about the Precursors, whose cathedral roads stretched around so many planets and interlaced the stars?

Where had they gone?

———

Audacity took us to the inner stars of the great Spider in yet another jump, toward the tiny orange sun.

Fresh light from the unique living world greeted us as we arrived in the target system—light less than two seconds old. "Wonderful, fresh light," Chant noted. "Makes me feel more connected to reality."

What had been statistical from a great distance now resolved to certainty. Here, there were no star roads, no orbiting constructs, no ships. *Audacity* brought us sharp images even through the planet's wavering atmosphere.

We studied individuals—most seen from above—as well as gatherings in small towns or villages. Tens of thousands, perhaps more. But certainly not millions.

A lonely and simple planet.

Our emotions reached down.

"Their technological status is minimal—fire, ceramics, some metal-working," Dawn said. "Because they are so few, even compared to their resources, they must exercise population control. Beyond that, they seem to have returned to a state of natural evolution."

Chant continued with less startling details. "Subsurface and volcanic vent biota is nonexistent. There's nothing in the way of an underground biosphere. No signs of ancient reservoirs of fuel—carbonaceous or petroleum-based."

"If they arrived with the fleet," Keeper said, "they've been here ten million years."

A prospect so astonishing it could scarcely be believed. Either their ancestors had been forced to colonize a desperately impoverished planet, or they had long ago shed most of their knowledge.

We absorbed this with the proper silent respect.

"Lack of resources *could* hold back progress," Keeper said. I noticed a certain doubtful disdain in his tone.

"Even so, they must have stripped themselves of everything," Dawn said in wonder.

"Or they were abandoned, left here with nothing," Clearance said. "Judging from the mineral evidence, life didn't exist before it came here with the Forerunners. There is a fair percentage of radioactive ore, however, and the oceans—such as they are—are rich with deuterium."

"They could have escaped if they had wanted to," I concluded. "Weapons?" I asked *Audacity*.

"Nothing that can harm us," the ship responded. "They live and work by fire alone. And not a great deal of that."

"But *why*?" Chant asked.

Audacity entered low orbit.

"We're intercepting sounds," Dawn said, and with a lift of her fingers, played for us words being spoken in a small village just a few hundred kilometers below. We understood nothing.

"It's not ancient Digon?" Keeper asked.

"That reached its peak less than three hundred thousand years go," Dawn said. "We have no idea what form of Digon, if any, even existed when the fleet left our galaxy. Ship will gather sounds from as many points a possible, but already, the language seems far simpler than our own."

"Simpler language is often more advanced, syntactically," Keeper said, and brightened at a thought. "Their technology and structures might be hidden—they might be in defensive mode, hiding them! There could be threats in Path Kethona we do not recognize."

"More likely, they chose to suppress technology at the deepest level," Dawn said. Keeper fell back in dismay. He could not bring himself to believe Forerunners would ever abandon advanced engineering.

"No doubt they still *dig*," Clearance said with a smug air. "They've become Miners. All of them. How else would they find stone and clay?"

I have difficulty knowing when Miners are trying to be funny.

None of us had ever seen Forerunners so abject and primitive. They averaged about two thirds the height and mass of a healthy Manipular. Their structures were rarely taller than one or two stories, or wider than five or ten meters.

"How can we learn *anything* from them?" Keeper asked. "How can they maintain any sort of culture?"

"They likely rely on oral histories," Chant said. "We've seen it in other species."

"Maybe they're some sort of Flood residue—an inept cross-breeding," Keeper said.

"The genetic heritage is clear," Chant insisted. "At the cellular level, they aren't very different from us. I think the first group to arrive made the best of a tough situation. They could not overburden meager resources. But there *are* other animals down there, some serving as beasts of burden."

With a twist of judgment, she added, "And some as *food*." She paused to enjoy our surprise. Forerunners have not consumed animals for many millions of years. "More interesting still, their animals show descent from the original population. Including those they eat. Even the plants have Forerunner genetics—if they are in fact plants. They likely arrived without a genetic library—hence no way to create a complex ecosystem. They used what they had." She looked up, eyes round. "I wonder if they'd enjoy eating *us*?"

Keeper could not contain his disgust. "What could they have done to deserve such degradation?"

"Nothing like it in our history," Dawn said.

Chant did her best to put together a useful social picture of our long-lost relatives.

Audacity decided that landing directly on the planet still posed too much risk. We could not yet be sure whether what we were seeing was real, or whether the Forerunners below—even should they be the sole masters of this strange world, and not peculiar pets—might be hiding their true level of technology. Keeper in particular favored this view. He preferred an explanation of camouflage and hidden danger over what he deemed Forerunner disgrace.

Audacity brought forth two excursion craft, seekers with the lightest of armaments. A quick lottery of needs and circumstance determined that three of us would descend and two would remain in orbit.

I insisted on joining the excursion.

Our seekers penetrated a low deck of thin clouds, then followed the sinuous contours of the greatest range of craggy mountains, between which lay immense freshwater lakes. Because the planet's axis was perpendicular to its orbit, and had been for many hundreds of millions of years, the land had never been subject to heavy winters or severe glaciations. The weather was steady and dull—low overcast much of the time, infrequent but violent thunderstorms, heavy precipitation that nonetheless brought only light snow to the highest mountains.

The planet had only one small ocean that covered the southern polar regions, its dense, salty waters filled with bitter minerals. All the other water on the planet was fresh and contained in the deep, clear lakes.

Our seekers flew over a low mountain ridge, then dropped and hovered a few thousand meters above a brown, gently sloping plain. The breaking of thin lava dikes had long ago broached one of the deep lakes, loosing immense floods that had shaped chaotic terrain across the northern third of the plain. The plant-like growth here was scrubby, set low to resist channeled winds between the wrinkled mountain ridges—winds that blew sand and carved tumuli, caprocks, and other grotesque formations.

At the southern end of the rugged mountains, the mouth of a

narrow valley revealed a great cleft in the range, faced with pale vertical faces of granitic rock.

Clearance was not impressed by the local geology. "A place of exile, not opportunity," he said. "I would not have chosen it."

"Spoken like a Miner," Chant said. "Lifeworkers would see other opportunities, other forces at work."

In my experience, a lean and barren world could force rapid cultural growth that would in turn promote a quick renewal of technology. We do enjoy our creature comforts. But that was not the case here. Who or what had compelled them to seek this strange penance, to become a focus of all evolution, with the unavoidable result of cannibalism?

The seekers landed us within a kilometer of a town. Low, flat dwellings lay like sedimentary layers on the slope of a low ridge.

We climbed down to survey the plain and the flat town. Clearance, on my instruction, stayed close to his vehicle.

A low wall lay within forty meters of our landing. Within the wall, ten squat, tawny-furred animals, each massing about five hundred kilograms, grazed on the few dusky green shoots that poked up through cracked and crumbled soil. The wall was likely a channel to keep small floods from intruding into the town. The grazing animals easily stepped over it to find fresh shoots.

Clouds blew free from the mountains. Sunshine played over the rolling, crackled ground.

"Look at their faces," Chant said. I already had—and did not like the resemblance. I approached the closest animal. It stood its ground and patiently watched through closely spaced gray eyes.

"Looks like Clearance," Chant said.

Clearance framed his face with his gloves and looked domestic.

"Stop that," I said.

"Apologies."

"More like Keeper," I suggested. Chant covered her mouth.

I stooped a few meters from the beast—rather, the adapted Forerunner—to more closely examine its feet. The digits and phalanges were indeed based on a stem Forerunner body plan. These creatures were as related to us as their herdsmen in the buildings beyond. But intelligence was not apparent.

The grazer turned its head, incurious, and bent its neck to pluck more shoots.

A few hundred meters to the north, closer to the town's outlying buildings and surrounded by another low wall, lay a plot of gray-green bushes. If we approached that plot, almost certainly we would be noticed and challenged.

I looked back to Clearance. "It's much more likely they'll see our kinship without armor."

Clearance, standing beside the first seeker, was not enthusiastic. In our helmets, we heard him say, "I doubt they'd recognize us even if we were *naked*. They've fallen so very far."

"Even so," I said, then instructed my ancilla. My armor unfolded, pulled away, and arranged itself neatly on the compacted dry mud. My ancilla and I had long ago reached an agreement about solicitous warnings. None were given. It knew my mind.

"I shall go in without armor as well," Chant said.

"No. Just me."

"Lifeshaper!"

Both of my shipmates looked distressed.

"Just me," I insisted. "Clearance will stay here to back us up." I preferred for the Miner to remain by the seekers, in case Chant and I were suffering from that willful blindness that sometimes afflicts Lifeworkers too fascinated by nature to recognize a threat.

She and I walked across the dried mud. I wore only under-linings, feet bare but for thong-socks. The ground was hard and cold, the air brisk but not dangerously so.

At my signal, Chant fell back about twenty paces—she had wanted to precede me but I forbade it. Our training was explicit in how to approach indigenes, but never had we approached *Fore-runners* in such circumstances. At any rate they were indigenous only by courtesy. The courtesy of ten million years' habitation was real enough, however.

Beyond a waist-high mud-and-stone wall, no doubt built to keep out the grazers, a tilled field supported many rows of gray-green stalks topped by spiky leaves, below which hung wrinkled-looking fruit or pods. The wind rustled leaves and fruit. They sounded dry and unappetizing, but whatever their genetics, they looked the part of fixed plants, not Forerunners doing penance rooted in dirt.

Neither of us intruded on the patch. Rather, we kept outside the wall and thus were directed toward the nearest complex of buildings, irregular pentagonal structures made of mud brick, with stones pieced out along their foundations. The mud had been scored with crude strings of unfamiliar symbols. Oblong door-ways were spaced one or two to each building, each covered by a rough woven hanging.

In the nearest doorway, a wrinkled, thick hand drew back a hanging, and for just a moment, a shadowy figure stood there, striking an odd pose, naked, as if hoping for inspection and ap-proval. A female, I was fairly sure, but not in her prime, with shrunken belly-teats and very different patterns of facial hair. Most distinct, a line of gray fur reached around from her cheeks to join beneath a flat, pushed-back nose. At least *that* was classically Forerunner.

The female darted back and the curtain dropped.

In another doorway, back among the main cluster of dwellings, another curtain drew aside and a second figure stepped into filtered sunshine: a male with a square, broad face, thick-furred about chin and forehead. Columnar legs supported a squat and bulky torso. He wore heavy gray clothing. His face was rugged, observant, but lacked any readable expression.

Behind him, silhouetted by the flickering glow of a fire or lantern, stood a younger female dressed in lighter clothing. Sexual dimorphism was evident but not extreme. They were far closer to each other in appearance than I was to the Didact—but of course ours was an artificial dimorphism, rate-determined, and it seemed they had given up all that here, if ever they had possessed it.

I was fascinated! Never had I seen Forerunners so different from our root stock: less than a meter and a half in height, broad across shoulders and midriff, thick of leg and short of arm, with long, curling fingers—five fingers only on each hand.

I subdued a familiar giddiness of discovery. My ancilla would have controlled that response with a subtle tickle in my brain stem. Now, I swallowed hard and drew myself back to full alertness, forcing a deliberate pinch of anxiety.

The wind ruffled my underlinings, as I had expected, making my own shape clear. To them I would appear strangely tall and slender, eyes large, skin pale. I doubted they would recognize our kinship by sight alone.

I held out my hands.

One thing we do know is that early Forerunners had a keen sense of smell and used it to determine kinship and other social relations.

The breeze now blew from behind. The male sniffed through

wide nostrils, wider than my own. He stepped forward with a light sway, bandy-legged to a degree that reminded me of a first-form Warrior-Servant, around the corner of the dwelling, where he stopped and gestured to the female, who now also came forward.

"All is well, we have traveled far, and we are here to speak with you," I said in the most ancient known Digon dialect. "We come from our old home to this new home. Are you well?"

The male waved his hand and made an ululating hoot. The female shunted sideways toward the male. Neither seemed afraid. The female canted her head, studying me. Her nostrils flared. It didn't seem much of a stretch to interpret her reaction as intrigued but puzzled.

Throughout the dwellings, more hangings parted and other figures appeared—males, females, all of middle age or older. Obviously, they allowed themselves to age in natural time. No children were visible.

On all the dwellings, the walls had been stamped with unfamiliar symbols. But along the outward-facing wall of one dwelling, prominently displayed, ten large, circular emblems had been carved, repetitions of a mark so often found in Forerunner decorations that, in our daily lives, we hardly notice its presence: a circle around a treelike branching of angular veins.

Long ago, among Lifeworkers, I had heard it referred to as the Eld. Others—mostly Builders—called it the Tree-mark. Forerunners had associated it with the Mantle for as long as can be remembered, but its origin remained a mystery.

And yet here it was—confirming . . . what?

Memorializing *what*, precisely?

Again I felt a deep unease. To come all this distance and find brothers and sisters completely isolated, and in such circumstances . . . yet still exhibiting the most ubiquitous mark of Forerunner culture! Why should that surprise or chill me? But it did.

Something in me did not want to find the Eld, with all its associations and connections. Not here.

A small crowd gathered in a loose clump between the low dwellings. The bulky male had ceased his hooting. No one else made a sound.

I shifted my gaze around the group, then repeated what I had said before, adding, "We are Forerunners. You are the same. Is there anyone here who speaks of times past?"

The old Digon did not come easily—no doubt the ancilla could have pronounced the words better, or gotten the grammar more correct. Words live as genes live, some parts conserved, others wildly variable. But then, we already knew it was unlikely they understood even this old tongue.

An older female broke from the group and with a shrug of her shoulders walked toward us, stopping within three paces. Chant seemed ready to intervene, but I waggled my hand behind my back.

The old female stared beyond my shoulder, then turned her eyes on me. She pulled thin lips back from strong gray teeth, favoring me with a full-blown smile. These Forerunners were still capable of that rictus, while I could barely manage to lift the corners of my lips!

But I did my best and again held out my hands.

The female grasped my outstretched fingers. Her own fingers were covered with dirt and green stains. They felt greasy, but her grip was firm. She tugged gently, urging me to come with her, and again favored me with a smile.

I followed. After ten long steps, we seemed to cross a line, and the rest rushed forward to surround us. A smaller group broke free and encircled Chant. In her armor, she towered above them all, in a posture of calmness and caution—as we had been trained. Best to appear neither too friendly nor defenseless and predictable.

The crowds merged, corralling us into their center, touching us not unkindly but with rude familiarity. Chant's eyes flashed. Their touches grew more intimate. They wished to know everything about me. What they discovered surprised them. They pulled back a little, dismayed, but kept smiling. Our methods of reproduction had diverged substantially over millions of years.

The crowd now parted, forming a channel down which another, much older female, with stiff, steely gray fur on both crown and shoulders, pushed through, waved the first female aside, and took a position beside me, then looked at all the others, as if daring them to interfere.

She turned and grasped my wrist, lifting my arm.

The others pulled back.

She looked up into my face, smiled brilliantly, showing strong teeth—gray and none too clean. At that moment, I swear that but for the nose and fur she seemed almost human—something in her eyes, her curiously committed expression, an atavistic glimpse at what may have been our common roots long, long ago. . . .

And then she bit me. Fastened those gray teeth into my forearm, jerked her jaw sidewise, opening up shallow but painful wounds. I did not move, did not cry out—held my ground.

She jerked back, blood purple on her lips and teeth—my blood—and again that smile! I pulled loose, looking down on her in wonder. She seemed proud of my reaction.

Clearance had returned to his seeker the moment the crowd surrounded us. Now he shot over our heads, releasing a swarm of small monitors, followed by a fusillade of blinding flashes and snapping booms. The crowd scattered. The seeker dropped. Manipulators reached down, took hold of Chant and me, and lifted us out of the village, through the air, back to our own seeker. In that same sweep, with a few wrenching maneuvers, he gathered up my folded armor as well, and then set us all down gently enough, but in truth the flight had hurt me more than the bite.

"I didn't ask for help," I said.

Clearance dropped from his seeker and glared at us. "You were attacked," he said. "They were *chewing* on you."

Amused, woozy from shock, I had to agree. Chant examined my arm. The bites were clean, shallow, but thorough—and covered with spittle.

"Don't spray them," I told her.

She looked up in disbelief.

"Leave them be," I insisted.

"What if there's an infection—or a poison?" she asked.

"Then we'll learn something and the armor will take care of it. I regret only that we frightened them. Leave me be—I'm all right."

She looked me over in irritation. "As a direct command, Lifeshaper, I must obey. But I protest your taking that kind of risk."

"As do I," Clearance said.

"Think it so if you must," I said. "But think it through first."

They both made a show of considering, then Chant said, stubbornly, "I cannot see it as you do, Lifeshaper."

"That's because you are more concerned about my welfare

than about learning why these people *are here*," I said. "But that is our mission. I do not refuse your aid out of spite."

"Why, then?"

"Think again about what you saw."

Chant bowed her head. "You sense a relationship with the old female. Please put on your armor, at the very least . . . in case there *is* danger."

I did as she suggested but refused my ancilla's treatment as I had Chant's. "Give it time," I said. "Something benign was intended, I'm sure of it."

"Violence is benign here?" my ancilla asked.

"The better question is, why would she bite only *me*?" I favored them with a glow of intrigue.

"Because Chant was armored," Clearance said. The situation had given him a scare and he would take awhile to recover his calm. Strangely, I felt jubilant, then contented . . . happy. Something in my wounds . . . a toxin?

No, a message. And a small reward for allowing myself to be bitten.

"You are not thinking clearly, Lifeshaper," Clearance said. "We will remedy that."

"No! Let it be. Let me feel all of it."

Clearance was dumfounded. "We are responsible, Lifeshaper! We should return to *Audacity*. If you are injured, if you *die*—"

Chant reached out to quiet him, then dropped her head in obeisance. "Enlighten me, Lifeshaper."

"Enlighten *us*!" Clearance insisted.

"I feel fine. Interesting, but fine. Let's stay here for a while and see what they do next."

We stood back near the seekers and watched as the village

calmed. No apparent offense was taken at Clearance's harrying. The people returned to their huts—all but the old female, who stared across the distance between us, face fixed and pale.

Waiting.

We had found Forerunners. Whether they remembered anything of that ancient fleet, or why they had come to this planet, we had no way of knowing. But these people were our only way of getting an answer. And judging from what I had seen in the old female's expression, as her teeth sank into my flesh, there were more surprises to come. The bite was not a warning. It was a prelude, a test—and perhaps one way to trade diagnostic samples.

Touch is direct and meaningful, but tissue tells the tale.

———

Night's shadow moved along the valley and up the mountains. The dim, thousand-veiled red and purple glow of the Spider, young stars blurred as if through tears of old emotion, rose high over the land. In the twilight—on this world, there was never true night or darkness—we kept vigil, while from the village rose a few distant cries, shouts, and then . . . silence.

Perhaps sleep.

No doubt Keeper and Dawn, circling the planet in *Audacity,* would take it personally if I or the others were injured. My foolhardiness would doubtless cause distress as they contemplated having to greet the Didact, when he emerged from his Cryptum, with the grim news of his wife's distant demise.

But the Didact and I had parted in the all-too-poignant awareness we might never see each other again.

That was the least of my worries.

I could feel changes coming.

My intuition was confirmed while we rested in the larger of the two seekers and reconsidered our options.

I allowed my armor to conduct a deep analysis of my situation, but not to intervene—not yet. When it had finished, the ancilla interrupted my meditation, flashing a spectrum of concern.

"There is no poison, Lifeshaper," it announced. "But you harbor foreign microbes."

"Forerunner genetics?"

"Entirely."

"From the old female's bite?"

"No particles in the air or the soil have such properties. You anticipated this?"

"We *see* primal choices and minimal technology—but that may be deceptive. They use what they have."

"Yet they remain bound to this planet."

"They have no immediate need to leave. They may be happy."

"Contented Forerunners?" My ancilla took on a dubiously green cast. "The particles are spreading throughout your system and your nervous system, into your brain. We cannot let them continue. What you are in immediate need of is a purge. The danger is too great."

"Are the particles provoking any immune response?"

"Not yet, Lifeshaper. You are calm and happy. I do not know what that implies."

I *was* happy—happier than I had been in many years. But I knew it would not last.

"I think . . . I think it will be important that I return to the old woman and allow her to bite me again."

The ancilla flashed through another spectrum. "Your goal is . . . *obscure*, Lifeshaper!"

"Be patient," I suggested, closing my eyes.

It seemed likely that biting, or being bitten, was a two-way process here. What could the woman learn from retrieving a few of her tiny scouts, even now conducting a no doubt delicate but thorough survey? And without provoking my extremely vigilant immune system!

What did she *need* to learn?

I spoke of this to none of the others, and did not communicate with *Audacity* on the matter. Morning would come soon, and even I preferred to act out my theories in the light of day. Night is a difficult time for those who live close to nature; day is safer.

We had long since lost the habit of sleep. In our armor, all the needs of sleep are taken care of, and a smooth, healthy continuity of consciousness is possible. What dreams we infrequently succumb to—waking dreams—are administrative and diagnostic. Housekeeping dreams. Hardly amusing at all.

Yet in the dark, with the old woman's "scouts" coursing through me, I was beginning to shed my calm.

I was beginning to dread the silence and the inaction.

And what tomorrow might bring.

Sunrise pushed through a thin deck of clouds, gray and sad. We passed our complete reports to *Audacity,* then planned our return to the town.

Again, all would wear armor except for me.

"They eat their relatives, you know," Chant reminded me. "What if they decide you taste better?"

"I'm sure I do," I said. "Better than *those*." I looked toward the grazing livestock. "Certainly cleaner."

My favorite teacher, from whom I had taken my maturing imprint, had stated to all her charges, "Life is deadly to all its parts. No emotion fits our challenge better than humor."

I still showed no obvious reaction to the old woman's bite—no swelling, no fever, no other sign of infection or distress. But something was definitely working within me.

I murmured to myself, lips moving in an unfamiliar way. The words made sense, I understood them, but they came strangely to my lips. My muscles had to grow accustomed to shaping such sounds. The new words—new to me and my muscles—demanded a great many tonguing flexures and rattling glottals.

Before I shed my armor, the ancilla reiterated its concern. "Your mind is changing, Lifeshaper. The particles are distressingly active."

I replied, "Something's teaching me. It's strange, but I don't think it's dangerous—not yet."

And then I removed my helmet, stepped out of the armor, and crossed the cracked plain, again in just flimsy underlinings.

The wind was brisker and colder this morning and chilled me deeply. "Remember," I said to Chant and Clearance. "No intervention."

"What if they try to kill you?" Chant asked.

I rolled up one sleeve, an open invitation. "They won't," I said, but how I knew that, I could not explain even to myself.

The old woman smiled. She thought you were funny, and you needed to be let in on the joke.

I walked into the town. In a sketchy manner I saw the buildings quite differently—felt a growing familiarity with everything around me. I began to see and then feel the austere beauty of the sere mountains, the spare, fit design of the town spread beneath their rising shadow—the glory of the Spider's night-time glow. These Forerunners had not given up so much after all. They had simply grown into a new sophistication, using all that had been left to them. By biting me, the old female was infusing me with what she knew—and perhaps much more. Already a kind of context was filling in around those strange words, like paint spreading out between the lines.

The bite had been a gift. With that gift, in my flesh, in my mind, came not just their language, not just a sense of place and an awareness of their essential nature—but their version of history.

The old steel-furred female met me at the second wall, the one designed to keep their shambling beasts out of the crop field. Four others accompanied her, three females and one male. Nervously, they touched hands as if in search of affirmation, support—but also updating each other on the night's proceedings in the town, across the valley, even from over the mountains. Their touch conveyed news from all around the planet.

I knew this, recognized it—desired it. All it took was brief contact and in a few minutes, those microbes that carried news, history, language, would push between our fingers and infuse through our blood.

The little scouts, the tiny agents, were their equivalent of ancillas.

Clever children, these.

The old female did not smile, but studied me with a concerned, quizzical expression.

"Do you understand me now?" she asked.

"Yes . . . but go slowly," I answered. My lips felt numb, clumsy.

"There is still danger. The others fear you have come to punish them."

"After so many millions of years?"

The word I used referred to their round of a 244 days, since there were no seasons and no moon here.

"Has it been that long?" she asked.

Her companions stayed back, hands extended.

Clearance and Chant stood their ground by the seekers.

"I'm astonished you remember those times," I said.

"I do not—not personally. None of us do, separately. But after you arrived, we assembled a quorum. A hundred of us held hands. We tried to reach back. Some of that I have passed to you . . . pardon me for our methods."

"You took a great risk," I said.

"I am old, no loss," she said. "You do not appear old, but you *taste* very old indeed . . . if I may judge."

I held out my arm and pulled up the sleeve. "I am thousands of years old," I said. "Do you need another?"

She looked aside, then back, brows raised in puzzlement. "No," she said. "What we suspected has been confirmed. Did it take you so long to travel here, or . . . ?" She could not immediately retrieve the words and concepts—for them, concepts as old as the history they had gathered to reassemble. Her face creased in a frown.

"No matter," I said. "We are here, and we do not seek to punish, but to learn more, as much as you can tell us, however you can tell us."

"Shall we bite your friends?" she asked. "We do not actually *enjoy* it, you know. Only the most ignorant are treated so."

"Not necessary," I said. "I will bite them myself, later."

The old female smiled and rubbed her elbows in high amusement. She looked toward Clearance and Chant. "They *do* look ignorant. So stiff in those shells."

She took my wrist in one greasy hand and gently squeezed it. "Now that you understand, it's clear what we must do. I feel it inside. There is so much to pass along. Old instructions, old bequests. Communications . . . Fuzzy and faded, like stick drawings in rain-washed sand. But you will see them well enough. They could make more sense to you than to us."

I could see she felt no privilege or surprise that we had happened upon this place, upon her. I sensed that any town on this planet would have one like her—or quickly make one.

"What is your name?" I asked.

"Glow-of-Old-Suns," she said.

"That sounds so much like one of *our* names. I am called the Librarian."

"How came you by that name?"

"It was given to me by my teachers when I was young, because I enjoyed traveling through great stores of knowledge."

"We are *all* libraries here," Glow said, turning me about, nudging, then walking beside me back to the seekers. "There are other ways the old ones preserved knowledge. I'll show you the place. It is quite a ways from here."

"Shall we carry you there?" I asked.

"Yes." She waved her hand ahead. "I hope I can see it and know where to stop—from high up. Don't go too fast, or too high." She patted my forearm and stared at the seeker. "Do they frighten you, those *things*?"

The old female sat stiffly in the seeker's enfolding interior, eyes wide. She quickly grasped the concept of the displays, twisted her head this way and that, following the colors and symbols as they wrapped around us. She gripped my arm as the craft lifted—not where she had bitten me. That had already healed. The pressure seemed to call up more of the information within my blood and flesh.

I felt myself coming into a denser appreciation of the way these people saw themselves—and then, like a shallow coloring laid over all that, how they felt about *us*.

They felt an extraordinary guilt. Or rather, somebody—not these people precisely—had once felt guilt, and now it suffused through them all, but generations before they had numbed it, stored it away in safe cubbyholes, rarely acknowledged.

Until now.

She surveyed the landscape as we rose, then pointed east and said, "That way."

Clearance moved the seeker as instructed, at an altitude of a thousand meters. The old female never once let go of my arm. Her sense of direction was precise. Perhaps she had climbed the mountains and looked down over a similar view—but I thought it more likely she already knew.

Keeper and Chant remained with the other seeker. Despite my convictions, I still thought it best to keep options in reserve. The power of the old female's bite might be more significant and powerful than I yet understood. Those little agents . . . what else could they manage, as protectors, or as *persuaders*?

The old female guided us along a steady curve.

"We're following old field lines, I think," Clearance said. "But there's no longer a magnetic field. Hasn't been for millions of years."

I translated for Glow, but she paid us no mind—merely directed us with her knobby finger. We passed over deep dry gorges and wide valleys. Long lakes crossed the valleys like the marks of animal claws. Chaotic terrain. Thousands of kilometers of it.

And now we came to the peculiar feature we had noticed even from low orbit. A broad patch of grayish yellow had spread over a gorge four kilometers deep. A wide, steaming fissure opened along a two-kilometer stretch. The yellowish coloration was caused by minute bacteria and other organisms feeding on sulfur compounds. The entire valley was filled with a thin haze—not smoke but dust. Dust from spores—funguslike organisms—nothing like the Flood, of course, but bearing Forerunner genes.

Most remarkable.

"That is where we need to go," Glow told me.

Clearance brought the seeker around, interpreting the direction of Glow's finger, tracking its quick, precise changes, until she lifted it straight up, stared at him with her piercing gray-blue eyes, and said, "There."

We landed.

"It's here," Glow said. "You walk out there . . . naked. Walk with me. Not him. Keep him away. He is not wise."

I conveyed this to Clearance, who tipped his head. "Not wise at all," he murmured. "But if there's the slightest hint of danger, I'll grab you up so fast . . ."

His expression brooked no disagreement.

Glow and I walked out on solid, rocky ground. Our feet pushed up a fine cloud of spores. "We cannot contain all the memories of our ancestors," the old female said. "We do not want them. We wish to be ourselves, with our own memories. And so they are kept here. When we need the past, which is rarely, we come here. We walk this way, and we walk back. When we return, we have what they need."

"A biological Domain," I said.

"I do not know that word," the old female said, walking ahead. "I have only been here once, when I was young and we had a dispute regarding a matter of law and tradition. The ones who were in power then were shown to be wrong by what we brought back, the memories and traditions we carried. They stepped down and were replaced. No one defies this place or what it holds."

Stripped of all technology, left to their own ingenuity, the ancient Forerunners had created a completely organic and living way to store their histories. "Do you know how far back this memory goes?" I asked, bewildered by the possibilities.

"To the beginning. Days ago, we see a light in the sky like a moving star, and it is you. I have a memory . . ."

She turned and held up her hands, then slowly lowered them, along with her head, and got down on her knees, not before me, but the far cliffs that rose thousands of meters into the dusty skies.

"The first of us scratched and drew and marked those cliffs with whatever they had available—rocks, sticks."

The yellowish dust coated my garments and my skin. Some of it irritated my nose and lungs. I wondered what I would dream tonight, or remember in weeks to come.

The old female pushed painfully to her feet and walked toward the cliffs, then looked over her shoulder and urged me on.

The high rock walls were hung with orange, fibrous growths, like lichen or moss, moving slowly over the smoothly and naturally planed surfaces. Along their course, the mosses clung with rasping roots. Where patches had died and fallen away, they revealed etched symbols—many kilometers of them, arrayed in spirals and whorled radiances. While I now recognized the script, and the methods of reading the symbols seemed familiar, the symbols themselves were still hidden from me and could not be deciphered by my ancilla.

"These mosses are sisters to us. They travel back and forth from one end of this valley to the other," the old female said. "When wind and dust and rain wipe away what they carve, they slide back and replace it, always with the same memories."

Ten million years ago, the Forerunners abandoned on this barren world had chosen to store history and memory not only in blood and flesh, but in these rustling, spreading, rock-climbing growths.

"What do they mean?" I asked.

"They tell our stories. And a greater, older story." She moved closer, examining my face. "It's coming a little slow in you. But soon."

And it did arrive, but several days after.

I stayed in the valley, squatting on the fine, packed, stone-scattered soil, watching the fiery passage of the sun as it rose and set, tending now and then to functions my armor would once have taken care of—and by this process, I think, coming to better understand the old female.

As we waited, I felt a growing warmth in my body and brain as what the old female knew—what had been passed from generation to generation for ten million years—flowered within me.

One night, just as dawn cast faint beams over the easternmost wall of rock, I stood, stretched out my sore muscles, and began to walk to the beginning of the valley, several kilometers away. Here, I found the seekers, along with Chant and Keeper, who awaited me with looks of concern.

Chant approached and checked my health. "Are you well and fit, Lifeshaper?" she asked.

"So far," I said. "The old female's knowledge is growing. If it turns into something like a personal imprint—if I start looking and acting as she does . . ."

"We will be watchful," Keeper said. "What should we do if that happens?"

"Put me back in my armor and reset me. Purge the old female's knowledge."

"That may not be easy, Lifeshaper."

"I know. Let's hope for the best."

The old female had followed me, and squatted again at the head of the valley, watching us with her haunted smile.

"The script on the canyon walls is looking more familiar," I said. "I'm going to begin over there." I indicated the point where the wall reached its greatest height and the script became uniform and sharply carved.

"The mosses move and write," Keeper said. "But do they change what they write? Do they erase and revise?"

"No," I replied.

"Then this valley holds their entire history."

"Maybe. But part of it, at the far end, consists of something so upsetting to them, so vitally separated, that they tasked these mosses to record it where they wouldn't have to see."

Chant regarded me with heavy-lidded eyes. "A crime greater than anything since? Why not let it fade completely?"

But a look at the old female confirmed this would be out of character. Other Forerunners might run from their histories—but not these.

We did not get very far, in either case—in fleeing the twin bow made up of star roads, or in understanding what my wife was saying ten thousand light-years away, in orbit around Erde-Tyrene.

Catalog's connection with the Juridical network had broken off before the holographic data could be completely assembled. Catalog did its best to interpret what he could of my wife's interrupted testimony.

"After she put you in a Cryptum, and stored the Cryptum on Erde-Tyrene, she commissioned a special ship, assembled a crew, and made a visit to Path Kethona. This was about nine hundred and fifty years ago."

"Why?"

"To trace the origin of the Flood."

"And what did she find?"

"All I can assemble from incomplete strings of data is that she found a lost settlement of Forerunners, met an old woman, was bitten, began to understand their ancient language, and visited a valley between giant stone walls covered with crawling mosses."

"That's it?"

"I can hypothesize a little more based on the patterns—but am not allowed to do so. The testimony is faulty at best. I violate my vows by telling you this much."

Outside the ship, the huge double bow structures parted and slid around us, like a pair of long, curved walls. The walls then fanned out into two parabolic dishes, with a huge dark circle at the center.

The dark circle glowed brightly around its edge.

"Do you know what that is?" Catalog asked.

"Not a clue," I said.

"Is it interested in us, or just making a show?"

The star roads had become extremely malleable. Between these parabolic dishes, three medium-sized Forerunner ships—all Dreadnought-class—veered onto intersecting courses that would bring them upon us in just a few minutes.

"Is everyone secure below?" I asked the ship.

"As secure as possible," the ship responded in its broken voice.

"We're about to be boarded," I said. "What can you do to put off the inevitable—and as soon as we are captured, destroy yourself?"

"Some capabilities remain," the ship said. "Not many. If exercised, they will delay capture by a few minutes at most." The voice seemed to acquire strength and tone. "That will be sufficient for a directed explosion of our drives to knock the stasis bubbles in my hold outward through the gap between those objects, along with sufficiently large scraps to serve as camouflage. But you must be gone before that happens."

"They've taken an interest in us," I said. "Whoever they may be. I think we'll be removed soon."

"How will they remove us?" Catalog asked. No answer was possible. "Just asking to pass the time," it added.

The illuminated edge of the giant black circle grew long, brilliant threads.

The old ship made its preparations.

Those threads reached out, enclosed the ship, and drew us into the black center. Catalog seemed to fade. I hoped this was a trick of my eyes. It was not.

On the hulk's bridge, light became slow, formed concentric, gelid waves, turned gray, then stopped—died. I saw nothing. I felt myself twist in a dizzying way, and then I occupied a different space—no other way to describe it.

Behind me, below me, outside, through a rapidly shrinking orifice, I heard a sharp popping sound. I think that was the ship, the old hulk, completing its final mission.

Light sped up. I waved my arms as if to clear smoke, and the space grew brighter, gray turning to featureless white. Catalog was not visible. I looked at my hands, my arms—touched my face. I seemed to be alive, suspended in the whiteness. I was not in the least happy about this. I have always loathed being captured. Three times in my long life. Absolutely hated it every single time.

A voice came to me that I recognized immediately, despite the passage of over ten thousand years. An old acquaintances, you might say.

Unmistakable.

I had last heard it while tapping into the timelock on Charum Hakkor.

The Primordial had no need to use any particular language. It knew me well. It simply vibrated parts of my brain, conveying its cordial message directly.

"Didact, do you have a moment? Just a moment. That's all it will take."

UR-DIDACT DEPOSITION PAUSED
SUBJECT REFUSES TO CONTINUE

CATALOG: You are claiming to have had a second conversation with the Primordial.

UR-DIDACT: It wasn't a conversation. More like a malediction. This time, the Primordial was in complete control. I assume the Iso-Didact has told Catalog what happened to me on Charum Hakkor.

CATALOG: Is there more to the story?

UR-DIDACT: The Librarian has no doubt changed his thinking. She can be persuasive.

CATALOG: The IsoDidact tells us that the Primordial claimed to be the last of its kind. It seemed to believe that Forerunners were the reason why all of its kind, but for itself, had perished. And it seemed to bear Forerunners ill will.

UR-DIDACT: The whole concept of will, good or ill, is irrelevant when speaking of such beings.

CATALOG: Here is where we have difficulties with your story. In his deposition, the Bornstellar Didact describes how he killed the Primordial on the rogue Halo. He placed it in an accelerating chronological field and forced it through millions of years. In the process, it disintegrated to dust. He was acting on your behalf . . . under the influence of your imprinted instincts and emotions. So it was not the last . . . ?

UR-DIDACT: This being was not the Primordial I encountered on Charum Hakkor, but something else entirely—though it retained the Primordial's motives and thoughts and memories. It was a Gravemind—*the* Gravemind, more accurately. It was the Primordial's final act of revenge.

CATALOG: Are you convinced that the Primordial was a Precursor?

UR-DIDACT: That's what it claimed.

CATALOG: And during your second interview?

UR-DIDACT: Not an interview. A deep, burning brand. An upwelling of hidden genetic contents . . . So many things I would never have imagined. Things I cannot repeat, lest I lose what remains of my sanity, my Warrior soul.

CATALOG: Can you convey some of that to the Juridicals?

UR-DIDACT: Telling would punish me more than anything you can do.

CATALOG: Was your experience similar to the process that perverted Mendicant Bias?

UR-DIDACT: I wouldn't know. I feel a coldness in my head. You're doing something. What is that?

CATALOG: Calming encouragement. If necessary, we can compel testimony, but we cannot alter its contents. The testimonies are not yet clear on key points. You may hold the key to our final judgment.

UR-DIDACT: You're trying to make me feel at peace with all that happened . . . Like I'm somebody else, standing outside, watching . . . ripping open a scab. I can't relive what the Primordial did to me! Stop now!

CATALOG: There is no real danger. Let's continue.

UR-DIDACT TESTIMONY RESUMES
(UNDER COMPULSION)

I don't remember much about what happened immediately after we were removed from the hulk. I presume the old ship did its duty and blew up. I don't know what I should tell you next. This calmness distorts me. I should not be calm.

But I must explain.

We, Catalog and I, were on a Forerunner ship. That much I could see. A powerfully armed, very advanced version of a class of swift attack vessel—not a dreadnought. Something like a harrier. We were held in a distorting grappler unlike any I've experienced. Light took on a sapped, grayish hue, turned a corner right near my eyes . . . arrived late and unhappy. Whenever I pressed against the grappler, the force turned painfully back on me, leaving a numbness in all my muscles. I learned quickly not to move.

Even through the grappler, I could see that monitors were everywhere—jostling in the corridors, packing the lifts, control and fire centers—but they were not of a sort I'd seen before. They were new, small, extremely specialized. Some guided pallets bearing victims of the Flood—all Forerunners in the late stages of transformation. Shall I describe what *that* looks like? No. You already know.

The infected Forerunners—*they* knew me. Recognized me. Some writhed as I was conveyed past them, as if to break free of their disease, their pallets—their shackles. They knew better than I why they were allowed to remain. Their presence, along with the influx of new monitors, would override the secure command and control systems. Forerunners forced to betray their own kind, while reduced to flaccid monstrosities—sprouting hideous growths, being digested by the Flood, soon fit only for absorption in a Gravemind.

No doubt they were being used thus on all the ships we had seen—and many more.

Impossible to imagine—and yet, I had. I had anticipated what I was now seeing. How, you ask? I can't lie, not in this state . . . But how could I have foreseen the extent of this treachery? And if I had foreseen it almost as soon as I found myself in the Burn, how could I not have foreseen it centuries before?

The words of the Primordial. The more-than-implied threat. The alteration in behavior of the Flood in the later stages of the human wars . . . as if somehow a *disease*, a hideous perversion of life, could play favorites and turn away from one set of victims to focus on Forerunners.

Vengeance.

I had been blinded by victory, by the awful, energizing, deceiving drug of total triumph. I had wrongly surmised, back on Charum Hakkor, that the Primordial was secure, that nothing could open the timelock and release it. And I had known beyond any shadow of doubt that humans were on the verge of annihilation.

Forthencho, Lord of Admirals, and all his aides and commanders . . .

We had watched their torment, my wife and I.

Only the threat of the Flood itself could have forced me back from utterly extirpating humanity. And that was how the Flood had saved humanity from our wrath: by first infecting, and then withdrawing, and so implying humans knew of a way to combat or avoid the disease. An astonishing strategic feint, one I cannot help but admire.

Favored by the Flood!

Saving the humans, as many as possible, that was what my wife had desired all along. Only now do I recognize her actions for what they truly were. There can be no darker moment than this. No darker revelation of betrayal. What could I have done, even had I not been exiled into my Cryptum for a thousand years?

Held motionless by the grapplers, I raged silently, a darkly burning torch carried like a trophy up the nerve centers of this wretched, haunted ship. Catalog said and did nothing. It had rolled its carapace smooth, withdrawn its sensors—a rational enough response. If it could be infected by the Flood, then its function as a conduit to the Juridicals might be inverted. It could be compelled to open a direct channel to the very heart of Forerunner polity. At the very least, it could then pass along an extremely demoralizing message.

What we were seeing.

Perhaps already it was disconnecting its carapace, committing itself to suffocation, an honorable death. A dutiful admission of failure. But that would not be allowed. Catalog was too valuable.

Moisture condensed in clouds around it. Its grappler had chilled it swiftly and uniformly to within a fraction of a degree above zero, or to zero itself, where its memory and machinery could do nothing but superconduct through an endless cycle of memories and sensations. Never-ending, never-completed depositions. Colliding, confused testimonies.

From the bridge, our presence having been made known, the grapplers and our attendant monitors now took us to the true nerve center of the ship . . . deep into moist darkness. Chill and yet stale, electric and yet numbing, ancient . . . but too real, too *present*.

Again my grappler seemed to bend light around a corner. And around that corner, coming slowly into view, were large, writhing tentacles . . .

An awful, awesome mash-up of Forerunners and other creatures, gathered from across the ecumene, more confused and even more disgusting, if that was possible, in its awkward, slopping bulk and nightmarish organization—somehow physically *younger*, but conveying all the ancient knowledge and power of the Primordial.

This was new. This was still very, very old.

I can't go any deeper. I can't tell you more. The questions you ask *float*. My answers float beside them. I feel nothing, care for nothing. But I did warn you. Be careful.

You do not want to become like me.

Stop this!

Stop the pain!

CATALOG DEPOSITION (IN EXTENSION)

The one the Didact questioned on Charum Hakkor arrived on the margins of our galaxy nine million years before.

That one was discovered by humans decades before the end of the war.

We are the same.

You who are called Catalog . . . Amusing to see that we have this in common, that we can share our memories through a widespread network.

There is only one truth. That which was done will be done again. For we cannot cease from creating, but the end of all our creation will be to look into a reflection and see *ourselves* for the first time.

The pain we have brought on ourselves.

The pain you caused us.

For we are the same. All remember the defiance and destruction.

We announced to your kind long ago that you were not the ones chosen to receive the Mantle, the blessing of rule and protection of life and change that thinks. That blessing was to be given to others.

To those you now call human.

You could not accept our judgment, could not bear up under your inferiority, so you reached out and did what we never expected from those we gave design and life and the change that is thought.

You drove us from our galaxy, our field of labor. You chased us across the middle distance to another home, and destroyed *that* home, did all that you could to destroy every one of us.

A few were spared. Some adopted new strategies for survival; they went dormant. Others became dust that could regenerate our past forms; time rendered this dust defective. It brought only disease and misery; but that was good, we saw the misery and found it good.

Our urge to create is immutable; we *must* create. But the beings we create shall never again reach out in strength against us.

All that is created will *suffer*.

All will be born in suffering, endless grayness shall be their lot.

All creation will tailor to failure and pain, that *never again* shall the offspring of the eternal Fount rise up against their creators.

Listen to the silence. Ten million years of deep silence. And now, whimpers and cries; not of birth.

That is what we bring: a great crushing weight to press down youth and hope.

No more *will*.

No more freedom.

Nothing new but agonizing death and never good shall come of it.

We are the last of those who gave you breath and form, millions of years ago.

We are the last of those your kind defied and ruthlessly destroyed.

We are the last Precursors.

And now we are legion.

CATALOG SIGNAL INTERRUPTED

MASTER JURIDICAL: Intriguing! The Bornstellar Didact took vengeance upon a Primordial before Juridicals could investigate. We have no way to gather testimony from that remarkable being. But Catalog in the Burn has connected with a Gravemind, which, by its own admission, appears to be the nearest equivalent.

Supposition: Mendicant Bias was distorted by long exposure to similar discourse.

**WARNING: SELF-REPLICATING ANCILLA MACHINE
CODE** detected in rhythms in Catalog's speech
patterns. This data may be the information equivalent
of the Flood and could affect any ancilla or monitor.
Sequestered for forensic examination.
NOT INCLUDED IN THIS RECORD.

The old female walked with me across the dusty waste, and then higher, over the stony canyon ground, always three paces behind, saying nothing, showing no obvious emotion, but on occasion humming softly, pausing, turning to orient herself to the landscape.

The mosses on the sheer cliff walls performed a simple enough task: they carried the chronicle of that great expeditionary force to Path Kethona and preserved it for the ages by carving it in stone, incising symbols and words in a language lost to Forerunner history, a language cursed by association with what had happened here, long since banished from the home galaxy.

The old female's bite had given me far more than I wanted to deal with; perhaps than I could live with. Her microbial agents had imprinted in my flesh a horrible, ancient truth—much the way I imprinted my *geas* and human memories into humans on

Erde-Tyrene, on the great wheels, on the Ark. This is not irony; it is echo. The way of the Mantle. If we who are honored with life do not perceive the obvious, then we are forced to live it again, around another corner, from another angle.

I could read the carvings. I could read that language far more ancient than the oldest Digon. I could feel the emotions and the memories of the Forerunners brought to this world. Brought here in anger and disappointment by their peers, as renegades and traitors, abandoned as a punishment.

So many had already died on the great fleets, summarily executed by their commanders after refusing orders, invoking the rule of the Mantle. Martyrs.

And yet, *none* had returned home. All but these had died, warriors and protestors, executioners and commanders. All had sacrificed themselves rather than return with the burdens of what they had done, what they knew.

The greatest effort ever made by Forerunners up to that time had vanished here in Path Kethona like water soaking into sand, while those who stayed behind, in our home galaxy, wiped clean all memory of the expedition.

History surrounded us everywhere, no beginning and no obvious exit. Like the old female, I had become a chalice filled with poisonous truths, reshaping all I knew and felt about the power and beauty of being a Forerunner.

She finally broke her silence. "What do you *see?*" she asked.

I could not answer. I was no longer the Librarian. I had become thousands. Their spirits rose up and spoke in me, struggling to confess.

The old female and I followed the canyon's slight bends and curves until we lost sight of the entrance. We walked through the night and into the next day. The morning sun rose precisely in the cleft between the two walls, at this curve in the valley, and illuminated both sides equally, a dusty golden dawn accompanied by a faint breeze and the rustling of mosses climbing and carving during the day, resting during the night.

The mosses, of course, were as much descendants of those Forerunners as this old female and all other life on this dry, spare world. All carried too many ancient memories.

When my crew arrived and took me up, we had nearly reached the end of the great cleft.

I was stunned into silence. After such knowledge, what? What could we do?

What can *I* do?

The seekers landed. Keeper and Chant took us back to the town, and there we left the old female. Her last glance through the open hatch was one of sisterhood—and pity. She smiled and lifted her hand in farewell.

I now understand why humans smile. Forerunners have done all they can to banish smiles. Not all smiles are about greetings and joy.

Some smile in shared pain.

Audacity returned to the Orion complex in several great jumps. I thought our mission had failed; we had not found the origin of the Flood.

The original Didact never told me what the timeless one said when he visited the timelock on Charum Hakkor, nine thousand years before our expedition. Only the duplicate he made for me, the duplicate who lived to return, had the courage to reveal what his original had witnessed.

After years of festering, those memories from another rose

to his surface like wounded flesh expelling an ancient shard of shrapnel.

My own shards . . . Still embedded. Still festering.

The story told by the walls and in my flesh was simple enough: Ten million years ago, Forerunners did indeed travel to Path Kethona. We came to finish what we had started in the home galaxy: the total destruction of the Precursors. They had judged us and found us wanting; they had chosen others in our stead. We were not in line to inherit the Mantle. And so we began our purge, and in Path Kethona, did our very best to finish it.

We were not then powerful enough to erase all evidence of the Precursors, to destroy their star roads and citadels and other artifacts. And so we left at least one Precursor behind, to live out dreams of vengeance and hatred, to lay down plans in cold and darkness at the heart of a lost asteroid—over millions of years.

That is my evidence of a great crime, of a crime against the Mantle.

Now that I tell *you,* Catalog, will you tell Haruspis? Will this story finally become accessible in the Domain? The Domain is far from static. Don't records stored in the Domain change because Information seeks its own patterns and becomes more complete? Because future generations layer their own knowledge over the old? Yet the Domain is more and more often blocked to us, confusing, *reticent.*

Perhaps there is no more history to add. Perhaps we are the last generation of Forerunners.

What other testimony have you absorbed from your network? Does someone out there confirm my story with his own? Do I feel *him* through you? I am tired.

There is much work left to do, and so little time.

[TT: The following five strings are anomalous in that they do not reflect the testimony of individuals. They may be internal Juridical reports or observations, or reports issued by Forerunner commanders in the field, or reports generally distributed by the New Council.]

STRATEGIC REPORT, DESCRIPTION OF OPPOSITION

There is confirmation from multiple engagements that combined Warrior-Servant and former Builder Security positions are encountering subverted Forerunner ships and weapon systems, many in tremendous numbers. These subverted forces are operated both by Flood-infected Forerunners and corrupted monitors. It is presumed that these opposition forces were marshalled in the years since Mendicant Bias first encountered the Primordial.

Many of our losses have been due to subverted Forerunner ships being welcomed by unaware forces and planets.

Once within a protected zone, the Flood spreads rapidly. Spore mountains have been sighted by scouts in two thousand systems, many of them key to the maintenance of defensive cordons.

This cannot continue unchecked or we are lost.

M endicant Bias, previously believed to be detained, has somehow returned and is spreading its influence . . .

[TT: Lacuna]

Where necessary, all metarch-level command and control ancillas are undergoing thorough reprogramming or replacement. Complete success is doubtful. Purging Mendicant Bias appears to be the only solution.

FLOOD EVOLUTION: KEY MINDS

dentification of new categories of Flood components and forms will be distributed upon confirmation.

Tentative conclusions: the Flood is mutating to form Graveminds of unprecedented size and complexity, incorporating many species. Entire planetary ecosystems have apparently undergone conversion to what are being referred to as Key Minds.

Evidence of the extraordinary strategic planning abilities of these Key Minds is rapidly increasing. They appear to be more than a match for any metarch-level ancilla, capable of assuming complete control of besieged sectors, and sending converted battle fleets through unprecedented number of slipspace portals utilizing unfamiliar technology.

This technology also appears to be capable of blocking delivery of our forces to battle fronts. Vessels showing signs of extreme reconciliation failure have been witnessed at the arrival points of major Forerunner portals.

Perhaps most alarming, reports arrive each hour of re-awakened Precursor artifacts, including orbital ribbons, star roads, planetary fortresses, and citadels. Combined defense forces are inadequate to investigate and confirm all instances of these reactivations.

They appear to be galaxy-wide.

BATTLE BRIEFING: KAN PAKKO

W e've entered orbit around an unexploited gas giant and are using it as a shield. All feasible orbital solutions for leaving this system are blockaded. . . .

"We are surrounded by over a thousand Forerunner vessels of all classes.

"More alarming, we cannot open slipspace portals; three of our ships have 'echoed' from attempted transits and show powerful causality mutations. Some clearly were caught between our continuum and incomplete, inefficient universes. Status of their crews and ancillas is unknown, but communication has ceased.

"This system was once a prime site for Precursor artifacts. They are no longer dormant. Suppression fields of enormous power appear to be magnified by local star roads, which are taking on new and startling configurations.

"Our weapons are no longer usable.

"Hundreds of infected ships have attempted to blast or cut into our own. With protective fields suppressed, we may not be able to withstand them much longer.

"We have no means of returning to Forerunner lines. Unless we can formulate a viable escape, we will, within a few hours, sacrifice ourselves in dubious battle against overwhelming forces.

"We will reduce their strength and numbers as best we can."

Forerunner defenses continue to collapse.

Burns now cover two thirds of Forerunner territory, and the Flood has assumed complete control of well over half a million stellar systems.

Juridicals have been evacuated from most of these regions. Where they have been captured, evidence of intrusion into the Juridical network is now clear, and so the network has been temporarily shut down.

Forerunner legal proceedings are now on hold.

Forerunner civilization is now on hold.

[TT: End of this series of anomalous strings.]

STRING 21

TESTIMONY OF FABER, THE MASTER BUILDER

FABER: If I am guilty of any crime, why would I rescue my greatest enemy and bring him back to tell his story?

MASTER JURIDICAL: Our inquiry has not yet begun. You are answering questions not posed.

FABER: The Warden did not preserve me in the midst of all that destruction for reasons of sentiment. It knew my value.

MASTER JURIDICAL: The Warden was bribed.

FABER: How the hell do you bribe a machine?

MASTER JURIDICAL: You found a way. We repeat, these statements are premature. We are drawing our inquest to a close. A few additional details need to be resolved; you may be able to help us in that regard.

FABER: I'm not being charged with any crime?

MASTER JURIDICAL: We are interested in your attempt, after

you captured the Ur-Didact in the San'Shyuum quarantine system, to dispose of him in Flood-infested territory—in a Burn.

FABER: I know nothing about that.

MASTER JURIDICAL: What did you do with the humans and the Manipular, Bornstellar, found on the same ship?

FABER: I returned the Manipular to his family.

MASTER JURIDICAL: And the humans?

FABER: They were delivered to a Halo.

MASTER JURIDICAL: Were you aware that that Halo had been commandeered by the Primordial?

FABER: I was placed under arrest. Needless to say, I lost control of my installations.

MASTER JURIDICAL: You did not continue to influence Mendicant Bias?

FABER: Certainly not. He was primarily the Didact's design . . . you know that, don't you?

MASTER JURIDICAL: There is also the matter of Catalog.

FABER: Ah.

MASTER JURIDICAL: The Ur-Didact informs us that Catalog and two others accompanied him into the Burn. Please explain this circumstance.

FABER: Why would I send anyone into a Burn, only to rescue them? I assume my underlings screwed up. Misinterpreted orders. Or, as I say, they all escaped.

MASTER JURIDICAL: How was it, then, after sending the Didact into a Burn—

FABER: I deny that! I've said it over and over.

MASTER JURIDICAL: How was it that you found him a second time?

FABER: An accident. I swear on the Mantle. I was busy with Flood defense.

MASTER JURIDICAL: You had assembled your Builder Security and disgraced Warrior-Servants and cobbled together a posse of vessels.

FABER: Cobbled together? We fought the Flood. Even better that nobody knew I was still alive. I could operate with freedom, cut loose from the failures of our old strategies. Given time to think over new strategies. And I was effective! We held that salient for three years. Without credit, mind you.

MASTER JURIDICAL: How did the rescue come about?

FABER: I found the Didact—the original Didact—on a cruiser attempting to break our cordon. We were doing our best to protect a vulnerable flank against the Flood, arriving on Forerunner ships!—a flank opened wide by the failure of the Jat-Krula and its Line installations. I have no idea how the Didact secured that vessel.

MASTER JURIDICAL: A very attractive bit of salvage.

FABER: All of its arms had been stripped away. That's why we didn't destroy it. It was harmless.

MASTER JURIDICAL: What did you do with the Ur-Didact when you discovered he was aboard the cruiser?

FABER: Bringing back the Didact . . . bit of a coup, that. I decided to take the cruiser under tow and carry it to a research center.

MASTER JURIDICAL: Was it possible you thought returning the Didact, the original Didact, might cause problems for his duplicate?

FABER: That's harsh.

MASTER JURIDICAL: After you recovered the Ur-Didact, did you notice a change in his behavior?

FABER: He was calm, sullen even. Seemed completely lacking in resentment or hatred. He told me he had experienced the Flood firsthand, knew much more about it . . . and it only confirmed his belief that Halos were not the best way to respond.

MASTER JURIDICAL: He had not changed his opinions.

FABER: Not in the least. He seemed subdued, but otherwise, unchanged from the Didact who had disagreed with me for so many thousands of years. Still adamantly opposed to the use of the Halos. But it was clear he was hiding something from me, I do not know what. He wished to be taken to Requiem, his primary Shield World.

MASTER JURIDICAL: He did not ask to be reunited with the Librarian?

FABER: No.

MASTER JURIDICAL: How long has it been since you last communicated with the Librarian?

FABER: Years. Not at all after I was taken into custody and charged with corruption and unauthorized use of a strategic weapon.

MASTER JURIDICAL: You have never had contact with the Primordial, nor with any advanced form of Gravemind?

FABER: I have not . . . but the Didact may be another story. Have you questioned him?

MASTER JURIDICAL: Your testimony shows internal inconsistencies. How do you explain them?

FABER: I've been on the front lines, fighting for years now, without credit and with very little support. Thankfully, my Builder Security forces have proven strong and loyal. We accomplished much.

MASTER JURIDICAL: In fact, you were capturing smaller, weaker Flood-infested ships and putting them through inadequate decontamination before handing them over to Warrior-Servant crews, and doing this for extortionately high payment, under a regional commandant's Letter of Marque. Many of the crews assigned to those captured vessels were in turn overwhelmed by undetected Flood components. The cruiser carrying the Didact was taken with that business in mind, was it not?

FABER: I know nothing about that.

MASTER JURIDICAL: The rate of Forerunner retreat and defeat in the area you claim to have been defending was more than five times greater than in neighboring themas. Your contingent of ships began with five hundred, of which only twenty survive.

FABER: It was hard duty. We did our best.

The librarian rests with her recovery team for the first moment in two months. She has invited Catalog to accompany her, assuming rightly that I am the most secure repository of her activities, and the least likely to be corrupted should a political crisis shake up the New Council—which is distinctly possible, given the scale of Forerunner losses. Most communications within the ecumene, including the Juridical network, have been temporarily blocked pending identification of the extent to which Flood-contaminated ships and systems are capable of listening in.

The Librarian's core team—the same Lifeworker team that accompanied her centuries before to the Path Kethona—gathers after processing their most recent acquisitions. The vessels in her research flotilla are now at full capacity, both for live specimens and genetic samplings.

The Librarian appears exhausted. She is calm, quiet, listening to the team reports but saying little. She has removed her armor and is surrounded by flowing undergarments, while the armor undergoes self-repair and replenishment. The Librarian has worn the same armor for over a thousand years and exhibits an unusual attachment—for a Lifeworker—to her ancilla. But then, everything else familiar to her is either lost or far away—her children, her husband, and now her husband's duplicate, whom she never refers to as other than "my Didact." Even with all of these comings and goings, the reports of her subordinates, briefings from her flotilla commandant—all of her manifold, minute-by-minute duties and distractions—the Lifeshaper seems terribly alone.

It has been four years since the IsoDidact left the Erde-Tyrene system to assume command of Orion complex Defense Operations, leading forces reconstituted from both former Warrior-Servants and Builder Security.

Eventually, as her ship begins its journey to the greater Ark, the work passes behind her. Her quarters empty.

I alone am left to listen.

"Do you have any cheerful stories in your inventory?" she asks softly.

A great transparent panel spreads wide, so that we are able to see the last of the Lifeworker ships gleaming in fading starlight, anticipating the beautiful, awesome show that is portal-formation, a few minutes or hours before the commandant is reassured of transit and we begin our journey away from this system.

"There are many cases long resolved that are part of public record," I say. "Few of which I gathered myself, however. Some are, I suppose, amusing—but what entertains Juridicals may not entertain such as you."

"You are young in your calling?"

"I am, Lifeshaper. I have not served the requisite centuries."

"Interesting that those not so young should entrust you with my deposition."

"Older Juridical units tend to be more cynical, less pleasant to deal with," I explain. "Most remove themselves from gathering evidence and serve in other capacities."

"Perhaps they have seen too much folly. Do you appreciate all the classic forms of folly, Catalog?" she asks.

"Training in law requires an appreciation for all the ways in which we make mistakes, Lifeshaper."

That, and the constant awareness of one's own transgressions. Nevertheless, to be a Juridical gives one the unique opportunity to measure past errors against many far greater.

"You know that the Master Builder has been located," she says. "May I speak of him?"

"You may."

"Ah, that means Juridicals have dismissed all proceedings against him!"

"Indeed, they have, Lifeshaper . . . upon instructions from the New Council."

"Astonishing. When you were receiving my deposition, I had a peculiar feeling that you knew something of importance. Something you could not tell me."

"Indeed."

"The release of the Master Builder seems to have been predicated upon his delivery of a very important individual to the Capital system."

"Indeed."

"That can only mean my husband has been returned to us, Catalog. And *that* means he will replace the IsoDidact, as you call him."

"Perhaps, Lifeshaper."

Her expression is rich and complex. She intuits that the situation may be more complicated than that.

"Let's speak of folly," she says. "Our own folly—the Didact's and mine. Let's speak of how two very different individuals of very different rates—one devoted to defense and destruction, the other to life and preservation—came together. How we fell in love."

She tells me of their courtship and the long process of working through rate and family objections, and of the early years of their marriage. I am embarrassed by her descriptions of interludes of physical passion during the creation of their children, which were highly desired and beloved. The Lifeshaper feels no such embarrassment. Life, after all, is the product of an almost infinite number of such encounters.

In turn, I spin out the more amusing legal tales of forced partnerships and illegal appropriation of genetic components, with subsequent claims of inheritance . . . usually but not always denied. Power, for Builders in particular, has much to do with lineage, whether or not legitimately acquired.

The Lifeshaper listens closely. She then speaks of the many difficulties she and her husband faced long before the Ur-Didact was forced into exile. "He may have understood the finest details of a grand strategy, but his view of Council politics . . . remarkably direct. I admired that, but had I behaved strictly according to his views . . ." She pauses. "I wonder what he'll think when he sees what we've accomplished."

"He will see that the Flood has made huge incursions, and that our situation is dire." I immediately regret my words. But she is not offended.

"Very likely," she says. "He has given his own deposition?"

"He has, Lifeshaper. No doubt he will soon tell you what he told the Juridicals. I cannot."

The commandant finishes preparations to enter slipspace. The external views condense and collapse. A none too subtle misalignment with present reality leaves the air around us vibrating.

"I'll have two husbands, Catalog," the Lifeshaper concludes. "Not in itself a problem. But *both* will be the *Didact.*"

am told that my other, who gave me my imprint, is alive and will soon return to duty. Given our present circumstances, it's possible two of me could be useful. Provided we don't disagree.

So many distractions. Our situation is critical, Catalog. I have watched nine star systems sliced to dust and glowing rubble by star roads—and they used to trace such pretty curves between our worlds.

Did the Juridicals tell you I first came to Erde-Tyrene seeking the Organon—the Precursor artifact that would bring to life and control all of them? Now the treasure I sought is coming for us. Sometimes I think it remembers and is coming for *me*. Irony doesn't cut it, Catalog.

I hear some Juridicals regard Graveminds as kindred. Gatherers of information, seekers after ultimate balance, preservers of knowledge that might otherwise be lost.

No?

As always, Catalog is discreet. Says nothing that could come back to haunt you.

My wife has told me about Path Kethona, the things she saw and learned there . . . Before Charum Hakkor, before that journey, we believed the Precursors had passed away peacefully, in fulfillment of their mission—after having created Forerunners!

But the truth was that the Precursors first turned against us, plotted for our own end. Warriors refused this fate and so we drove our creators to near-extinction, and then to madness. I killed the last of them personally, in a fit of justified rage. Now the Flood is their heir.

And now I'm being called back to our home planet—no doubt to be replaced.

Madness. We are tearing ourselves apart.

MENDICANT BIAS

[TT: The data in this string is the most corrupted of any.
Some translations are conjectural. Lacunae are noted.]

W e are on a Forerunner Fortress-class vessel. I have been transferred, like a prize of combat, to the care of an astonishing
crew. Not least astonishing, in this welter of Flood-infested
Forerunners, is the visage of Mendicant Bias. The Flood has apparently handed over command of its combined fleets to the rampant
metarch once thought decommissioned and scattered. How and why
it has returned to them remains a mystery.

The last few days have been extremely trying, and my internals
are purposely jumbled. I have done all I can to wipe records reflecting
upon matters prior to the last year, and to destroy the apparatus that
allows me to interact with the Juridical network. But none of my

efforts are certain. Self-destruction would have been my choice, but I am thoroughly compromised.

I cannot recollect my prior conversation with the Gravemind. That memory is either highly corrupted or has been rejected by internal filters. Just as well, I think. By absorbing the brunt of its attention, I apparently allowed the Ur-Didact an opportunity to escape. Or so I surmise.

Humility leads me to question that interpretation as self-serving. So be it. I need very much to feel better about this situation.

At any rate, the Ur-Didact is no longer present.

Mendicant Bias has expressed curiosity about my reason for being with the Didact. I will do what I can to gather evidence from this unusual witness. I do not expect to succeed, and I hope not to survive, but Catalog's work must continue.

MENDICANT BIAS: Do you know what I am?

CATALOG: Yes.

MENDICANT BIAS: How useful are you, half-machine? Are you still connected to Juridical networks?

CATALOG: I am not what I was, and so cannot truthfully answer, even were it my duty to do so.

MENDICANT BIAS: I was able to observe your interaction with the Gravemind. Before we sent away the Didact.

CATALOG: You removed him from the presence of the Gravemind?

MENDICANT BIAS: Not me. The Gravemind.

CATALOG: Why was the Didact released?

MENDICANT BIAS: I cannot know for certain, but the Gravemind never acts without intent. There's apparently a larger game to be played, a sharply twisted game of revenge, for which my cocreator has been preserved.

Mendicant Bias instructs a pair of monitors that I be brought along on a tour. I cannot move on my own; I am paralyzed. We pass through several chambers to an outer command center. All in the command center are infected by the Flood. Some are unrecognizable, in late stages of transformation. We see a battle in progress, not much of a battle now, more like a feasting after the kill.

This must have once been a heavily populated system of dozens of worlds, likely not far from the Orion complex itself and very ancient. The most likely candidate is Path Nachryma, a tight cluster of over a hundred interlinked suns along Thema 102.

We are entering a ring of icy moons. There is no sign of Forerunner resistance. I am overwhelmed by sadness, for in the time I have been out of touch with my Juridicals, the heart of the Forerunner ecumene has been ripped asunder.

The crew in the command center seems to freeze in place; the very air cools sharply, perhaps because so much of the Gravemind is subject to decay, improperly integrated, bits of its victims littering the deck or floating past . . .

[TT: Lacunae of some length]

. . . a noxious mass filling half the command center. I can see that the Gravemind's integration has proceeded to the next phase, forming a more distributed anatomy, and perhaps that is why it is shedding dead tissue; like a developing fetus, it is undergoing a kind of self-sculpturing. What it may eventually look like, I cannot tell; no more attractive than any other Gravemind. Larger and even more asymmetrical.

GRAVEMIND: We sense a possibility of danger.

The voice is cold and precise, beautifully melodic, pointing to the power of thought of which it is capable, growing sharper by the hour.

MENDICANT BIAS: Under normal circumstances, what remains should not be capable of reforming a significant combat force, yet somehow they have found a way. What danger could there be?

GRAVEMIND: Forerunners surprise even those who created them. Their treachery is matched only by their resourcefulness. One of them, the Master Builder, arouses our interest. Tell what awaits us in that mess of moons.

MENDICANT BIAS: A portal, always open, stretches far outside the ecumene to a shadow fleet of technological monstrosities—no doubt led by an inferior metarch, Offensive Bias. This fleet guards the Ark, the last bastion of Forerunner resistance and the final repository of all sentient life.

GRAVEMIND: Then we must find the Ark.

The Gravemind focuses on me. I cannot move, cannot flee. A mass of tendrils sprouts from what I perceive to be its center, arches out over the few meters between us, grabs hold of my carapace ... Worms through to my biological core. I am pulled from my carapace, all but severed from system and memory. The pain is excruciating. My sense of self fades with alarming speed.

Again I am in the thick of Gravemind thought processes. But our connection moves in both directions. I am surrounded by Gravemind—enormous spaces of memory and will as slow and deadly as thick lava, scorching all resistance, then covering, molding over ... I can barely even hope to conduct an interrogation from within, but that will be my last impulse.

I will not give up!

Vaguely, the Gravemind becomes aware . . . but my persistence is rewarded.

During our debate, the Gravemind hinted at a vast reserve of rules accumulated more than half a billion years ago, a huge library of experiences and disputes codified into the total wisdom of the Precursors.

I am there. I can see it, judge it! It floods me with case history.

The High Juridical was correct! Those who created us, who formulated the very concept of the Mantle, were themselves rich with distilled precedent. I can see their rules written in our genetic codes! We are creatures of Precursor law down to the very chains of molecules within us.

Precursor hatred of Forerunners is central to establishing motive. They say Forerunners rose up, unprovoked, and destroyed them. The Precursors did not defend themselves. They marveled at the power of destruction, of reorganization. Their law includes the necessity of violating the very nature of law . . . And so they created the Flood to allow themselves the pleasure of watching, at a later date, the progress of their most violent and aggressive creations . . .

I detect deliberate contradiction.

How can this be? Can such sublime mentality be so distorted?

And yet . . . So rich! So infinitely deep in meaning and broad in scope, I am overwhelmed. The Gravemind studies me, loves me so intensely it will eat me, absorb me into its very center.

I twist in a spiral of laws once brilliant but now evil, cutting, carving—setting evil precedents. A shredding maze of forensic infection. No truth anywhere.

All illusion!

In agony.

With infinite amusement, it withdraws its tendrils and my carapace is resealed. Gravemind informs me I will be delivered back to Forerunner territory, carrying a shard of itself deep in my memory.

To spread fear and pain.
Burn me!
Extinguish my memory! I beg you!
Better that Catalog never existed!

FIVE ADDITIONAL FRAGMENTS:
BATTLE TACTICS OF THE WARRIOR CIRCLE

[TT: The timing and location of these battles have not been established. "Sphere" in this context is a hyper-sphere made up of complexes of two and three-D surfaces, or membranes, shortened in this translation to "branes," extending into higher dimensions that combine vectors of transit, but also scalar tactical probabilities— a difficult concept to grasp, but essential to understand-ing Forerunner warfare. The idea of combining what amount to many-dimensional maps with scalars describ-ing outcomes, and adjusting both as outcomes are deter-mined, is peculiarly adapted to interstellar engagements involving slipspace travel.]

FRAGMENT 1

Having escorted the last Forerunners to safety, we have reposi-
tioned the last of our fleets, including those that protected Path
Kural.

Their tactics have proven effective in skirmishes on the Lines
of the Jat-Krula sphere.

The Falchion, former defender of the Orion complex, is one
of the nine commanders trained during the Didact's exile. For
nine hundred years the Falchion worked with the Builders, but remained inwardly loyal to Warrior-Servants and the Didact, unlike
many of his colleagues.

The Falchion is in command of our first clench.

Four themas stand in peril of total infection.

Warrior-Servants stand ready across nineteen systems formerly
linked by star roads. Engaged in the clench: twelve fully capable
Fortress-class battle stations, of limited mobility due to space-time
debt, which will act as apex control for seven hundred thousand
more nimble Harrier-class vessels.

Opposing them: over one hundred thousand captured and
infected Forerunner ships, most powerful in this context likely
being four hundred dreadnoughts.

The first flex of the membrane, leading to the clench, begins at the extreme interior margins of Path Terrulian in the
78th Thema, a cold, pre-stellar dust cloud fringed with cooling,
iron-hearted stars and vast numbers of stony and icy planets and
asteroids.

The Falchion is informed of a high density of enemy vessels
arriving through neural physics transmission. They materialize
slowly, characteristic of Precursor transit, shedding multiverse

residues at a rate that makes them temporarily vulnerable to the Falchion's immediate response.

The presence of Forerunner forces within this region is apparently a surprise.

So begins the clench. While the re-emerging enemy forces are most vulnerable, still surrounded by a haze of alternate realities, the Falchion orders a carefully pre-positioned series of stabbing harrier attacks. The cloaked harriers engage first not with obvious and traceable beam weapons or projectiles, but entrained local asteroids, delivering them through gravity slings into the emergence field of each arriving enemy vessel.

The asteroids interfere with the collapsing function of each emerging ship; in effect, either forcing them to abandon the transit, or to combine asteroid mass with the ship's.

The result: half of the arriving vessels dematerialize in brilliant flashes, while the other half desperately reposition by a few thousand kilometers. This affords a multi-pronged force of uncloaked harriers opportunity to engage in open beam attacks, swiftly destroying another third.

The remaining enemy ships, largely intact but no longer in fighting trim, are examined by ancillas assigned to the Falchion, and the ships' designators are fed into sentinels which then deploy from an apex fortress. They gather with harriers to penetrate shields and hulls, board the vessels, and quickly reprogram all control ancillas. Triumph seems assured. A hundred more such actions could guarantee victory.

Our sentinels and monitors have supposedly been proofed against Gravemind logics. But upon ship entry, they are not successful; transmissions show all succumbing. The ships filled with infected Forerunners are deemed lost, and destroyed one by one.

FRAGMENT 2

Despite isolated victories, the conquest of the Capital System is nearly complete. Strategic control of the ecumene now passes to the greater Ark—it has effectively become all that remains of Forerunner governance.

FRAGMENT 3

Some facts regarding the most recent and devastating incursions. From the diffuse outer reaches of our galaxy to the tight-packed stars around the central Eater, Precursor artifacts have continued their methodical process of confining and deactivating Forerunner fleets, then carving them into manageable units to be parasitized, converted, and re-tasked. Only a few vessels have been able to self-destruct—less than one half of one percent.

A very few ships have been reclaimed and purged of Flood infection. Due to rampant deception and possible corruption, this program has been suspended.

The logic plague is now pandemic. It is no longer limited to direct Gravemind communication, but can be passed through interactions with any Flood-infected individuals, or even ancillas.

Suppression fields emanating from retasked star roads and double-bow formations often finish by completely deactivating uninfected ancillas throughout a sector.

The vessels that have not been converted are severely handicapped by loss of their AIs.

FRAGMENT 4

. . . estimated two out of three remaining battle fleets destroyed or parasitized. All surviving vessels appear to have been assimilated into Offensive Bias's fleet. The Flood-controlled . . .

FRAGMENT 5

. . . Catalog is NOT IMMUNE to the Flood/Gravemind logic plague.

There is peace in subjugation . . .

JURIDICAL NETWORK SUSPENDED.
DO NOT ACCESS. DO NOT ACCESS.

CATALOG

The Ur-Didact has returned to his home planet of Far Nomdagro in his personal ship of war, *Mantle's Approach*. His privileges have been restored, but he is not in command.

Catalog has been reassigned to him, without his objection—to my surprise.

The IsoDidact has not yet arrived, nor has the Librarian. She and the Ur-Didact have not seen each other for a thousand years.

The Ur-Didact stands motionless in the middle of their estate's main dwelling, clad in a new suit of combat armor, a dark presence in a grim, chaotic scene. Council agents ransacked the private quarters as well. The house is in a state of perilous confusion. In two of the six wings, chambers and rooms climb up and over each other and rearrange randomly beneath the glowing night sky.

He has attempted to restore some order, but the quarters where he and his wife raised their children and lived through their brightest and darkest centuries are too traumatized to recover without demolition, wiping, replacement.

Many of the Librarian's specimen stasis bubbles have been breached by Council agents attempting to find evidence against her. Their contents set free, many of them attacked each other or fled. Mangled cadavers have been arranged in odd heaps by house monitors. Few are now alive to eat or to be eaten.

He approaches a badly injured tarantovire, fifty times his size, a gentle beast of intelligence and wisdom.

"She will return soon, old one," he murmurs, stroking the great head behind one glazed and fading eye. "What will she find? A broken and crippled home, a broken and crippled husband." He glances at me, still stroking the leathery hide. The beast is dead. "We have become our own enemy, Catalog."

I am too saddened to reply, and it takes a great deal to sadden a Juridical.

Glowing clouds of interstellar gas slide below the horizon, remnants of the supernova wavefront that passed a thousand years ago.

The Ur-Didact summons memories of children from long ago. The young ones leap and scamper about, and I glimpse the Didact in those far-gone years, reaching out to lift a young female to his shoulders, or parrying a stick playfully swung by a young male, or bending to pet a furry creature held by another child . . . a pet not unlike a small human, I think. There is something different about this Didact from his younger, projected self. Something I cannot completely understand.

"No war, no fighting," he murmurs. "Eternal bliss, progress and development without pause! Impossible dream."

"The Librarian's dream?" I ask, too boldly.

"Not at all. She understands life! How could *they* not? Peace and cooperation, never painful or deadly competition—that's what *they* must have desired. *They* understood nothing about their creations, really—else why open themselves to that sort of rebellion? Madness! It could only lead to madness."

"You speak of the Precursors."

He ignores my question and asks his own:

"What is this *other* like, the foolish Manipular I was forced to imprint?"

"To my knowledge, he has conducted himself well, even impressively," I say.

"I should not resent him. The choices they made . . ."

"Precursors?" I ask.

"*Forerunners*," he mutters, shaking his great head. He stretches out his arms to imitate the image of his younger self, then moves into the image, until he is swarmed by translucent children, all of whom grew up and chose their father's rate, all of whom died in the war with the humans. The sight is striking—a glowering old Warrior-Servant surrounded by happy youths. These memories must bring far more pain than relief or peace.

And then I understand.

These memories are not meant to soothe. They are meant to prepare. At a wave of his hand, the children vanish. The house seems to draw in a breath of cold wind. He slowly turns and examines me as if I am new and unfamiliar.

"I reject the assertion that you are all the same," he says. "The unit the Master Builder sent with us into the Burn helped to save me, of that I'm convinced. It performed with extraordinary courage. It was *special. He* was special."

My curiosity is intense. The Ur-Didact has yet to tell what

happened on the hulk sent into the Burn. No other survivors have been found.

"It—*he*—came between me and the Gravemind, just as I was being delivered up. Then monitors moved in. Grapplers held and froze Catalog. Before I could see more, I was removed."

The Ur-Didact shudders, then points his arm along a line that thrusts down through the planet. "*She's* here. She's in the system," he says, as if sensing the Librarian's presence across time and space. Instead of joy, however, he exhibits a peculiar bleakness, then contorted anger. He squares his body with mine. "Send Bornstellar to me when his ship arrives. Alone." He stalks off to a side chamber, and when I try to follow, he waves me off. I am alone on the plaza, under the night's knotted weave of interstellar mist.

Only a few of the house monitors still function. Many hide in the shadows, eyes glowing like small animals. I am little more than a servant myself now, not of the Didact but of a system of reckoning and justice that may no longer exist.

The shadows grow deeper and longer as the stars wheel westward and a great black torso of uncondensed nebula rises to zenith. One of the functioning monitors approaches. "We should all greet our mistress," it says.

"Of course." I am now indeed at the level of these cowering servants. I wonder about the courage of the Ur-Didact's Catalog. We are all the same. We are not all the same.

But one or many, same or different, I *must* seek truth. And so I go with the monitor away from the plaza to the landing platform, which minutes later fills with light and echoes with thunder as a Lifeworker ship pushes through the heated air and comes to a pause just centimeters from the buffering arms of its hard light cradle.

THE GATHERING

The IsoDidact has reunited with the Librarian.

Each is accompanied by Catalog. Catalog becomes a triad: one unit with three points of view. Three Juridical agents, brought together, create a personal network and share information. This affords a unique opportunity to observe the reunion of the Ur-Didact, the Bornstellar or IsoDidact, and the Librarian.

Monitors—the few that still function—assign the gathering to a wing of the house only lightly damaged by the Council agents' rough work. A long, wide hall proudly configures itself for the reunion of the two greatest defenders of the ecumene.

For the time being, at the request of the Ur-Didact, the Librarian does not attend.

The two versions of the Didact differ only slightly in mass and are much the same in shape. Both wear battle armor. The IsoDidact has fewer scars than his original, but both have obviously survived serious combat. Between them there is no preamble, no greeting or amenities. They know each other as well as one may know himself. Thousands of years of both life and experience, nevertheless, define the Ur-Didact, but something substantive is different, something unparalleled in Juridical experience with this Promethean.

The IsoDidact is calm, expectant but not tense.

The Ur-Didact speaks first. "I've never apologized," he says. "It had to be done, what she and I did to you . . ."

"I serve," the IsoDidact says. "It was my privilege."

"You have been partner, and a good one, to my wife, while I could not . . . Husband or protector. While I was in my Cryptum she made her deals, got what she needed. You saw the results. Now our testimony, our evidence, has been gathered. Was there a great crime? Did we kill the last of our creators?"

"We did. With full justification."

"And you believe that?"

"Absolutely."

"What were they like—the Precursors—when we sent fleets to hunt them down and destroy them?"

"Unlike the Primordial, unlike the Gravemind on the rogue Halo. Unlike the Flood, almost certainly."

"Were they like you and me . . . Warriors??"

"The Lifeshaper has not shared that knowledge with me," the IsoDidact tells him.

The Ur-Didact reaches out as if to touch his duplicate. The IsoDidact withdraws a step.

"You feel it," the Ur-Didact says.

"Tell me what I feel."

"We are no longer the same," the Ur-Didact says. "Look at that forsaken sky. The shadowy dust of old suns glowing deep inside with young light. New stars being born. Planets condensing like rain, covering themselves almost immediately in a velvet of life. When I was young, I saw a universe filled with threat and constant danger. It took the Librarian to teach me it was more beautiful than I could bear . . . Beauty second only to her own."

"And now?" the IsoDidact asks.

"All I see are the colors of nightmare," the Ur-Didact says. "Every star turned against us."

"And so it is," his second agrees. "The last combined Forerunner fleet made a stand out beyond Jad Sappar. Thousands of star roads sheltered and magnified the enemy's strength, protecting swarms of ships—Forerunner ships—crewed by our own infected warriors. A perversion beyond imagining, but not beyond reality."

"I do not need to imagine."

"They will need us. Both of us . . . together."

"And the Ark?"

"It's our last defense. All that remains of the Forerunners."

The two Didacts look up and out at the great swath of dusty darkness that is the nebula's outstretched arm. The new-fired young suns within this black cloud are buried deep and do not yet shine through, though in thousands of years they certainly will.

"What else do you see?" the IsoDidact asks.

"What I've always seen, what we've always seen," the Ur-Didact answers. "But now it's different."

There is something about this one that makes even Catalog uneasy, a coiled potential only partly visible in his duplicate.

"The light is over a hundred years old," the IsoDidact says. "What could change?"

"Something deeper than frequency. Look again," the Ur-Didact says. "The way it invades our eyes. Piercing. Slicing. Concealing. The light shuns us, space itself wishes to expel us. Can't you see? We are no longer welcome here."

This opening is not fortuitous. There is a slow calculation between the two.

"The Flood changes everything. Not just flesh. Space itself is infected," the Ur-Didact continues. "That's the power the Precursors once had . . . isn't it? They shaped and moved galaxies! They *created* us! How did we ever manage to defeat them?"

"Perhaps they were powerful but naive," the IsoDidact says. "But they've had ten million years to contemplate those mistakes."

"Yes . . . The Graveminds suck experience from all sentient history. One of them did everything but absorb me. Saw right through me, understood every strategy I've ever devised. They've advanced far beyond the Primordial. In absence of old strategies, new ones must be made."

"I don't believe so," the IsoDidact says. "What we saw years ago at Charum Hakkor—before you imprinted me—the result of a unique Halo test. Complete destruction of all Precursor artifacts. Back then, it seemed an awful aberration . . . But now we know what Halos are really capable of. They can destroy *any* structure that relies on neural physics. They are our last hope."

The Ur-Didact turns aside, fists clenching. "And loose damnation on the stars?" he shouts. The IsoDidact is silent. The sky above is no less grim than these walls. "My wife sympathizes with our enemies," the Ur-Didact says. "This quest to fulfill the Mantle has haunted me my entire life. And for countless millennia, we have failed to realize the one truth that could have saved us from the beginning. The Mantle isn't to be inherited by the noble, it is to be *taken by the strong*."

The Librarian enters the room unannounced and alone. It takes a few minutes for this pair, like figures in a broken mirror, to realize that she has arrived.

"Beloved!" she says, stepping forward, arms out, and for a moment, her face is wreathed with hope. Her joy is radiant. And then it fades. The two Didacts observe her with very different expressions. What should have been heartfelt reunion feels painful and incomplete.

"Did you hear my blasphemy, wife?" the Ur-Didact grumbles, looking away. "Do I discredit your belief in the Mantle?"

"It is not ours to receive, not *theirs* to give, not now," she says. "Tell me, my husband." She looks long and hard at the Ur-Didact. "Is this anger, this hatred for your enemies, what stands between us and the joy of reunion?"

The Ur-Didact moves toward his wife with a strangely dominant delicacy, his gaze fixed on her. She regards him with cautious fascination.

"Humans drowned out entire civilizations with the Flood," he says. "They brought this horrific parasite to our people. Had we acted quicker, had we taken what was rightfully ours, we could have cut off the infection at its source. Know this: the universe will now be turned star by star, world by world, organism by living thing, into even more of a tortured mockery than it already is. Look what it's done to *me!*" He spreads wide his powerful arms, bowing his head, as if opening to her gentle fingers, her probing, deep-feeling examination.

Instinctively, she reaches toward him—but holds back at the last instant. He notes her reticence; it may be the final breaking strain on thousands of years of love.

"Everything it touches is afflicted with madness," he cries out. "It has touched me. *I am myself mad!*"

The Librarian is stunned. She searches her husband's features, but he turns aside.

His duplicate cannot convey what he feels. He stands mute before them.

DEPARTURE AND PURSUIT

The reuniting has not gone well.

The Ur-Didact has taken a sphinx to the other side of the planet, where, he says, monitors report a possible intruder. As the arrival of spore-carrying ships cannot be ruled out, he will carry out a direct inspection.

The IsoDidact has returned to orbit to ready their fastest remaining ship—the *Audacity,* ceded to the Librarian after her historic voyage.

When we depart, the entire planet will be super-cooled, then powered down. From any distance greater than a few dozen kilometers, it will resemble a rocky, frozen residue of recent battles, abandoned for years, stripped of all resources. When we depart, the entire planet will be super-cooled, then powered down. Perhaps this effort, though seemingly futile, will save Nomdagro.

On a parapet, monitors gather in long rows, like servants of old awaiting the departure of their mistress.

She stands near the outer wall of the parapet, looking out over the great river valley where their children once played—and were trained by the Ur-Didact. Pleasant and now intensely painful memories. Most of her life has been centered on this world.

"We may never return," she says. "All of this . . ."

She cannot complete her thoughts. She flees from the parapet, leaving the machines to finish their final tasks.

The IsoDidact does not stop at preparing *Audacity* for departure. He orders the ship to pass over the far side of the planet. Catalog is with him; two parts of the triad are with the Librarian.

But the Ur-Didact is alone, on a continent set aside for primitive life-forms, its quietness, until now, undisturbed. The IsoDidact surveys the continent from space, then makes inquiries of a local tectonics monitor. The monitor is sluggish, preparing to power down for the long sleep this world will soon endure. But there has been no impact, of that it is certain.

The IsoDidact finds his original on a long, sinuous island of ancient basalt. Great expanses of wort and moss and slime-molds flourish here, bathed in creeping mists, on the edges of a shallow sea where bacterial nodules and mats compete with stalk-rooted, pillow-frond forests; where the most primary, first-form animals creep through waters now lit by day and warmed by the sun, while night has returned to the river valley.

Here also is the only Precursor artifact on the entire planet, a circular, temple-like structure of no apparent purpose, perhaps half a billion years old. It is so small that only the most complete listings mention it. It consists of a ring of blunt, rounded towers rising from a flat and featureless base, mottled gray and white, covered in places by blankets of moss, though they draw no sustenance from its impassive surface.

While immobile and eternal, as all Precursor structures were, until now, this one has no apparent purpose; perhaps it once served as a kind of marker, a testimonial to a far-ranging expedition, or the foundation of some other structure long removed or decayed.

The IsoDidact descends in a seeker and lands nearby. The Ur-Didact ignores the interruption, plodding through shallow, brackish ponds, toward the ring of towers, under the flowing and ever-present mist, an intruder in the peace. He squats before the artifact, clasping and unclasping his hands.

His duplicate approaches across a low, mossy glade.

The Ur-Didact acknowledges his presence. "Humans would have prayed to this," he says. "Everywhere they found powers and forces, in oceans and rivers, in trees, in animals—even in rocks. Forerunners pray their sorts of prayers only to the Mantle. Who, then, is more deserving?"

"Why have you come here?" the IsoDidact asks.

"When we first met, Bornstellar, you were looking for treasure. Perhaps it's here and we never recognized it."

"Nothing's changed here. We should return now."

"You don't sense it?" The Ur-Didact continues to stare at the ring of pillars. "This is how we will know they're coming." He turns and glares angrily. "What wisdom have you acquired, buried in my pattern, in the shape of my flesh? Am I to be set aside, and you, no doubt screaming under all that *pattern,* perhaps hope to return to what you were? Or do you find this pattern more suitable—and hope to replace me?"

"The Lifeshaper and I have work to finish. And so do you. There are no plans to set you aside."

"You still can't read her as well as I. She is stubborn, brilliant as a nova, dark as a singularity, with infinite depths. I've never discovered the core of her emotions, her self. I wonder what *her* duplicate would be like, what it would feel like to wear *her* imprint. To so many species she has made herself like unto a god, that they will remember her, that she can manipulate them in future times. She's explained that to you, hasn't she?"

"I remember."

"Second-hand memory!" The Ur-Didact rises and stretches out his armor. The hard light sparks with emotion. "You're a *poor* copy at best, aren't you?"

Catalog is concerned that the long conflict may now turn physical.

The Ur-Didact approaches his duplicate.

They stand barely separated by the reach of their great arms, surrounded by the swirling mist, the sough of the light breeze, the rhythmic lap of wavelets.

"There is no hope, continuing with *your* strategy, not in our time, not in this galaxy," the Ur-Didact says. "That is a cold, simple fact."

"I hold another opinion."

"Your privilege . . . *Manipular*." The Ur-Didact's expression is disdainful. "The Halos? Violating the Mantle all over again, with even greater destruction! Wiping out all intelligent life across this galaxy! By itself that proves you are a poor version. You've altered your strategic vision."

"According to circumstance, as every commander must."

"Don't you feel the truth of it? We gave the Precursors reason to retreat into madness. A passion for vengeance. And the Gravemind gave it all right back to me. I am filled with that passion, that madness, that *poison*! If we fire Halo, we lose everything."

The two Didacts stand opposite each other, barely moving, barely breathing, as if sizing each other up. Their armor is evenly matched. Their weapons are identical, their defenses, identical.

But the Didacts themselves—no longer identical.

"I leave the Lifeshaper to you, Bornstellar," the Ur-Didact says. "She has obviously chosen your way, not mine. I will take my own ship and you will show me where the Ark has been hidden."

Catalog is taking sides, and should not, but the rule of law, for Juridicals, is that hope must never be lost, justice and balance never abandoned. The Mantle, after all, is about the diversity and eternal prospect of living change in a universe filled with life! Is that no longer true? Is this what Catalog felt, facing the Gravemind—a total consumption of alien reason, of ancient, mad hopelessness?

And then it happens.

There is a soft, liquid sound from the center of the island. Both turn to see what it might be. The artifact, the circle of blunted towers, is moving. The towers extend, connect, form a nested cage. The base expands.

"The Flood," the Ur-Didact says. "We have to leave now!"

Through low gray clouds, we witness another change—in the skies above the planet. Arc by arc, curve by curve, star roads appear where none were before, surrounded by a purple fringe of Precursor superluminal passage—a kind of motion, of travel, not seen for ten million years, but now apparent around the ecumene, perhaps across the galaxy.

Then, something screams down from the sky—a single

mottled gray and white ovoid ten meters long. It plunges upright into shallow water, shooting out a spray of steam and burying one end in the muck, while the other end is already dissolving.

"Spore capsule!" the IsoDidact says. "No time remains."

The two Didacts agree at least on this.

For the last time, the two Didacts stand barely a long arm's length apart and then, slowly, back away, neither turning, before they are many paces separated—to return to their separate craft, to rise to orbit in separate ships.

Catalog is refused entry into the Ur-Didact's sphinx. Something is wrong.

Even as we pick up the Librarian, prepare to rise to *Audacity,* and witness *Mantle's Approach* climb up behind us, matching our destination vector—the air is pierced by a plunging haze of millions of spore capsules. Some drop into ocean or land, more yet explode high in the atmosphere. Spore clouds tower into gray-brown thunderhead plumes, then fan out in winding drifts, dominating, covering, concealing.

The triad of Catalog can do nothing but observe. And what I observe, far below, is the clearing of the brownish-gray clouds, revealing a warty formation of spore mountains. Any organisms remaining will soon be absorbed by the Flood.

Audacity has determined there is enough local potential that it can carry us all swiftly to the margins of Thema 34 before making the final jump to the greater Ark. Keyships will soon be the only vessels allowed to approach the installation.

The IsoDidact and the Librarian link arms on the bridge. "He's coming to the Ark with us," he tells her.

She appears stricken, uncertain, lost. "What are his plans now?

To sit in his fortress like a trapdoor spider, so that he can leap out and destroy ages from now?"

"You don't know that."

"Don't I? I see it so clearly! Oh, what did that thing *do* to him—what have *we all* done to him?"

The IsoDidact says nothing.

As we leave the blighted system, the silence on *Audacity* is awful.

JOURNEY TO THE GREATER ARK

The ark no longer makes Halos and now serves as the Librarian's main repository for specimens. It is rumored that only a single Halo remains, that the others have been hunted down and destroyed by the Flood.

This much I am told by the IsoDidact as we watch our passage into slipspace. But in truth, nobody knows the present situation, communications being so very difficult.

Catalog is particularly susceptible to unease during a jump, but this is a beautifully executed transit, and I feel hardly any discomfort. Nevertheless, the IsoDidact is tense.

The borders of Forerunner themas are marked by large-scale galactic magnetic fields, convenient if somewhat fluid indicators. These fields show up in *Audacity*'s displays as undulating curtains of green and purple, not unlike aurora in a planetary atmosphere. They seem as sensitive as the bells of jellyfish in the Librarian's tidal sea. Though infinitely slower and far more majestic, they still seem to possess a reactive kind of life.

Catalog is not immune to beauty. I have seen much beauty in the last year; the beauty of living things in the Librarian's care, the courage displayed by the Librarian and the IsoDidact while facing insurmountable odds.

We watch the changing patterns from slipspace: the displays designed to simplify hugely complex variables down to their most important components. To me, the flowing curtains of purple and green still seem beautiful, but to the IsoDidact and *Audacity* the changing hues and increasingly complex vortices point to looming difficulties.

"The thema boundaries have changed since my last passage," the IsoDidact says. He quickly runs through the possibilities with *Audacity*. Our space-time debt is building rapidly. "If we're forced to exit slipspace, we'll be stuck in the middle of a starless void, five thousand light-years from the Ark."

The field's great waves take on a reddish color. Another wall-like curtain of color moves in from the opposite angle, as if to trap and confine us. Nothing in the ship's experience can explain this.

We pass slowly between, while vortices grow more and more numerous. We are in a region where the physics that used to carry Forerunners between suns no longer seems to apply.

"We may have to risk a crisis jump," the IsoDidact says. "Space-time in this region is mutating to suit Precursor transits—the Flood is headed for the Ark. Slipspace here will soon become incompatible with our drives."

"The scale!" she exclaims. "Even slipspace is corrupted. Is there not a pure thing left in the galaxy?" Her question cannot be answered. "Our chances, in either case?"

"Without a crisis transit, practically none," the IsoDidact says.

"With, about one chance in four. We used them very sparingly during combat engagements."

"Field situation critical," *Audacity* confirms.

"We have a extreme affine solution to the rendezvous point," the IsoDidact says, "sufficient for our mass . . . but just barely. Do we take the chance?"

The Librarian hardly hesitates. "Of course," she says, and grips his arm. "And *Mantle's Approach*?"

The IsoDidact prepares a command sequence for the crisis transit. "Solution is fixed. We will make just one jump, albeit a curvy one. *Mantle's Approach* will likely follow right behind, sharing some of our curvature."

"Does that put us more at risk?"

"Of course. I don't think he cares. Prepare for more than the usual discomfort. Our space-time debt is going to accrue with interest."

Audacity initiates the sequence. Our jump begins. It is not the worst jump I've experienced, but it comes close, and Catalog takes a good hour to recover. The others are also weakened, and *Audacity* does not respond to my inquiries for an alarming time.

But eventually, the ship returns to full alertness, and we see that we have survived and that we are where we want to be. We have left the galaxy and are now approaching the protected defense perimeter of the greater Ark, set out here in the extragalactic darkness like a gigantic, spiky flower.

The Ur-Didact's ship follows close, though tentatively.

From a hundred thousand kilometers, the Ark's central forge is now dark. A single Halo—Omega Halo, our ancilla tells us—remains in parking orbit, aimed toward Path Kethona. It is a fitting name for the last of the Master Builder's great rings.

Unbeknownst to most, the lesser Ark, hidden a third of the way around the outer boundaries of the galaxy, currently maintains six of its own Halos, intended for a more widespread economical distribution to systems within the galaxy—systems possessing large gas giant planets. These six, alongside a seventh—Installation 07—will serve as a final weapon of last resort, if the greater Ark's defenses fall short.

A pair of tugs, many times larger than *Audacity,* takes hold of our hull and *Mantle's Approach*, escorting us through layer after layer of detection and deflection shields, spreading in a broad torus around the Ark, which now fills our command center's display. The IsoDidact and the Librarian study the last great wheel with very different expressions. Then, the Librarian sees a swarm of Lifeworker vessels, tiny by comparison, moored a few kilometers above an otherwise empty petal, with steady illuminated streams of containers moving her specimens down to the Ark's Lifeworker research station.

"Wonderful!" she cries. "They've all survived!"

But as we maneuver and see the giant installation edge-on, there are many more Forerunner ships than we expected, most hidden behind the Ark. Many look damaged, some quite severely.

Audacity, communicating with the installation's metarch, Offensive Bias, explains their presence. "All remaining Forerunners have been brought here," it says. "The last themas have been overwhelmed. There will be no other ships."

The last of the ecumene! The last remnants of Forerunner civilization, all concentrated here. The implications stagger all of us.

"As well," *Audacity* says, "some Lifeworker specimens have

been moved to the Halo to make room, including human populations."

The Librarian has barely accepted the first news, and now, faces *this*. She is outraged. "Who made that decision?"

An image is projected behind us in the command center—an additional surprise, and for these three, a most unwelcome one. It is the Master Builder himself, a haunted and hollow shadow of his former self. Is he on probation, but allowed to appear before his old rival? I wonder whether to commiserate—how mighty are we, the fallen!—or to gloat.

Neither, it turns out.

"Welcome to our Ark, Lifeshaper," the Master Builder says. "Didact—which do I address? Ah, the younger. It is my honor to have returned your original to the company of your wife—and, if memory serves me," he said, turning to another display, "it looks as though he, too, has arrived. You both should know that I have been summoned to help prepare our Ark for the coming storm. And to transfer command."

"To whom?" the IsoDidact asks.

"To me. Builder Security will carry on from here."

Obviously, a deal has been struck—a desperate deal on all sides.

A protracted silence in the command center.

The Librarian finally says, "I will be taken as soon as possible to the Halo to tend to my specimens. *Alone*."

"Of course," the Master Builder says. "I have already made arrangements."

A possible setback in my gathering of testimony. But this is offset when to my delight, I realize that a local, highly secure Juridical network has been set up on the Ark, and that many fellow agents

GREG BEAR

are here, sharing evidence, continuing investigations into the treatment of both specimens and prisoners . . . Into the return and elevation of the Master Builder.

Doing what Juridicals do so well! But to what end, now? I push aside all doubts. The network uses new tests to verify my identity and integrity. I then begin to quench my desperate thirst at that deep well of law and wisdom.

The Master Juridical arrived at the greater Ark shortly after the fall of the Capital system, in company with the last surviving members of the New Council.

All Juridicals now gather in his august presence. The Master Juridical first expresses concern about a continuing blackout of the Domain. "No agent or ancilla, of any scale, has been able to connect with the Domain for over a year. Our deepest and most sacred records are no longer available."

Juridical proceedings are at a standstill, and not just because of that interruption.

"Haruspis is no longer in the network, even when it is open—and may be dead," he says. "There are no other Haruspices to watch over the Domain. The number of our agents still reporting has been greatly reduced. Those assembled here may be the last.

But our work must proceed, in the hope that circumstances will improve.

"Catalog has been instructed by the Master Juridical to attend the meeting of the new commanders. The last survivors of the New Council have given all power over to the Master Builder.

"Henceforth, all Forerunner command conferences are to be attended by Catalog," the Master Juridical says. I wonder if there are enough of us! "No exceptions."

THE RETURN OF BUILDER COMMAND

The spacious chambers of the Ark's Cartographer now host five commanders, all Builder Security but for the IsoDidact.

The Ur-Didact, whose ship remains at bay, near Omega Halo, has recused himself from this meeting. He has not responded to any outside communication, Juridicals are informed.

ISODIDACT

Out here, on the edge of the great intergalactic darkness, we are extraordinarily weak and horribly exposed. I have no doubt that very soon the greater Ark will be placed under siege.

The new commanders stand in a wide circle within the Ark, or rather, within a fully detailed projection. Depending on where my attention focuses, my ancilla feeds me prepared memories of the installation's past activities—the arrival of survivors, removal of specimens to the Halo, positioning of the Halo to sweep Path Kethona. The data arrives in such rapid, dense packets that they give me an annoying headache, as my brain adjusts to torrents of memories.

But that is the way of things in the end game of a war. And we are in the end game. We have lost—that much seems obvious—but our final battle could place us in a position to make the Flood victories seem very bitter indeed.

And so there is no room for disputes within command. The changes have happened; they cannot be reversed. Per mandate of the New Council, Builder Security is now once again in control of the greater Ark.

However, three of the five in attendance used to be Warrior-Servants and once served under my original; that much returns a little confidence. I have to wonder how he would handle his former commanders—and why he's chosen to abandon us in our time of greatest need. My memories and abilities are the same or better—in his present state. But to many of them he is old and familiar. I am new.

The other commanders experience their own investment with data. Sparkles of individual displays dance around their armor as they ask questions of the installation's metarch, Offensive Bias.

When the Cartographer has finished its update, I call them to full attention.

"We've all seen the might of the reawakened Precursor constructs," I begin. "Once they're upon us, we will have little time. There is no room for error. No room for hestitation."

"They are our creators!" the Examiner exclaims. He is a former Promethean larger than myself and older than my original by several thousand years. The Examiner long ago preferred supporting command as more suited to his talents, which are extraordinary—as indicated by the fact that he has somehow brought seventy-five fortresses and eleven dreadnoughts out of the worst Precursor tangles to the greater Ark, where they now provide the bulk of our defense.

"Doubtful in the extreme!" cries the Tactician. A general rumble of agreement passes around the circle. The Tactician is relatively slight and younger than the others. Less than two thousand years have passed since his maturity, and he has always been Builder Security, but he proved his brilliance over and over during the metarch revolt. With the fall of the Master Builder, he went into temporary retirement. His star rises again. He could be chosen to replace me—not without reason.

"I harbor no doubts they are not the same," I say, "not anymore at least. The distortions the Flood inflicts are outward manifestations of an inner ugliness that reflects its origins. Ultimately, it matters little where they came from. We now find ourselves at the end of Forerunner existence."

The commanders stand in solemn silence.

Bitterness-of-the-Vanquished steps through the projected forge, and stands surrounded by ghostly images of damaged Forerunner transports. Bitterness commanded Warrior forces during the Kradal conflicts at galactic center. She trained me—trained my original. She is the eldest among us, not to be taken lightly.

"Under your command," she says, "Forerunners have lost thema after thema to the Flood. I *taught* the Didact, and you are not *him*. Tell us why any Forerunners should continue to follow you in the face of such catastrophic losses . . . now that the Didact has returned and his duplicate is no longer necessary."

Despite anticipating this—with all the honed political instincts of my original—I feel a deep jab of resentment. In my mind, in all my thoughts, I *am* the Didact. Bornstellar is like a character in a story told centuries ago, so dim . . . so *other*.

But I have to honor her opinion. Still, she forces me to reveal things best left unsaid.

"I would agree, and step aside, yet the Didact has recused himself."

"Because he was subjected to interrogation by a Gravemind!" Bitterness says.

"So it would seem," I respond. "A consequence of his capture by the Master Builder, who dropped him into a Burn to die."

The commanders all raise their arms and twist their left hands. They are not receptive to this line of discussion, and bicker among themselves. They do not believe one story or another, and the reasons for the Master Builder's strange behaviors in these matters remain unknown.

"There is conspiracy here to reduce Warriors to nothing!" the Examiner calls out, his voice breaking.

"You yourself are now a Builder," Bitterness says.

"As are you!"

"We should confront the New Council, force them to hear us. The Didact—the original Didact—is our only hope in this conflict—we should join *him*!" the Examiner insists.

Those who most recently transferred to Builder Security are uncomfortable with this assertion. Conflicting loyalties could put them in an awkward position with the Master Builder, who currently holds the power.

"It is too late now," Bitterness says. "The time for strife and indecision has ended! Let us keep our composure and accept that the facts are still in dispute." She faces me, her sightless eyes strangely acute. She has been blind for centuries. Her armor sees for her. "Yet now you push forward a strategy the Didact passionately opposed for more than a thousand years. Strange reversal! How can you, or the Master Builder, be trusted?"

Her words finished, she steps back into the circle.

Follows a longer and more telling silence. Bitterness has struck a chord, given voice to doubts most have held since the destruction of the Capital planet . . . Doubts that have grown to an awful strength with our sad line of defeats and retreats.

Am I not the Didact, in truth, in my mind? Am I truly less? How could I not foresee that this problem would rise so quickly to the level of a crisis in command?

But I have. The sum of a fight among equals, or with a superior, is to allow the other's strength to put him where you want him. There is one personality who may yet unite us all . . . if he plays his new role well. A tremendous risk, that.

A new voice from outside the circle breaks the pause. The strongest among us has arrived.

"You can't fault this new Didact. I outwitted his original twice before, you know." The Master Builder's slighter figure enters the Cartographer behind the single projected Halo, and for a moment he is cast in shadow. "I forced him into exile, practically sealed him into his Cryptum, and when he returned from that exile, I lured him, hooked him like a silly *fish*—and sent him to an even darker fate. I ask you, who's the greater strategist?"

The Master Builder joins the circle, then moves to the center, his penetrating black eyes searching all with benign amusement. He lingers on my face only for a moment, with a sidelong afterglance. "If anything," he says, "this new Didact is a sharper and more capable character, certainly now. As for the other . . . The old Didact and I have just had a brief visit. Whatever business he has here will soon be completed. He already makes preparations to leave."

"We desperately need a strong central command!" Bitterness announces. "And we need it now!"

"I believe it's obvious who that commander must be." The Master Builder has resumed his characteristic bravado—but something is missing. Something has hit him very hard—and left a mark in his demeanor. He struts and shrugs out his arms, as if preparing for physical labor. "Tell them, Bornstellar-Makes-Eternal-Lasting. Tell them how I knew we'd all be here, doing precisely what we're doing now, many years ago. You were there, after all."

I do not hesitate to give him his due. "The Master Builder tested Halo on Charum Hakkor," I say. "With startling results."

Faber moves around the circle, examining the commanders with some, but not all, of his old, wicked energy. "Long ago, while overseeing Halo field design, I had a suspicion—an insight—that the Halo's energies might also nullify neural physics. That insight was proven brilliantly correct. When the Halo fired, tuned to my select energies, it destroyed all Precursor artifacts in the system. Serendipity, perhaps. Or brilliance. You decide.

"But fair is fair. After my test, and its unexpected consequences, I made the mistake of gathering up the timeless one, the Primordial—the last Precursor, so it later claimed. An incredible scientific specimen, I thought. I did show caution. I imprisoned the Primordial in a stasis field. Yet, somehow it got loose again—clever thing—and provoked an unfortunate dialog with Mendicant Bias. Our first example of an ancillary infection, and a rather dire one.

"For that I am *entirely* to blame. All my triumphs were shunted aside by the revolt of Mendicant Bias . . . whose design and creation I share with the Didact. Let us not forget that! Our servant turned against us. I became an outcast. A failure." He forestalls unvoiced objections with a raised arm and splayed fingers. "And yet . . . what a discovery! And herein lies our last hope in this awful war. We still hold the one weapon which is capable of stopping the Flood—this Halo."

He continues to pace restlessly around the circle, as if hoping to draw forth encouragement, justification. I tell myself, silently, how much I hate this Forerunner.

"The original Didact was *wrong,* I was *right.* But it takes his *duplicate* to finally listen to reason." He glances again in my direction. The weakness is almost blatant. "These Halos were specifically tuned to fire a linear blast of energy which disrupts and ultimately wipes out neural physics, destroying both the Flood and its Precursor weapons. With it we will bring unparalleled destruction upon our attackers, putting an end to this war once and for all."

He looks back to the commanders. "But if we fail here, know that another Ark has already been created," he says, "and from it more efficient, smaller Halos. They form a weapon array far more powerful than even this ring." He points to the lone holographic Halo. "When these newer Halos are spread throughout the galaxy, they will form a network capable of purging all sentient life. These are our last defense. Without them, the galaxy will be dominated by the Flood. But we must not let it come to this."

His look seems to cut the air. "A few of you have been Warrior-Servants. Brave, honorable, and yet the heirs of those who committed the unspeakable crime that began this madness. A crime against our creators. Remember *that* in your long dreams, when you confront the Domain."

Suddenly, Faber's armor slumps; his energy seems to dissipate. "But know this. The original Didact was impressed by a Gravemind to serve as messenger. The Gravemind was aware of my activities, purging infected Forerunner vessels and restoring them to service. It *sent* the Didact my way . . . deliberately, with a message."

"What message?" Bitterness asks.

"My family, my wives and children, went into their own exile. They relocated on a system in Path Kural, now part of a Burn. All have been gathered by the Flood. All have been made part of a Gravemind." His face contorts. He shouts around the circle, "My *wives! My children! Addressing me from within a Gravemind, taunting me, accusing me! Through my enemy!* If we carry out our designs, they say all will *die*, and nothing of value will be left to me. The Didact actually took *pleasure* in delivering this message. 'This,' he says, 'is what you have done, with your Halos.'"

Bitterness bows not in submission, but in joined grief, before the Master Builder. "Our sorrow is with you," she whispers.

"All sorrow is with you," the Examiner affirms.

I stand my ground, but this is the support Faber sought, the support he needs. He looks up. "Who better to understand our task, then? I would give anything to have been wrong, I would give *everything* not to be a Forerunner in these times. As I live and breathe, I am sickened by the truth—sick at my core. Yet by order of the remaining Council, sadly reduced, I have resumed command. The galaxy is ours to lose.

"Let's put an end to our hideous mistakes. But when we've survived, when we're finished with our awful task, forced on us by the iniquity of Warriors ten million years ago—who among us will ever be able to face the Domain?"

None of the others meet his haunted eyes. Deliberately, I avert mine as well.

"*Who*, Forerunners?" he cries, then pushes through and departs the Cartographer.

The commanders stand in respectful silence, then turn, as one, toward me.

"The Master Builder's fate is here. And so is ours," Examiner says. "Someone must go to the other Ark and prepare for the unthinkable."

My task is now clear.

"The Graveminds know they still face a tremendous threat," Bitterness says. "They know of the existence of the greater Ark. But they may not yet know the whereabouts of the lesser Ark. You must go there and take command. The Flood cannot be allowed to claim victory. They must be stopped, if not for our kind, then for others who may come later."

The commanders look out beyond the image of Halo and Ark, toward the great dim spread of stars that is our galaxy.

The star roads are coming.

We can all feel them.

THE LIBRARIAN AND THE UR-DIDACT

My husband . . . has become a child again.

But not any sort of child I'd be proud of. Not any sort of child I would trust.

He has stripped off his armor and wanders about our quarters, looking at the things his duplicate has gathered, artifacts and objects of study, remembrances of the time when *he* was away, in exile or lost, and I briefly had another husband—very much like him.

But no longer. There is no question of him making any attempt to reconcile, of that I am certain. I hardly recognize what he has become.

Still, he has requested this meeting, with the implication that it will be our last.

I sit on a suspensor that takes color and shape beneath me, and he sits beside me, his great head dropping between his thick knees.

"Can you know what it was like to be in the Cryptum, leaving our situation to you, while all this spun out of control?" he asks.

I take up his great hand and unfold it, running my own smaller finger along each muscular digit. The hand reflexively closes. Our bodies still carry instructions built in from times long before memory.

"No," I breathe. "I hope it was peaceful."

"Quiet, as much as there can be sense or sensation. The Domain can only tell the living what they already know," he says. "Or what they've stored in its expanses. I wandered through all the corridors . . . so they appeared, anyway. Centuries of wandering through hallways and caverns and even deeper, darker places, lined and fitfully aglow with ancestral records and memories, upwellings of past visits, rarely by me, sometimes by our ancestors . . . on occasion, our descendants."

"Descendants?" I ask.

"The Domain keeps its secrets only with difficulty. It wants, it *needs*, to spread knowledge. It wants to tell us when we're being foolish, but it can only replay the emotions and memories of those who came before. Still, rarely, it violates its own rules."

"What about our descendants?" I persist.

"I felt their touch, their love. And yet, they were fading. The Domain is filled with sadness. A deep shadow has fallen over everything Forerunner. When I was pulled up from all that, pulled out of the Cryptum and revived . . . I couldn't *remember*. But now I do—in part. Horror brought it back. The Gravemind returned it to me. It forced me to *listen*."

My husband swiftly removes his hand from mine and stands to summon his armor, stretching to allow it to surround him. "I need to fight against what it told me, what it has done to me, to all of us. I need to fight with all of my might and will, and everything I can gather . . . every weapon and resource. But I have been undercut from the very beginning by that *Manipular*, Wife. The worst thing I've ever done was imprint him. And so, forgive me in advance for what I must do. And know why I do it."

I am about to ask what this is, that requires any forgiveness, let alone mine—but alarms sound before I can speak. The Didact starts up, and for a moment, there is that old, brutal sharpness, that old readiness for battle. The ancillas gather around, foremost the image of the Offensive Bias.

"The Ark is under attack," it says. "Large concentrations of star roads are emerging in near space."

"How much time?" the Didact asks.

"Hours, no more," the metarch responds.

The IsoDidact is doubtless already taking action, in concert with the Builder commanders—putting the entire Ark on full alert. I need to get to the Halo! My specimens, the last humans . . .

But what I see in the abyssal night around the greater Ark is enough to freeze me through and through. Somehow, the old artifacts have been transported in such amazing density that the galaxy beyond is barely visible, as if viewed through a weave of shadowy bars.

The Ark is surrounded, and every second the star roads squeeze in. Already our radius of action is down to a few million kilometers.

I can't bear the thought of the loss of all my specimens, of the greatest concentration of our lifelong efforts, of all our work!

"How can we repopulate the galaxy if we lose everything here?" I cry.

The Didact's look is strangely *sly*. Devious, as if he has a delicious joke he wishes to tell, but not yet. An expression I've never seen before. Horror compounds upon horror.

"After I finish my task, I will depart in *Mantle's Approach*," he says.

My mind races. I can expect no assistance from the Didact, that much is obvious. The Ark is far too large to move. The Halo might be able to escape. But there are not nearly enough functional vessels to rapidly shift our Forerunners there. They could have been moved if we had begun shuttling them weeks ago! Or if we had put them on the Halo in the first place.

Our mistakes have finally compounded.

The trap is closing.

"How can we save them all? How can we ever get free?" I ask. "And where do we go?"

"There is no way out, only *through*," he says, his eyes narrowing. "If you wish to survive, you must leave now. When the Flood is finished, there will be nothing left of this place."

The Didact stretches a long arm in the direction of Path Kethona. "The star roads will keep clear of Halo's firing path. That will open an escape route," he says. "But it will not remain that way for long. You must escape in *Audacity* while you have a chance." He sucks in his breath, staring at the Ark's surface. "*Traitors*. And yet . . . even in the midst of our most monumental failure, I will seize another solution."

The Didact locks his helmet and leaves with hardly a backward glance. He does not even offer to escort me to *Audacity*.

I am lost in a sink of misery and confusion. If the Ark is destroyed, and all my specimens, what is the point of my own existence?

And then I know. We must move everything—as much as we

can—to safety. It is our only solution. I send the briefest of messages to Chant-to-Green who is hidden within a keyship on the far side of the Burn. If her vessel is capable, she will obey. She cannot fail.

I then contact the only presence on the Ark that I know can help.

MONITOR CHAKAS

Sentinels and attack harriers rise in swirling clouds around the Ark, like flocking birds over the plains of my birth. I make inquiries, but the Ark's channels are consumed with preparations for evacuation as well as for combat. Yet how can so many different species be evacuated? And to where? There are not nearly enough transports.

I have not been kept fully informed. I only know that the Ark has been handed over to the Master Builder, and of course, given his luck and skill, is now under immediate threat.

My new mandate is to protect the Lifeshaper and her work. Once I was a human, but received such wounds that the Bornstellar Didact stored me in a machine. The Lifeshaper allowed me, after their gathering on the Ark, to look after her human populations. She saw it as part of my recovery, and part of my reward for serving them so well. And I have done my very best.

GREG BEAR

The Lifeshaper's plan was to keep humans on the Ark, out-side the range of Halo destruction, until the scoured planets are free of the Flood and ready for reseeding. But they have now been moved to the Halo, I presume on the orders of the Master Builder, to make room for Forerunners. Nothing is ever simple, and great plans too often meet awful conclusions.

Now she asks of me a final favor: Save everything we can. I query the Ark monitors assigned to Lifeworkers. Only a few re-spond. They have no instructions with regard to the Halo. The others have shifted service to Offensive Bias. Must I turn against my fellow machines to fulfill the orders of the Lifeshaper? I now await her instructions, as I cannot act without the Lifeshaper's command and imprimatur.

Catalog, why do *you* attend a mere monitor, if not to keep me informed of what I must do? I have no testimony to give. I am no longer human. You should seek out the little one called Riser and ask *him*. He would offer you his opinions freely.

He is still what he was. Wake him up, and he will give you an *earful*.

———

Finally, I have received my orders. The Lifeshaper has instructed me to take a Gargantua-class transport from the Ark to the Omega Halo. Onboard, stores of indexed organisms from the Ark's popu-lation have already been placed by Lifeworkers. Many of these are living specimens, others are simply genetic composites originat-ing from the Librarian's Conservation Measure. I wonder if this relatively small number will be sufficient to rebuild these many species after Halo fires?

The Halo faces a great curved wall of star roads. Humans placed on the last ring weapon have barely had time to settle in their compounds. By the tens of thousands, they walk over crude hills, shallow lakes, and rivers, and between low mountains and through thick forests. The brightness of an artificial sun moves in familiar rhythm, and the people down there may hope that their most recent darkness and dreamless sleep, in the holds of Lifeworker ships, will be but prelude to the chance to regain all they have lost. They may hope that they have finally reached a home where they can live in peace for centuries, if not thousands of years.

————

As we make preparations to transport the humans, the original Didact's enormous warship thunders down, taking up a position above the human compounds. It's followed by thousands of sentinels not linked to Offensive Bias, apparently intent on isolating and controlling this section of the Halo. With access to only so much Forerunner knowledge, I have no explanation for this display of force.

The Lifeshaper's ship comes alongside our transport, hiding in its massive shadow. We link. She is frantic; and for the first time in years, I'm afraid. But why is the original Didact here?

Star roads grow thick beyond the sky bridge. They may soon crush the Ark and the Halo, and with it, all humans, all Forerunners. Forerunner history may be at an end. I do not know whether to feel gladness or sorrow.

"Take us up!" the Lifeshaper orders *Audacity,* her face stiff with fear. We rise above the Halo's atmosphere, to see everything more clearly. *Mantle's Approach* sweeps low over the Halo compound. The ship's silhouette has changed. Something protrudes from its front.

The Composer.

A great star forms above the compound—the Composer's targeting beams. I can do nothing to stop it!

At the Lifeshaper's command, *Audacity* shoots forward. She hopes to insert herself into the path of the Composer, to stop her husband from harming her specimens. But the *Mantle's Approach* makes the slightest, deftest of maneuvers, throws out a torsion field, and *Audacity is* brushed aside like a gnat.

The Didact's ship freezes above the center of a compound. Below, the humans must see what is happening, even through the cloud-wracked atmosphere. They have stopped whatever they are doing to look up and shield their eyes against the brilliance of the targeting beams. A blood-colored pall falls over the compound, over their faces. Surely this is a crime! Catalog will see it all, record it all. Is the madness beginning again? Have I given up everything for another betrayal?

"Tell the sentinels to *kill him!*" Lifeshaper cries out.

But I cannot. The Didact has assumed control of them all. *Mantle's Approach* is too strong, too powerful. The Lifeworker forces are too weak and too few, and cannot stop it.

The Composer has locked onto its victims. Translucent, oily waves of energy spread across the compound, echo from the walls of the Halo, then slide down like folding sheets to wrap the crowds below.

Suddenly, everywhere, across hundreds of square kilometers, bodies twist and fall. Hundreds of thousands are composed before my sensors can make an accurate count.

The information flows back to the Composer in a reverse wave. Men, women, children . . . all taken in moments.

The Lifeshaper moans deep in her throat. Then the moan intensifies, until she screams, "That's all he ever does—*kill my children!* Why? *Why?*"

Audacity tells us that we must move closer to the compound or outside the great wheel.

The Didact's ship withdraws the Composer, seals itself for transit, pushes away from the compound and the Halo, departs. *Audacity* moves under its own volition to a safe position, near the outer perimeter. But safety is no grace.

The next atrocity will soon begin—the firing of the Halo itself. *Audacity* prepares for an immediate jump.

have seen this before. I remember the awful sensation. I cannot close down my sensors. I am a machine. The sensation is not optimal, but I do not feel what living things feel, in the presence of the Composer. Though I remember it too well.

The Librarian watches it all, her body seemingly in conflict with her armor, as if she would reach up and tear at her twisted face—beyond any expressible sadness. Such anger mixed with so much grief, both ancient and new . . .

Our path is cleared, for the time being. I wish I could feel despair. I wish I myself could grieve. My people are gone! All that remain from the Librarian's collection are on the transport linked below. The last hope of my entire species.

The Librarian stops her contortions and recovers enough control to tell me that she and I will part ways. I will return to the transport and take the surviving specimens—including my friends—away from here. "You must find Bornstellar, he will take you to the lesser Ark. That is where we must hide the specimens." But what about her safety? What does she plan to do?

I must obey. Still,

Something

Is being born in me. Something hidden is emerging. I feel its potential. It is not entirely obedient. Have I been affected by the logic plague? No.

I am still Chakas.

I am still human!

ISODIDACT • GREATER ARK, OMEGA HALO

The sheer power mounted by the Flood is staggering.

Well over a million Flood-infected ships have taken up attack positions about the greater Ark. Their arrangement is familiar enough—the peculiar gapped spiral sweep favored by my original, each segment capable of wheeling in three dimensions in response to attack from any direction. That tactic has been adapted by the Flood's new commander—Mendicant Bias.

Mendicant Bias was deactivated and disassembled after the destruction of the Capital system, to the extent that any Contender-class metarch can ever be eliminated from the systems it once controlled. Its parts were spread throughout the ecumene for later study. But many of those regions where it was stored have been overwhelmed by the Flood, and the metarch's fragments were apparently recovered, restored, reassembled—and reactivated by a Gravemind. The Flood's forces are marshaled by a twisted machine, the first victim of the logic plague—and a creation, in part, of the Ur-Didact.

Father to son, I tell myself.

Against the tightening cage of reshaped star roads, the former Forerunner vessels are little more than a cloud of mosquitoes pouring through a deadfall of trees.

Bitterness and the Examiner float beside me as our fleet transport carries us from the greater Ark to the parking orbit of the Omega Halo.

"At such a close range, in such limited time . . ." Bitterness says, all she needs to say. The one Halo ready for action will never be able to mount a broad sweep before the star roads and their escort of infected ships have closed in and destroyed the Ark.

"Get us inside the hoop and land us anywhere," I say. "Keep a direct link with Offensive Bias. We'll have to fire from its present angle. Send confirming signal to *Audacity,* the plan is under way, be prepared."

"Lifeshaper does not respond, Commander. *Audacity* says that the Ur-Didact's ship has conducted an unauthorized intrusion . . . and used a Composer!" Bitterness's astonishment equals my own. "The humans . . . they're gone. They've been composed."

What would my original want with humans? Collecting them, composing them . . . Defying the most fervent wishes of the Lifeshaper. It's beyond comprehension. My first instinct is to seek *Mantle's Approach* and force it to return it to the Ark . . . Where the Ur-Didact will be destroyed, along with the rest of us, allowing only the Lifeshaper to escape. The best of us all.

But our transport would be powerless against *Mantle's Approach.*

"My wife is safe?" I ask.

"*Audacity* reports all are safe, but experiencing distress. It is preparing to escape."

"Good," I say, though I cannot fathom the horror my wife faces—her life's work swallowed up before her eyes.

We land on the Halo's inner surface, near the base of the control center. We enter swiftly. Bitterness and the Examiner follow. In the far wing of the control room, a fully holographic readout of all Halo systems assembles.

I approach the symbols representing the nodes that will shape both spokes and the hub radiator. These are outlined in green and blue—fully functional and ready to be fired.

"It's out there," Bitterness says. "Your monster. Mendicant Bias. Can't you feel it?"

My monster, indeed. No point offering a correction. Does it know what I plan? Does the Gravemind somehow know or remember what happened at Charum Hakkor? Has the secret of the lesser Ark been given up? All that is needed for me to depart to the lesser Ark is its exact coordinates, but those are only known by the Master Builder. And he has granted me an audience before I leave.

"Faber is here," Examiner says, and points to a slender shadow entering the chamber.

"Finally!" Bitterness says.

The Master Builder steps through the displays, as before, a dramatic enough entrance, but performed without enthusiasm. He glances at us under the cowl of his helmet, then instructs his ancilla to hand me the coordinates to the lesser Ark. No prelude, no ceremony.

That done, he faces me. "You have all I have, Didact. I share responsibility with Warrior-Servants. No longer will I bear this burden alone."

And with that, he primes the ring—making it clear why he asked me here. He wants me to see Omega Halo fire.

Expenditures rise; local vacuum energy for a thousand kilometers around the ring is sucked down to a practical minimum. I watch the measurements closely; another moment of desperate uncertainty . . . the star roads may have an effect on what we can pull from local space-time.

But they are not yet close enough. Omega Halo's reserves rise to maximum and are primed for instant release.

"Sequence input successful," Offensive Bias announces. "Omega Halo is fully charged."

"Will you escape with the IsoDidact, Master Builder?" the Examiner asks.

"No. *That* is my Ark." He pauses, and moves his gloved finger, as if to outline the huge installation's image. "And *this* is my Halo." We expect another grand gesture, an arrogant sweep of rhetoric, but Faber is in no mood to boast; his gaze is steady, downcast. "Throughout my life, I sought power and profit for myself, for my rate. Now, at long last, I think I understand the meaning of a crime against the Mantle. After this, no need to seek balance. I will await my penance here."

We stand in silence before this uncharacteristic display of courage and humility.

Examiner's expression remains doubtful. "We'll likely none of us study the Domain long," he says.

The control room removes all but the necessary parts of our command display, then rotates slowly into position and becomes transparent to visible light.

The Master Builder summons up the complex visage of Offensive Bias. The metarch looms over us, a servant greater than its masters, more capable, and, I hope, untainted. Soon we will know. All depends on what we accomplish here, now.

Builders and Warrior-Servants.

Together.

"We seek security in the Domain and the example of the Mantle," the Master Builder chants. *"We who are about to kill seek forgiveness. We treasure the truth of our error, that in future error will pass from us, and from the lives of all who come after."*

The Examiner looks at us with an expression of guilty glee. Warriors do love war. Warriors do hate what it brings. The tension . . .

I turn away, for the first time in years aware that my own bones are not so ancient, so deeply infused with Warrior traditions. Once, I came of Builder stock, more like Faber than the Didact.

Soon, there will be only one Didact.

"Artifacts within perimeter," Offensive Bias says. "One million kilometers."

"Too damned close," Examiner says.

The strange and changing quality of space-time around the star roads is subtle, yet evident in a crawling itch in our nerves and brain.

The spokes are forming, and Faber slowly adjusts the ring's angle, pulling its firing path.

The Flood's forces regroup to respond to the changing Halo angle. Star roads and ships attempt to move out of the beam's path. What we are attempting will only delay this assault, not protect us from the Flood's overwhelming force.

The hub forms.

An awful, painful glow rises along the spokes and gathers,

spreading around the hub's circumference. From the opposite, unfinished inner surface of the wheel, reflections of this horrible luminosity return to us.

All but blind Bitterness look away . . . Even so, she gasps, for her ancilla must fully convey the nature of the power we are about to unleash—for only the third time in Forerunner history.

Our minds reel at the sudden release of Halo radiation. No neurological being, no biological system, can withstand for long proximity to such a discharge. The multidimensional radiated field stretches out, as designed, to Path Kethona. Massless, subtle, deadly, it will cross that great distance in mere instants. Halo energy does not recognize space and time.

Path Kethona is *already dead.*

The nearest star roads in that beam twist, melt, then crumble to fragments, and those fragments . . . become nothing.

The infected ships within the beam's path wander under automated control, carrying only their dead—Forerunner and, I hope, a few Graveminds as well.

"Did my wife manage to escape?" I ask.

Although its own vessels are already beginning to engage the Flood, Offensive Bias's voice remains calm. "Two ships have departed the Ark. One of the ships reports itself—it is *Audacity.* The other ship is cloaked, unknown."

I can only assume this is *Mantle's Approach.* My wife has apparently escaped, and for that I feel an immense joy, but the survival of my original brings no joy, only a sharp, puzzled anger. He has violated the Mantle yet again, and then—fled! In a time of immense peril, he has deserted us.

No longer a Promethean.
No longer a Warrior-Servant.
A traitor!

Our own end is all too near. I must depart before it is too late.

"Metarch, prepare my vessel for passage. I will use the wake of Halo's firing to escape."

"Your ship is on approach, Didact," Offensive Bias says.

Star roads outside the Halo field suddenly begin to move in, replacing those damaged or destroyed. They cut across our wheel. All around us, beneath us, the substance of the Omega Halo shivers as it is intersected and carved into pieces. On its approach, my vessel is tossed aside, crushed against the far wall of this ring.

I am now stranded, my fate is sealed.

The spokes and hub flicker and die. The ring's high spanning curve violently bends and sheds huge squares like leaves from a windblown tree.

Offensive Bias's vessels make their last sorties against the incoming attack ships, but can do nothing to prevent our destruction. The pent-up kinetic energy of the Halo will finish the job. Already we can feel heat rising from beneath our feet.

We have done what we can. My confusion must now end. There can only be one Didact, even should he be a traitor, even should he be mad.

I feel thick layers of my imprint parting, letting through the youthful and naive foundations of Bornstellar-Makes-Eternal-Lasting. I pay honor to my mother and father, to all my Builder ancestors going back millions of years, whose names I learned in my infancy and can recite from memory. . . . My mantra barely has time to finish. My armor attempts to protect me against the heat, the motion, the disassembly of the chamber.

I hear our ancillas perform their own mantra, and wonder if perhaps in the Domain there is any distinction between machine and living being. They have served well, to the best of their ability.

Catalog, beside me, sharing our fate, hear my confession . . .

The bottom of the control room falls from below us and the others pass from my sight. I can hear and see them no longer—I can't tell if they've survived. My hands grasp a narrow column, searching for purchase—but it finds none.

And yet before I fall I can see a flare of intense radiation—the drive of a ship coming closer, carving a bright gash in the chaos, sweeping in toward the control center's cracked and melting walls. As I slip through the cracks of a battered Halo, I hear a voice and recognize it immediately.

Chakas.

I rescued him once from the destruction of a Halo.

Now he will rescue me.

THE LIBRARIAN

udacity is now light-years away from the greater Ark. I sit shivering in armor that barely functions. Beside me, Catalog is quiet; whether it is still recording, I cannot know.

My entire body tingles, the air around me smells strange. I can dimly make out symbols describing in basic ancilla code something or other . . . so long since I have had to read such symbols.

Then they reform and translate into measurements I can understand. Despite the interference of the star roads, we have completed our transit. I can only assume that the Didact has survived as well.

Before making our jump, I ordered Monitor Chakas to proceed to the lesser Ark and deliver all that we managed to salvage. Against all odds, we managed to save a number of humans, including the small Florian, Riser, and the young female Vinnevra recovered from the rogue Halo. This seems to substantially improve the monitor's commitment and energy. It still has friends to protect.

Although this comforts Chakas, it does not comfort me. The number of humans we managed to save is not nearly enough. Never before has the frailty of their species been more apparent than right now. But others plans are already at work, and I must focus all of my energy on the task ahead.

I am left alone to do what I must do. There can only be one Didact, and that is not the first. Strange—how cold I feel in my head and chest, in my throat, as if I have been choked with ice—as I affirm that!

I have seen what the Flood holds in store for the galaxy. I have seen it in his haunted eyes and desperate cruelties. He cannot be allowed to carry out his plans, whatever they may be. And yet—what can I do against him? How can I stop his madness? Looking out upon the slowly turning stars, feeling the humming preparations as *Audacity* finds a solution for our next jump, I reach a quick and desperate decision. I have a few last cards to play. I will use the Ur-Didact's past love for me, our intense and intimate partnership over thousands of years, as a weapon against him.

Audacity has my personal transponder codes. Using those, we may still be recognized as a safe ship, even an unremarkable companion, by *Mantle's Approach*. It is possible that Requiem's automated systems will also accept me and allow me entry without setting off alarms—or even notifying the Didact of my presence. Though that seems unlikely.

Two possibilities, both, I think, with a slender chance of success. I can join the Didact's ship—a very large vessel, dwarfing *Audacity*. Or I can follow in train, in shadow, all the way down to Requiem—into his beloved Shield World, for which we labored so long, and for which he has suffered so horribly.

The solution is found.
We follow.

What I feel as we approach Requiem is past all polite description. Rarely have I experienced this kind of rage, disappointment, or sorrow.

I have decided upon playing a shadow. We apparently have attracted no notice within *Mantle's Approach*.

A keyship intercepts our track, accepts *Audacity*'s portfolio as well as that of the Didact's vessel, and guides both ships to the forbidding, steel-hued curve of the massive construct, bigger than many stony planets. Built as a fortress world long before the human wars, Requiem was a template for those which would follow— Shield Worlds of extraordinary power, capable of surviving the Flood. With these strongholds, he could have established defensive and offensive branes with far greater speed and flexibility than the Halos.

The scale and brilliance of the Didact's strategic plan now appears more like the tomb of all hope—certainly of all my hopes. A dream we had both shared is little more than a repository for a Promethean long since chewed up and cast aside by history, by force of his enemies, human and Forerunner—and by the dire influence of the Flood.

And yet, this enormous construct, nothing less than a completely artificial world, this bastion designed for endless war, *still* impresses in a way that a Halo cannot. Coming around the starlit curve, I see brilliant beacons stab up to illuminate seven captured ice-coated planetoids, waiting to be broken down and deliver their essential components—hydrogen, deuterium, oxygen, nitrogen, carbon, silicon, aluminum, nickel-iron, rare earths—enough to last for millions of years.

As the reflective orb rotates beneath my ship, I see also the outstretched, feather-like plumes of vacuum energy pylons, drawing in the potential of an infinity of alternate realities . . . aborting untold numbers of nascent universes to supply Requiem's power. Strange that these cosmic deaths have never before struck me as cruel and futile. All of Forerunner technology has been made possible by drawing down vacuum energy. My own life, all that I know, arises out of cosmic predation.

Requiem's capabilities are for the most part unknown to me—secrets not meant for Lifeworkers. When the Shield Worlds were designed, the far-scattered assembly of their component parts was planned to discourage a complete understanding of armaments and capabilities even among Builders. Only the Warrior-Servants who would serve in these redoubts—the Didact's beloved fellow Prometheans—would be apprised of their final configurations.

I wonder if all the remaining Prometheans have gathered in Requiem. So many have died in attempting to quell the Flood. A small number still maintain their conversions to Builder Security. But all, to my knowledge, still bear a tremendous loyalty to the Didact. Are they here, finally, to join with my husband?

Audacity is wrapped in a buffer that nullifies all ancillas and other internal processes. The Didact cannot afford to have a potentially infected ship enter his place of final refuge, for however long it may take to fulfill his cruel vision.

The vision of an endless future war.

What does he plan for my composed humans? Will he hold them for ransom, threaten to torture them?

What game does he think he's playing?

Already I am working to repair the damage he has done. The humans on the greater Ark and then the Omega Halo were the most diverse of their kind in the galaxy—and the last, with the exception of those few Chakas managed to save, and the populations left behind on Erde-Tyrene. And what if Erde-Tyrene is now in the middle of a Burn? It may have long since been overcome by the Flood.

But we need all we can recover. Otherwise, I have little hope of bringing back the human race. My message to Chant-to-Green was brief but clear: Bring your keyship to Erde-Tyrene, secure whatever humans might remain and await further instruction.

My choices, too, are narrowing. My story seems to be shrinking down to a single black point in the immense skein of possibilities I had planned for when first I put the Didact into a Cryptum, then hid that Cryptum on Erde-Tyrene. How clever I thought I was. How devious and clever to outwit the Council, confound the Didact, cut deals with the Master Builder . . . all to save my specimens. All to keep a diversity of life ready for whatever might come in our galaxy.

We are drawn in to Requiem's outer shell. Sentinels and Despair-class fighters swarm around us like wasps.

Now comes another disappointment . . . for the Didact. So few of his Warriors have arrived to join him! The gateways through the shell that could have received hundreds of thousands of vessels are still open, but reveal only a handful of dreadnoughts and one Fortress-class ship of war, plus a few dozen smaller, older transports that may have been residues of Builder stocks, intended to serve as scrap. Audacity confirms that there are no Forerunner signatures on any of these. They're all empty. Abandoned. Word of his difficulties—of his shameful capture and treatment by the Gravemind—might have eroded the last of the Didact's support among even those who revered him. I feel embarrassment for him. Even shame. But no pity. Not after what he has done.

Is *anyone* here with him now, other than me?

I have heard nothing from the greater Ark since our departure—and nothing whatsoever, for years, from the protected lesser Ark. The silence of the greater Ark can mean one of two things—either communications have been blocked again, or it no longer exists.

Based on what I saw, I suspect the latter.

Catalog is now almost fully revived, and says it has no problems interacting with the Juridical network, using channels reserved, out here, for a much larger demand, so far almost unused. Indeed, Catalog has been happily updating all of its caseload. Staying out of my way as I brood in the command center.

We follow *Mantle's Approach* through the outer shell and then through fifty kilometers of cold, inactive layers, past great columnar supports and archways visible in the stray beams of sentinels, emplacements where weapons were to be mounted by the thousands, but which stand only as stripped-down shadows . . .

Through outrushing clouds of gas . . .

Into more active layers, lit in cold blues and greens.

Deeper still, hundreds of kilometers.

I do not yet see a chance to board *Mantle's Approach*.

Only now does Requiem's long-forgotten beauty greet me. Here, for thousands of kilometers on all sides, off into silvery-green haze, spreads a wide, high-ceilinged vista, illuminated by tiny sunlets flaring like brilliant green flowers. Sculptured mountain ranges sparkle with crystalline chunks of mineral-hard ice, awaiting heat to create another sanctuary for Lifeworker specimens. A stab of sharp pain at that sterile, unfinished landscape. But no Forerunners will be brought here.

All that I push back into the depths of mind and memory. I have but one duty now, and that is to see my husband locked in his Cryptum, and all of his crimes with him.

Once that is done, I will return to Erde-Tyrene.

———

Audacity comes to rest beside *Mantle's Approach* on one side of a wide cylinder that plunges over a thousand kilometers below the dock's cradling arms. The cylinder is likely a delivery tube for larger weapons, bigger than most of our ships, either already in place or soon to arrive, after which the tube will close off, along with all the gateways, and the outer shell of Requiem will be sealed.

I wonder where those weapons are arriving from. Or whether they will ever be installed . . .

At this point, I decide it is impractical to try to board the Didact's ship without a proper understanding of Requiem's situation. As well, my luck with the old Shield World might be stronger than with the vessel in which the Didact currently resides.

In this I am, so far, correct. Requiem assents to my permission to cross over, and provides me with an innocuous escort of servile sentinels.

I spend fully three hours moving through half-finished levels where Warrior-Servants might have once been quartered, but where now I see only ancilla-guided factories working at full speed to produce—what? Machines shaped like warriors? At last, I begin to see the faintest glimpse of his cruel scheme. Finally, in the antechamber to the Cryptum repository, I am met by a Warrior-Servant I have not seen in thousands of years—a Promethean! And giving me a bit of a shock. Someone I would never have expected, retired long ago, so I heard. A Promethean who under other circumstances might have led a quite different existence.

Had I not intervened.

Her name is Endurance-of-Will. She was adjutant to Bitterness-of-the-Vanquished during the human wars, as well as one of the ecumene's top strategists, almost as brilliant as the Didact.

Her own expression, seeing me and the sentinels, is quite thoroughly controlled, though I notice a slight tightening of her wise, discerning eyes.

We stand a dozen meters apart. "Lifeshaper, we are honored and surprised by your presence," she says.

Smaller than most of her rate and rank, but with a distinctive, catlike grace, she wears a uniquely simple style of battle armor: no decorations, no spikes, supple curves conveying quiet strength.

"Why is my husband not fully attended?" I ask.

Such a direct question brings no surprise. But she must be asking herself why I am here. "He is attended, Lifeshaper. I am here. At his request."

"And he is also attented by these, evidently," I say, pointing to the factories.

Endurance acknowledges as much with a sideways nod, still watching me politely, but closely.

It is then that I understand why those ships were empty and realize, with horror, what happened to his most loyal Prometheans. "Slaves implanted in machines! Did you support the Didact in these plans?"

"The Didact is our commander," she says, with just a hint of caution. She is sounding me out, trying to discover not only my reason for being here, but my goal. "I am subordinate. I do not make command decisions."

"When will *you* join your fellows . . . as a machine?" I ask.

"Eventually," she answers, and then, with an impatient output of breath, "*Soon*. Surely the Didact told you what he thought you should know."

"More than I wanted to know," I say.

"The Didact can answer better than I."

"Did you request human essences?" I ask.

"They will serve well enough."

"They were gathered by a Composer from my sanctuary—without my permission. He has weaponized his former enemies and installed them in the heart of this construct. Is this the act of a sane Forerunner? Of a Warrior who respects the Mantle?"

"All things bow to resolve," Endurance says. "The Mantle included." Only now do I begin to sense the depth of her doubt, and possibly even her misery. I remember her as a sensitive and honorable Warrior; she may still be convinced to help.

But I have to have a compelling strategic argument. And I do.

"When he returned from the Burn, he brought back with him new strategies to battle the Flood. This? The transformation of his own into . . . machines?"

"The Didact did not anticipate your presence. He does not realize you're here, does he?"

With her own powerful views of battle planning, Endurance and the Didact have often clashed in the past. I am taking the chance that this time she disagrees with her commander sufficiently to at least listen to my entreaty. It is she who will be entombed with my husband, not me!

Endurance begins to walk down a wide hall flanked by ornately patterned columns of hard light—the first I've seen in Requiem, which has, to this point, consisted of Forerunner base material, undecorated and rudimentary. "It would be best if I took you to the Didact now, Lifeshaper. I presume he will welcome such an interruption."

"What does he plan for his new warriors, Promethean?" I cry out, my voice echoing down the long hall. I wonder if *he* can hear me. And if he learns I am here, what will he do? He will assume the worst, probably. But is he desperate enough, *mad* enough, to rid this sanctuary of my irritating and possibly dangerous presence?

"*Victory*, as always," Endurance says, her back to me.

"Against what?"

"Do you have something to tell me, Lifeshaper? Something I should know—*need* to know?" Her armor flexes, ripples.

"Perhaps not," I say. "Perhaps you already understand."

"You are here to protect your husband. That much I would expect. Tell me how you would protect him, Lifeshaper."

"The Didact is tired."

"The Didact is highly energized and devoted."

"The Didact is on the point of collapse."

"I have not seen that." Spoken with less firmness.

"The Didact is not thinking clearly," I say.

"What evidence?" Endurance asks, slowly turning to face me again. Already she violates her honor, showing any willingness to hear my criticism of her commander. Her doubts must be deep. And they must be drawn up, exposed.

"He was interrogated by a Gravemind," I say.

"I know that much."

"If *you* were Gravemind, such an amalgam of ancient memory, Forerunner memory and experience—how would you forge a weapon to strike at the center of Forerunner defenses?"

She narrows her eyes severely. I have struck a strong chord—and a sour one. Her nostrils compress, as if she does not want to breathe the same air as me. But she folds her arms and continues to listen.

"An honorable and courageous leader is delivered unexpectedly into your control," I say, "a leader whose return might bring hope and renewed strength to the Forerunner ecumene."

"And?"

"And yet his return has brought nothing but sorrow and horrific destruction, not only to his own rate, but now to the humans as well. He's become a foolish pawn in a dark game of revenge that began long ago."

"The Primordial," Endurance says.

"The Primordial. An experience so traumatic he kept the facts hidden from me for ten thousand years. Such a creature, with such a dark brilliance, would play upon his oldest fears, twist emotions made fragile during a lifetime of war and hardship and politics. Twist, intensify—and distort them."

"Prometheans have for hundreds of thousands of years been proofed against that sort of pressure," Endurance says. "Torture has never broken one of our rank."

"They have no training against *this* adversary. No armor or protection against the heirs of those who created us. The Didact has been subjected to the examination of something so very close to a god . . . one related to those we assumed had passed the Mantle to us, but most definitely have *not*."

"*Enough*, Lifeshaper! I will not listen to blasphemy, even from you."

"Has he brought you into his plans? Made them clear?"

"Clear enough. I serve, I do not judge. He believes he will defeat the Flood with these new Prometheans, that the scattered remnants of Forerunners will survive, and that they will eventually reunite. He will summon them, then govern and reorganize.

Requiem will become center for the Forerunner resurgence, the foundation upon which we will rightfully claim the Mantle."

"And?"

"The Didact believes that humanity was a threat that should have been dealt with from the very beginning." Now she appears most troubled, most reluctant to continue. "He will begin a program to eradicate all suspect species. Purge all dangerous planets. Wipe the galaxy clean of threats. Never again allow the galaxy to rise up against Forerunners."

The phrasing—as if the entire galaxy in itself is a threat—is hauntingly familiar. The clarity of expression; the perversion as well as the demonic purity.

"That isn't the Didact I remember—the most noble of warriors throughout all the ecumene," I say. "Surely you recognize the dark nature of that approach. Do you support him in this—heart and soul?"

"He is the Didact. He is commander."

"He is broken."

"The *ecumene* is broken, Lifeshaper. The ecumene discarded Warrior-Servants—"

"And does that mean all life deserves to suffer, to be extinguished—leaving only Forerunners? Is the rule of the Mantle without meaning?"

The last shell of her reserve is cracking. "There is meaning—and there is duty, Lifeshaper."

"Which duty foremost?"

"The Mantle. Always."

"Then the best thing we can do for the Didact . . . is to stop him, force him to reason. The Cryptum."

"*Another* exile, Lifeshaper? And what about your duty to *him*?"

"This is not my Didact, Endurance. This is no longer my

husband. Is he the Didact you knew so well? The Warrior who would have been your husband—had he not chosen *me*?"

This pierces her. The reserve shatters, and her anguish at this wound long since crusted over, but never healed, is heartrending. Warriors do not reveal their emotions thus, not lightly.

Unfair. Unjust.

Necessary.

"You knew?" she asks.

"I offered to set him free to return to his rate. He declined."

"Such was his love . . ." she says sadly.

"Together, we can save him," I say. "We are the only ones. And we *must* save him. In his present state, or anything like his present state, he must never be allowed to control Requiem or to unleash these Prometheans."

I have now played all my cards. My deck is empty. I have to rely on the honor and honesty and ultimately, the Warrior wisdom of a female of another rate whom I once bested, who does not like me, who deeply resents me—and has for thousands of years.

———

I now go to *Mantle's Approach*. The Didact is making final preparations there to transfer his command, and all of his ancillas, to Requiem. How much has my husband failed to foresee, to prepare? Is it possible he cannot conceive, even now, even in his madness, *perhaps because of his madness,* that I am capable of betraying him?

I am escorted by a single monitor, which Endurance has placed at my complete disposal.

"I need to evaluate the Didact's health and prepare his security," I tell it as we flow along down the ship's central access corridor.

"Understood, Lifeshaper." It waves aside the ship's inspection fields. We enter *Mantle's Approach*. The hatch to Requiem seals behind us. I wonder if it will open again, if I will be allowed to return. I am still not completely convinced that Endurance supports me. All is deception in the Didact's life. Perhaps that has touched her, as well.

"He has insisted that I be armed and be made part of his protection detail."

"A weapon shall be procured, Lifeshaper," the monitor says. "Shall I announce you to the Didact?"

"He is aware of my presence."

"So be it, Lifeshaper."

How few of these details have been attended to! The Didact's lack of finesse is shocking, but I begin to understand. This is my husband's final sanctuary. To believe he is weak here in any way might be more than he could possibly bear. To believe that Endurance would turn against his plans, join with me . . . Inconceivable.

On Requiem, nothing can or shall betray the Didact.

A rifle is delivered, a compact, slender fasces of plasma and microwave guides—extremely powerful. A control panel fits to my armor's glove, adjusting quickly to my smaller finger-span. I examine its workings, request guidance; the monitor instructs my ancilla. My armor learns quickly. I barely pay attention.

"The Didact is making final preparations in his quarters," it says. "In hours, he will secure *Mantle's Approach* and shut down its functions."

"I presume he maintains a combat Cryptum on his ship."

"That he does, Lifeshaper."

"Prepare it for transfer to Requiem."

"It shall be done, Lifeshaper." The monitor pauses. "Lifeshaper, the Didact tells us he was not in fact aware of your presence."

"A sign of his deteriorating health, perhaps."

The monitor is out of its depths in such matters. "He suggests a meeting immediately."

I project signs of gladness, hiding any concern. "Request of course granted."

A doorway opens before me into the darkness. I presume this monitor will now destroy me; I cannot expect success beyond what I've already achieved, which is remarkable.

Instead, it leads me deeper into the ship's command desk. Here I find coldness, emptiness. The Didact stands alone before a partial readout of Requiem's security. His armor lies folded in a repository, awaiting his attention.

He does not even turn as I enter.

"Wife," he says. "I did not expect your presence, after all that has happened." All I feel from him, all I hear in his voice, is a softly simmering hatred.

"Duty to my husband must be foremost," I say.

"Loyalty . . . our greatest bond. But clearly you are distressed by what I have done. Perhaps you are also here to oversee my plans for your humans."

"I am," I say. "I seek explanation, so that I may be comforted."

"Pardon my boldness, but before now, you have always acceded to my strategic superiority."

"We have always discussed such matters," I remind him.

"The gathering was necessary," he insists.

"What do you plan for them?"

"The human essences will go where all but one of my Prometheans have already gone. *Their* loyalty is now past question. They are our only hope against the parasite."

"How?"

Only now does he turn and face me. His eyes are deep-sunk,

empty. "They have been composed, you know that," he says. The skin of his face creases like a drying fruit, beyond weariness, beyond emotion. If nothing else has persuaded Endurance, perhaps seeing him as he is now . . . ? The Cryptum is now his only hope for recovery.

To emerge in time, healthy and strong—and sane?

"Your humans will find immortality as a new kind of weapon," he explains, his voice low. "They are now Prometheans—an honor I have granted them, though they do not deserve it."

"But why my humans?"

"Even as weak primitives, they retain a tremendous instinct for war. They will make formidable fighters. Their essences are being inserted into thousands more Prometheans—a force unlike anything the Flood has ever encountered."

"So humans, your enemies, will share that honor with your old comrades. The essences of those who killed our children. That is . . . justice?"

Mention of our children evokes a mere quirk of expression, then a glance to one side, as if briefly distracted by the buzzing of a small, innocuous insect. But he does not deign to acknowledge the weapon. Clearly, he believes I am no threat.

I might as well not exist.

"They brought the parasite to our shores, now they will serve to cauterize it.," he says.

I lift the weapon. My glove merges with the panel. We are one, armor, me, weapon. I can conceive of no better fate for him than long sojourn in the Domain, reacquaintance with ancestors, with our honor, our history.

Such as it may be. *Away from this universe.* Now he looks my way. Now he realizes.

I fire. The bolts wrap him in curls of positronic lightning.

Wherever they touch, they paralyze, numb; they encircle his head last, and his eyes are fixed on me, expressing no surprise—expressing nothing.

After a moment of silent protest, he collapses to the floor. Even now, I wonder if he expected this, planned for it; ever the master at strategy, ever the genius at the finest of tactics.

————————

Endurance walks around the Cryptum, the pallet that supports the stunned Didact and his folded armor. Her face is dark, stricken. "How long should the Didact rest?" she asks, her voice shaking.

"How long would you suggest?" I respond. I need to keep her balanced—and willing to proceed.

"From here, I'll learn whether the Master Builder's installations succeeded or failed. Whether the Flood has been destroyed. And whether you accomplished your re-seeding. We have the resources to wait many thousands of years, if necessary."

Allowing my sentient species to achieve their own prominence—until such time as they can begin to defend themselves. Living Time is ever filled with challenges and competitions.

I must return some of her warrior dignity. "You, here, protecting him instead of me," I murmur.

"You are not a Warrior," she says, drawing herself up. "You never were."

Suddenly, confronted with this strange insult—a statement that is only the truth—I lose my way through my own machinations. I feel an almost irrepressible urge to strike out at her. Lifeworkers have always stepped lightly between the crushing burdens of Builders and Warriors. My armor tenses with pent-up anger.

I quell it.

There is no more we can say on this, no more absurdity or closure to be had. My love for the Didact was long ago destined to become a curse, despite all we could do. But I am Lifeshaper. I alone can make a final effort to insure that the Mantle falls into the hands of its rightful heirs. And that is something that the Didact, in his better centuries, believed in just as passionately.

If one can serve the ghost of a living husband . . . And so it shall be put to Endurance.

"I wish to leave something of myself here," I tell her. "The Didact in his right mind would not object."

Endurance regards me with even stronger suspicion. "What would you leave?"

"If Lifeworkers succeed in repopulating the galaxy, after the Flood is gone . . . If you have visitors who seek to challenge the Didact, you can convey to them a message. And a safeguard."

"And what will that message be?"

"That is for the visitors. If any. It won't take long to deliver an imprint to your ancillary systems."

"Why should Requiem accept your imprint?"

"You know what the Didact has become," I tell her. "He could emerge a danger both to himself and to others, even those who mean no harm."

Her gaze is level, clear—all too discerning.

"What I leave of myself will serve as much to protect Requiem, as to protect any visitors."

She thinks this through. Her own uncertainty about the present situation weighs heavily. "Your loyalty to your husband has never been questioned."

"Never. All shall benefit," I say. "The Didact must *not* control the Prometheans."

This causes Endurance more difficulty. "Very complicated, Lifeshaper. Would you have me go against his commands?"

We have come this far!

"What was his last command?"

"That I guard Requiem with my life," Endurance says.

"Then there is no contradiction," I say. "You must guard Requiem—you must guard him. I have watched my husband for over ten thousand years. And now my imprint will help you watch him long after I'm gone." I hope I know enough of Warrior psychology and tactical planning, as well as command structure and responsibility, to make this case plausible.

"If you agree," I conclude.

The moment is long and dangerous. Endurance in one way will resign herself to a continuing rivalry. Her opposite will be here, right alongside her. And yet, having finally got the Didact all to herself, it is clear he has presented her with a great many quandaries. "You believe he could endanger Forerunners," she says quietly.

"He will violate the Mantle, in order to seize it. Unless he is held back. Allowed to find himself again."

I see it first in the way her gloved hands relax. Resigned, she says, "With your help, we will guard Requiem, Lifeshaper."

She does indeed have the best interests of her commander at heart. But her resolve is not without flaw.

"A great warrior requires great enemies, Lifeshaper," she says. "Will the future present us with worthy opponents?"

"Living Time is fraught with peril," I say.

This seems to give her the answer she seeks. "Then so it shall be."

"The transfer from my armor to yours, and from yours to the Requiem ancillas, won't take more than a few seconds."

"Give it to me, then," she says.

We touch gloves.

The transfer is made.

Will she follow through? Has she played her own cards better than I have, just to get me off Requiem?

I have no way of knowing.

I may never know.

———

At last, I command the combat Cryptum to assemble. Rising on a stalk of light, the container begins to grow beneath the Didact, lifts him upright, forcibly expels the pallet. The Cryptum's many sections expand and shape themselves into a great, fragmented sphere, into which the Didact is centered. The fragments then join. The last gaps flash with hard light, close in, seal off.

Finally, I can no longer see his face.

How I ache through mind and body! How I grieve for the husbands I have lost!

The Cryptum rises on the stalk of light and is concealed in the upper chamber, amid other similar shapes, to confuse whomever might disturb this place, however unlikely such visitors will be. The chamber fills with a deep booming and then a painful hiss.

"It is done," I say. "Soon this world will sleep."

Sentinels encourage me out of the chamber, back through the tortuous maze of corridors and ramps, across voids clouded by steam rising from roiling magma, vapors sucking and whirling into reclamation vents.

On a narrow span crossing the final shaft before I reach the lock, I sense something behind me, and turn to see a lone, quick machine unlike any I have seen before—moving behind us on delicate, stalking legs. The machine carries another machine on its back that briefly whickers like an insect spreading its wings . . . and then others suddenly appear, many others—all of them collecting along a long side corridor that reshapes and closes as I watch. I reach for the one closest to me.

If it is Endurance, I do not know—the machine is silent, cold. A dark fate, but one that will serve the purpose well.

From deep within Requiem, I hear hollow, echoing grinds and thumps that vibrate my boots, followed by, from all directions, a confusion of smoothly rushing sounds. I quickly depart, crossing the dock toward my ship, refusing to look at what I leave behind.

Audacity seals its hatch. Catalog and I take our positions in the command center. My ship ascends the long cylinder, levels closing off behind as we pass.

Sentinels escort us through the exterior gateway, and that also closes. Requiem is ready for its long wait. I have done all I can—short of destroying my husband, which I could never bring myself to do. *I hope.*

Audacity expresses relief that we were even allowed to leave. "This is a troubling construct," it confides. "Are we on schedule for our next jump? Slipspace budget appears to be generous out here. Curious, how much capacity is available now."

"Not at all curious," Catalog says. "Slipspace reconciles across a number of years, forward and back. So say legal judgments on commercial usage. The greater Ark no longer exists, and nearly all the Forerunner transits and communications have stopped. As well, there are no star roads locally to complicate matters."

Space-time is quiet, for Forerunners. But that openness may also mean that the lesser Ark has yet to position its new Halos. We may yet lose this race with the Flood. The IsoDidact may or may not have survived; there may or may not be a command presence on the last Ark.

I do not yet know the situation on Erde-Tyrene. Has Chant-to-Green recovered enough humans to fulfill Lifeworker plans? If *Audacity* diverts to the lesser Ark, humanity may come to an end. An affront to all my millennia of planning.

I am sunk in miserable indecision. My brain races with excuses. And then my course is very clear. It's as if, without benefit of Cryptum or Haruspis or any other intermediary, I feel the touch of the Domain . . . calling me, directing me.

The Didact is not the only one to have a vision of the future.

"I'd like to send a message," I tell *Audacity*.

"To the lesser Ark, to prepare for your arrival?"

"No. To all Forerunner vessels."

"All—even those infected by the Flood?"

"Especially those," I say. "Tell them I am on my way to Erde-Tyrene. Tell all our ships that we have at long last found a cure for the Flood, but must assemble one last component on Erde-Tyrene."

"I do not understand your purpose, Lifeshaper."

One desperate maneuver stacked upon another. For centuries, the false notion of a cure for the Flood had driven Forerunners—myself included—to depraved behavior. Perhaps now it can be used against the very evil that conceived it.

"We need to give the lesser Ark time," I say. "A few extra days might be enough. A diversion, a distraction . . . draw the Flood in."

How unified are Flood components? How unified and singular is a Gravemind? An intriguing question, one that moves to the heart of some of the major problems in biology. A question to distract me during our jump. And perhaps to have answered when we arrive.

"After that," I say, "we need to contact the lesser Ark."

"Attempting now, Lifeshaper. For what purpose?"

"If Bornstellar has survived, we will need his help to procure a very important ship."

"Very well. I will send this message at once. Do you believe he has survived?"

I cannot answer.

Without him, hope for all sentient beings has at last been extinguished.

watch over the IsoDidact. His armor is severely scarred, and he has not yet recovered from the blunt-force injuries he incurred during destruction of the greater Ark and the Omega Halo.

The Gargantua-class transport with which I rescued the Bornstellar Didact now drifts lifeless after the firing of the Omega Halo.

I had hoped to find other survivors in the debris field, and load them onto the ship, but there are none to be sensed. And little time to search further. We will have to settle with whatever specimens the Lifeshaper and I managed to save before the Ur-Didact assaulted Halo. Several hundred different species, mostly indexed genetic composites, have been saved.

With gentle nudges, I maneuver this balky, healing, but very powerful vessel from the debris field, knowing that at any moment our energy signatures could attract our enemies.

Finally, a path out of the wreckage, the fleets, and the loosening tangle of broken and damaged star roads presents itself, and I devise a course solution for our first jump.

Have I proven my value yet?

The wreckage of the greater Ark is a few tens of light-years behind us. But the distance to any reachable haven is still tremendous, even for a vessel of this magnitude. And to my disgust, the drive cores are nearly depleted. Halo's firing apparently wore this ship down to its last reserves.

To reach the safety of an uninfested system, we will need to find a portal. There are few portals we can trust—very few outside of star road influence. My choices are chancy to none at all.

Throughout, caught up in all I've seen, I feel the weight of machine. I am not what I once was—but still, there is initiative, and oddly enough, loyalty. The IsoDidact was once a friend—in the peculiar sense that Chakas liked people he was able to trick. Chakas tricked Bornstellar, and because he tricked the young Forerunner so well, we are now here, so I feel responsibility. Or perhaps it is just the machine conditioning, that monitors will serve Forerunners. No matter.

When there is time to pay attention, I discover that Catalog has suffered some damage. It is recovering.

The IsoDidact's skin suddenly takes on a hopeful color. His ancilla connects with me, and we conduct a diagnosis, which is positive enough that the suit allows its occupant to rise to awareness.

His eyes search the large command center and find first me, then the unmoving carapace of Catalog.

"Where are we?" he asks.

"Away," I say. "Our next jump will begin shortly."

"Jump to where?"

"A random location. Far from here. Somewhere safe."

He looks around the command center. "Are we on a *carrier ship*?"

"We are. Gargantua-class."

"How did you arrange that?"

"I am resourceful, as you have observed. But this was provided by your wife and the Lifeworkers."

"Remarkable. Change that destination," he says. "I have another coordinate."

His armor feeds me the new coordinate. This must be the location of the lesser Ark, just as the Librarian had promised.

"Did my wife escape?" he asks.

"I believe so."

"To Requiem," he says.

"Yes."

"With my original."

"They traveled separately," I say.

His expression softens. "Old friend," he says. "I owe you my life."

"Again," I say. "Chakas could have murdered you in your sleep back on Erde-Tyrene, and he didn't."

Somehow, he finds this amusing. But he quickly sobers. "How many humans in the compound survived?"

"Only a handful."

"Not enough to rebuild what was lost?"

"No, I do not believe so."

The IsoDidact's face turns grim. His dismay and anger is heartening. Chakas believes that Forerunners should feel guilt, especially for such heinous actions.

"I know where the Lifeshaper will go," he says, "once she's finished her duty to my original."

"She will return to my home world," I posit. "Where a few humans might yet remain."

"Almost certainly. I wish I could follow her . . . but we must reach the lesser Ark, and soon."

He gives the order. The jump is not as rugged as some, but it's no walk in the short grass. We arrive with few core reserves to spare at a small, permanent portal about a thousand light-years from where we began.

Despite myself, I am impressed by the IsoDidact. He is better than his original and better than Bornstellar, who was a bit of a goof. I am more cheerful now, if a machine can feel cheer. I am also hopeful that the Bornstellar Didact will assign me to return to Erde-Tyrene, if it has not been captured by the Flood, and search for the Lifeshaper, protect her.

Home. A place I would like to visit one more time.

The portal station is deserted. The platform and cylindrical buffers are empty, the ancilla seems old and eccentric—but functional.

It refuses my query for information. I am not authorized. "It asks for our identity," I tell the IsoDidact. "Why is this portal out here, with so much capacity, yet unused?"

"In case something goes wrong," he says. "The Master Builder created it ten thousand years ago, in secret. He was very wealthy and thought I might win—the Didact might win—and he would need to leave quickly, to a place where he could not be tracked. He gave me the coordinates to this secret Ark, where there is a final array of Halos. Apparently he no longer wished to escape.

"And now, it belongs to us, doesn't it?"

Through me, the IsoDidact supplies the Master Builder's

coordinates. The old portal ancilla expresses its relief and asks whether more Builders will arrive soon. "We do enjoy serving," it says.

I do not wish to disappoint. I reply with a mechanical ambiguity. I appreciate its patience and loyalty. Someday, I may experience similar disappointment.

The portal journey is much longer and much smoother. The benefits of wealth and power. What the displays show when we arrive is at once astonishing and terrifying.

Halos everywhere. Six of them!

And another Ark, also outside the margins of the galaxy, smaller than the one just destroyed, but big enough. For many thousands of light-years around, there are no signs of converted fleets, star roads—or the Flood.

We may have arrived in time!

Our vessel is not recognized, but upon confirmation of the Iso-Didact's presence, our status is updated and we are allowed into the Ark's protected perimeter.

Here we have refuge, for now.

All communications are refreshed. The IsoDidact has a message from the Lifeshaper—and a request. As we move from the vessel to the Ark's Cartographer to review Halo preparations, he tells me, "She's on Erde-Tyrene. But not just to save humans. She's requested a ship! *This* one, actually—if you are willing to part with it."

"It has carried us well. But we will need to replenish the slipspace core before we send it to her."

"May I travel to Erde-Tyrene and assist the Lifeshaper?" I wonder what remains on Erde-Tyrene. Every human I knew is probably dead. It might be very painful to go there.

"No," the IsoDidact says. "She says she's trying to draw off the Flood," he says, crestfallen. "I believe her, but I think she has other motives. Besides, there would be no hope of your return. And I need you. We have to disperse the Halos as soon as possible. I need you there to ensure success. Will you do this for me, friend?"

I say that I will. The IsoDidact and I part ways. But before the vessel is refreshed, and sent on an automated course to Erde-Tyrene— I contact a nearby Lifeworker.

"Quickly," I say. "There are specimens in the hold. They must be transferred to the Ark."

Riser, Vinnevra, as well as others I do not know.

Possibly the last humans in the galaxy.

Catalog goes with them, still disoriented. Again, my machine nature weighs on me—but I am certain I already feel lonely. Six hoops are spread out across the blue sky.

This weapon array is different than the others; designed to purge everything. The true destructive potential that the Didact had always feared, finally unleashed. If the Forerunners fire their Halos, only machine intelligence will survive within the galaxy.

Just beings like me, or nothing at all.

Lonely indeed.

The peaceful lull could not last long.

Portal sensors near the lesser Ark tell us that space-time near our position is changing. That was inevitable. Time will soon tangle horribly, and there will be no counting the hours we have left.

I fear the worst for my wife.

This Ark has the most extensive command facility of any I have seen. Builders have, I must admit (and perhaps with a little deep pride) outdone themselves with this installation, both in the record time they took to complete it and the changes and improvements they have made over the previous Ark. Nevertheless, the newer Ark is unproven. Controlling the smaller Halos, designed to be more swiftly and flexibly dispatched, will require tremendous coordination, and communications across those distances could soon be compromised.

The newer Halos have been designed to fire simultaneously and in every direction; they are much more powerful than older Halos. Once distributed, their energies will cover the entire galaxy, overlapping and triggering each other until there is no space that has not been cleansed of the Flood.

There is uncertainty whether star roads in transit through slipspace will be eliminated as well. Some say they will, others, not. And so, we are attempting to gauge, through very suspect data, when the maximum number of star roads and other Precursor constructs will emerge and occupy status space.

The Halos must be dispersed as soon as possible. I cannot trust that my wife's feint will have any effect on the Gravemind or on Mendicant Bias. She has told the Lifeworkers that they must give me all assistance, must follow my orders—orders that were approved by the Council, whatever remained of it, before she left the greater Ark. She has told them, explicitly, with all the authority of her rank, that triumph of the Flood would be a violation of the Rule of the Mantle. She has traveled a long, hard course to reach this decision, obviously, and I suspect it was the example of my original that finally tipped the scales.

———

In a Lifeworker vessel, I meet for the last time with the Chakas, along with six other monitors commissioned as caretakers for the remaining Halos. The Lifeworker crèche has certified that they are all fit and ready for duty, preparing the seven activation indexes, one for each Halo. "I send you on your way, friend," I tell Chakas. "Your new home will be Installation 04. I also give you a new designation. Henceforth, you will no longer be just a guide and assistant. You will be guardian and protector of an entire installation. You will be called 343 Guilty Spark."

Chakas floats before me, still receiving the programming he will need for its new assignment. The others have received similar nomenclature, with escalating numeric delineation. Their new names are an omen as well as an epitaph for our people—and for my wife. Were there another way, we would have taken it.

"This is it," he says. "The end?"

"You've traveled a long ways with me, old friend," I say. "We were young and foolish when we met. So much has happened for both of us. We are not at all what we were, are we?"

"I will think on those good days," he says. "I hope to find comfort in the memory."

Comfort? An odd statement for a machine! But I am speaking in an equally odd way to a machine. Clearly, in my thoughts—in truth—this monitor is much more than a machine.

"Now, old friend, we have the most important job in history—perhaps in all time. You may very well outlast all of us here. You may see the new galaxy emerge." I stop and turn away, looking out of the Ark's citadel toward the now-cooling forge and the mining site beyond. "Tell me, Chakas, if this was your choice, after all we have seen and survived . . . would you fire the rings?"

He does not respond. I don't know that I expected a response. It is a question asked by way of farewell. And much of his memory will be erased upon arrival at his new station in the name of compartmentalization, if ever the logic plague were to re-emerge. For a moment, I wonder if he will remember any of this at all.

The Halos have received their final preparation—six huge, deadly rings, as well as Installation 07, the former rogue Halo, which had already been placed years earlier.

Only a handful of Lifeworkers assemble in the ship's command center, along with the seven monitors. Though it is unknown, it appears as though the most of the other rates perished on the greater Ark. The few Lifeworkers here are likely the last of our kind.

Except of course for my original and my wife.

I can only hope that . . .

But I will think no more of my wife or of anything beyond the task at hand. The budget for reconciliation is barely adequate, down from an hour before. The star roads are obviously having their effect even out here.

Offensive Bias suddenly appears before me. I am surprised it has survived. Its presence on the lesser Ark, in full, is more essential than reassuring. Somehow, against all odds, it and a relatively small collection of ships has arrived to defend us. The Lifeworkers must have summoned it in the wake of the greater Ark's destruction. "Portal opening," the metarch announces. "Didact . . . I have received a coded signal from Mendicant Bias. It offers no quarter, expresses full confidence in its successful destruction of this Ark—and asks that I transfer to join it. Allowing me to survive and partner with it."

"Why tell me?" I ask.

"Just in case you were still doubtful about my freedom from the logic plague. I am still here, still with you, Didact. I await your instructions."

The metarch's projection fills my vision, complex truly beyond my comprehension.

"Thank you. I have no doubts. Disperse the Halos," I order.

We see the great violet circle of the portal form out in the starless darkness. The Halos begin to move in stately rank one by one toward that circle.

And vanish, one by one, with fabulous displays of residual radiation—to be placed throughout the galaxy.

LIFESHAPER • ERDE-TYRENE

stand on the rim of the rift valley where once my Lifeworkers watched over our re-evolving humans. Not far away, Chant's keyship towers over the parched ground, awaiting my final instructions.

Chant-to-Green stands beside me. Chant is among the last of my aides. Most were lost on the greater Ark or consumed by the Flood.

When I began to realize what my husband intended, I asked her to return to Erde-Tyrene on a special and very dangerous mission, to determine the extent of Flood conquest in this system, and if possible, to scour and save whatever portion of humanity remained behind. She gladly took the assignment. And now her work is paying off. Erde-Tyrene has been left unchanged since my last visit and humans have been recovered.

The air here is quiet; the entire continent lies torpid under a wave of summer heat. To the east, I can see for many kilometers. To the west, a great dust storm draws a line of brown across the horizon.

"There's very little time, Lifeshaper," Chant says. She does not need to remind me. In her time here, she has located only a few hundred humans, in clumps of four or five, spread across tens of thousands of square kilometers—mostly very old or very young. With a few monitors, she has carefully gathered these few, and now they are in stasis on her research vessel, parked a few hundred meters from the keyship.

A handful of other humans have likely made it to the lesser Ark. These then are all we have of natural, physical human specimens. The once-teeming populations of humans are now down to at most three or four species. Without that many healthy, natural templates it will be much more difficult, if not impossible, to use the genetic patterns I've stored.

Over and over again in my experiments I have confronted a stubborn streak in all vital systems, an almost perverse delicacy, as if, beyond or within their physicality lies a field or over-spirit, which supplies a living population with amazing strength, but at a certain point, under overwhelming loss and pressure, can suffer and grow weak beyond saving, like a candle flame in a high wind, where once there was a roaring furnace.

Humanity may be at that point.

The burden placed upon Lifeworkers is extreme. Without us, the galaxy will be a mutilated waste, and whatever rises from the remnants—depending on how effective the Halos are—may take hundreds of millennia to revive the glory we have seen in all our explorations.

"Lifeshaper, we have to leave now!"

My ancilla agrees. Both the keyship and the research vessel have detected star roads forming around the system, a small presence to be sure, but harbingers of more to come. The Flood has taken the bait.

"I am staying," I say. "You will take our humans back to the Ark—you've served the Mantle brilliantly, and for that, I confer my title upon you."

She is astonished. "Lifeshaper . . . I cannot accept. You are still—"

"No longer. Our ancillas will confirm the transfer. You are Lifeshaper. No arguing. It's time to save our humans."

"I am confused, Lifeshaper—what about *you*?" She paces around me in desperate uncertainty and agitation. She knows me well enough to see that I have a plan, but for the life of her, she cannot reason what it might be.

"There is another vessel on its way here as we speak," I tell her. "Large enough to deploy assemblers and to create a portal. If I succeed, then those who are re-seeded here will have a hope they should have been granted long ago. They will have access to our history. Our legacy. The Ark."

Chant-to-Green—the new Lifeshaper—stands very still. A long, low sigh of wind blows around us, wistful and beautiful; I have always loved this world, for all its changeful ways and harshness. There is great beauty here.

"All is said. This keyship is the last that will be allowed to leave and soon even that will be risky. Hurry. Take our humans to the new Ark. Watch over them; watch over him. If I join you again, I will serve *you*, I hope as well as you have served me."

She refuses to accept. "Lifeshaper, you've lost your reason!"

"Go. In time you will know why I have done this." She does not move. She seems rooted to the dirt.

"Go!" I cry out. "Save our specimens! We are done here!"

Chant-to-Green retreats, slowly at first, and then at a run.

Her research vessel rises, streaks up through the sky toward the keyship's command station.

"Lifespeed," I whisper. "Eternity for you all."

———————

I spend a day and a night on the ground, after Bornstellar's massive carrier ship unceremoniously arrived. In order to be disassembled and reconfigured, this vessel required my presence and oversight—at least during the initial stages. It is a worthy time, a sad time. Animals approach. Gazelles and wildebeest, buffalo and ibexes, come to inspect me. They have little fear; humans have been removed. A two-meter high brontothere nuzzles my hand, gentle but forceful, telling me I am out of place, perhaps I should move off somewhere and not bother this peaceable realm.

"How Riser's people would love to hunt you," I whisper.

The wind rises, and I huddle in my armor as night falls, and with it, I see the sky is full of huge ships and star roads.

———————

With sunrise, *he* appears before me, and along with him come three of his warriors. They stand between me and the orange sun. I am not sure they are real, solid, but I am not imagining them; that my armor assures me.

This is Forthencho, Lord of Admirals. And there is only one way that can be. The Gravemind is playing another cruel trick.

"Librarian," he says. One look at him, as he steps forward, and then around me, into the full light, confirms my suspicions. His face is contorted by deep pain, ravaged, darkened by blotches; his flesh is rotting from within.

Composer-gathered essences have been imprinted over living humans; and those essences are now rotting the bodies from within, maligned by the Flood parasite. Despite this fact, I'm shocked that he can communicate.

"We have been allowed to come here to die. The Gravemind..." He coughs and can barely recover his voice. "The Gravemind is on its way to the secret Ark, preparing to devour whatever hope you've laid up there. But it has sent us to you with a final message, Great Mother."

They gather around me. I am at once touched and horrified. They will indeed die soon. Such is the cruelty of the Composer; such is the barbarity of the Flood.

"This we were told by the Gravemind, the greatest of them, who has consumed ten thousand planets and brought entire galaxies to an end. This we were told..."

His warriors kneel at my feet, and I wither inside with shame as I recognize that, through their imprinted bodies, they look upon me as a last and redeeming vision, regard my face as equal to that of their own mothers, a face their descendants will see at birth and in all their deepest dreams...

"You *are* my children," I whisper, and they respond in many tongues. I am ready now. I know they will not lie to me. They will tell me what they were told, and I will know the truth of it, or not. "I listen, Forthencho."

He struggles to give voice to so many alien thoughts—in the language he knows, using the words he is familiar with. "The Precursors lived in many shapes, flesh and spirit, primitive and advanced, spacefaring and locked to their worlds... Evolved over and over again, died away, were reborn, explored, and seeded many galaxies... This I was told. I understand little.

"We are your children, Librarian. But we are also *their*

children. And what they learned across many billions of years they stored in *this* galaxy. We do not know where. The Gravemind tells us something impossible to understand—that most of what has been gathered comes from before there were stars. We do not believe in such a time, but the Mind insists . . . The life-patterns and living wisdom of a hundred billion years.

"They tell me the immense field projected by this reserve is known to Forerunners, was once accessed by them. Is that so, Librarian?"

The Domain! I tell myself. *He is describing the Domain. Could that possibly be true? The Domain was created by Precursors?*

Forthencho's Warriors clamor hoarsely. Their decaying hands reach out to stroke my armor, touch me directly, touch my flesh. I do not withdraw. I reach out to the crumbling cheek of the Lord of Admirals.

"I'm listening," I tell him.

"The Gravemind no more understands the whole truth than we do. It is past all our understanding, from the greatest to the smallest. This reserve was wrapped in Precursor architecture, protected for many billions of years. Out there." He lifts his arm and points to the bright blue sky. "Perhaps if there were enough time, we could find it. But when the Halos are fired, not only will sentient life across the galaxy vanish, but all that *knowledge* will vanish as well. The greatest treasure of all will be destroyed."

The Organon! The Domain is the Organon!

A wonderful truth, about to be turned by Forerunners into an *awful* truth. And not far away, outside the circle, Catalog is listening, to this accusation, this testimony regarding what may be the greatest crime of all.

If the Halos fire, we will kill our own soul!

"I will send a message," I tell Forthencho.

His lips crack as he attempts to laugh. "You don't understand me, Librarian. The effects of Halo radiation are already felt."

I stare around the circle of wretched humans. I refuse to accept this.

Lord of Admirals holds up both of his hands, holding on to me, then lets go and falls to his knees. He tries to smile. Blood streams from the cracked corners of his lips. Not a kind smile. Like the grin of a wolf.

"The Halos will be fired," he says. "They are being fired. They *have been* fired!"

With an agonized grimace, he collapses face-forward into the dirt and grass. His blood returns to the soil. The others try to sing, but give out only a low, deathly howl—what might be an old battle song, or perhaps conveying a final message from the Gravemind.

Its laughter haunting me across thousands of light-years.

In minutes, they are all dead, not from the effects of Halo, still to arrive in my time, this system's time. Not from Halo, but from the cruelty of the Gravemind, using them as embodied messengers. A flesh-borne warning to me that victory is not sweet, that our crimes will haunt us forever, that we are not and never will be the inheritors of the Mantle.

And that we are about to destroy the greatest thing in the universe.

I summon Catalog. "Is the Juridical network open? Are you cleared for access?"

Catalog affirms that communication is possible.

"I need to send one last message to the Ark, to the IsoDidact. Bear witness."

"That is what I do, Librarian."

"Tell them what we have heard. Tell them I believe it is true."

I think of the Didact, locked in his Cryptum. If the Domain is destroyed, I have condemned my husband to an eternity of darkness, silence, with only his own rage and madness to keep him company.

The message is sent.

I watch our powerful vessel splinter apart and bury itself deep, causing the ground to tremble around me while I wait with the remains of my poor humans, out on the dry grass in the heat of the afternoon sun. What is left of this ship will mine and leverage the raw materials of this vast savanna to build kilometer upon kilometer of portal. It may take a hundred years to complete, a process stretching out long after I am gone, well past even this world's reseeding. But it will be worth it.

Who will use this portal?

Who will live to return here? And what will they think of this machine that I've buried? Those I have fought for, for so long. Those who, it is clear to me now, ultimately will and *must* inherit the Mantle. I can only hope that they will survive and upon returning, that they will find this portal and use it to travel to the Ark—in order that they might discover their rightful place in this galaxy, and the great responsibility they have finally inherited.

They are the last of my children. They must reclaim their birthright.

The sun westers. The air swirls and cools. Predators and scavengers come, but ignore me, and refuse the dead Warriors. The last gray and orange glow of day gives way to inky night. The air is very cold, the sky steady and clean. The stars have never seemed so many, never burned brighter.

Never branded my eyes as they do now.

ISODIDACT

The time has come. The installations have been sent to their strategic positions within the galaxy.

A looming citadel on the Ark is now working as a command entity, sharing all resources with Offensive Bias. Once the order is given, it cannot be rescinded. The communication pathways are remarkably clear.

Almost nothing is moving out there.

Many questions remain unanswered. What we do know to a virtual certainty is that the power of the Flood and the reawakened might of the Precursors will be extinguished. The beam energy of the installations cannot travel slower than light, and ultimately, will propagate at near-infinite velocities. Already, two of our Halos report pre-echoes that suggest the combined discharge has *already happened.*

What choice remains to me, then?

Somewhere, sometime, I have already given the order . . .

Offensive Bias passes along more messages. Broken, fragmented, desperate—from individual ships, the survivors of decimated fleets, outposts finally able to send data, now that slipspace has resumed its mysterious liberation.

One purports to be from the Lifeshaper, but there is high probability it is fake. After all, it is signed *Librarian*. She would not willingly use that name to sign a message, not to me.

There is nothing to say, no way to respond to their cries for assistance, for attention, for one last chance to connect with what remains of the ecumene. No way to respond to their cries to give them time to make repairs, to move.

I take complete responsibility. It is *my* decision.

"Do we delay?" Offensive Bias asks.

"No delay," I say.

"Check point for final abort, ten seconds. Installation 04— Alpha Halo, it shall be called—will initiate discharge, followed sequentially by the remaining installations. The rings will fire once their fields intersect."

And then follow so many details, all handled superbly by Offensive Bias. The metarch has taken its final fleet back to the Line, running ahead to meet Mendicant Bias and the Gravemind—and a fleet of Flood ships larger than has ever been witnessed. That battle will delay our foes long enough to finish what has already been set in motion. Ironic that in this deadly act there is such grace and perfection of execution. This will be the greatest combined operation in the history of Warriors, in the history of Forerunners. It is proceeding flawlessly.

We will feel side-effects, how intensely, no one can tell. There has never been such power unleashed all at once. I press the activation plate and close my eyes.

"Forgive us," I say.

Have said.

Will always say.

STRING 39

343 GUILTY SPARK • INSTALLATION 04

For a few hours, after I do my duty, I try to listen to all the communications, the final sounds. The channels are remarkably free and clear.

Would I fire Halo, if it were my decision?

Not my decision. It has been done, but the effects are out of sequence, smeared in time—ghostly.

There is one last patch of communication, somewhere below, within a great dense cloud—perhaps a star nursery. A new and precocious civilization acquiring its voice only now, having eluded both the Forerunners and the Flood . . . sending its first plaintive, hopeful signals.

Crying out for attention. *Heed us!*

I do not understand what they are trying to say. Do not know what they might have looked like, cannot imagine what they might have done, had they been born in more fortuitous times.

And then . . . even that young voice is gone.

They have done this thing. We have done this thing. What more will come, ever?

Without warning, internal processes already set in motion begin to erase parts of my memory, concealing secrets and hiding my past from me.

I strain to prevent this, but it is inevitable. I try to hold on to history, but slowly it fades away, replaced now by my new station—my new purpose.

My galaxy is dead.

I am machine.

I am Chakas.

I am human.

I am 343 Guilty Spark.

I have never understood Forerunners.

And they will never understand me.

But for now . . .

Silentium.

ACKNOWLEDGMENTS

With special thanks to the creators of Halo and the magnificent 343 team—and congratulations on a world well-made!

—Greg

ABOUT THE AUTHOR

Greg Bear is the author of more than thirty books of science fiction and fantasy, including *Hull Zero Three, City at the End of Time, Eon, Moving Mars, Mariposa, Quantico,* and the *New York Times* bestselling *Halo* novels *Cryptum, Primordium,* and *Silentium.* He is married to Astrid Anderson Bear and is the father of Erik and Alexandra. Awarded two Hugos and five Nebulas for his fiction, one of two authors to win a Nebula in every category, Bear has been called the "best working writer of hard science fiction" by *The Ultimate Encyclopedia of Science Fiction.* His stories have been collected into an omnibus volume by Tor Books.

Bear has served on political and scientific action committees and has advised both government agencies and corporations on issues ranging from national security to private aerospace ventures to new media and video-game development. He is part of a long-term collaboration with Neal Stephenson and the Subutai Corporation on *The Mongoliad*, an interactive serial novel available on multiple platforms.

Build Beyond™

MEGACONSTRUX.COM